Crucifixion

V Plague Book Two

Dirk Patton

Dirk Patton

Published by Voodoo Dog Publishing, LLC
2824 N Power Road
Suite #113-256
Mesa, AZ 85215

Printed in the United States of America
First Printing, 2014

ISBN-13: 978-1511492232
ISBN-10: 1511492236

Crucifixion
Table of Contents

Crucifixion
Also by Dirk Patton

The V Plague Series:

Dirk Patton
Scourge: V Plague Book 14

Other Titles by Dirk Patton:

36: A Novel

The Void: A 36 Novel

Author's Note

Thank you for purchasing Crucifixion, Book 2 in the V Plague series. As you've probably already guessed from the title, this is the second book in the series. If you haven't read the first, I would encourage you to do so. Otherwise, you may be lost as this book is intended to continue the story in a serialized format. I intentionally did not do much to explain comments and events that reference Book 1. Regardless, you have my heartfelt thanks for reading my work, and I hope you're enjoying the adventure as much as I am. As always, a good review on Amazon is greatly appreciated.

First and foremost, I want to thank you, the reader, for having parted with your hard earned money for this book. Without you, this wouldn't be possible and certainly wouldn't be as rewarding. You can find me on the internet at www.dirkpatton.com and email me at dirk@dirkpatton.com Like the V Plague Facebook page www.facebook.com/FearThePlague and follow me on Twitter @DirkPatton for info on upcoming books as well as some behind the scenes details on the series and characters.

Being an Indie author is both wonderful and a pain in the ass. I enjoy the freedom of not having to force my work into a mold that will satisfy a publisher, but I sacrifice the marketing and publicity that being with a major publishing house brings. I'm not a marketing guy and am probably failing to do a lot of the things I should be doing to get publicity, or just plain doing them wrong.

That's where you, the reader, come in. The best marketing in the world is word of mouth. If you are enjoying the V Plague series, PLEASE write a good review for me on Amazon and Like the V Plague Facebook page. Tell your friends and family. There's a lot more to come in this world I've created, and I hope you'll help me get the word out there to as many people as possible.

Last, and most importantly, I want to thank my biggest fan, my beautiful wife, Katie. Yes, the same Katie I'm fighting across the whole continent to get to! Without your support, encouragement and unwavering faith in me this never would have happened. I hope you know I'd fight just as hard for you in real life. I love you!

Sappy shit aside, thank you again for reading.

Dirk Patton

Crucifixion

1

What a bag of dicks!

Colonel Crawford, commanding officer of the Army's 5th Special Operations Group, stood there and smiled at me. Smiling like the fucking cat that just ate the fucking canary. He'd just imparted the news on me that by Presidential order I was being reactivated into the US Army. I understand this can happen in times of national crisis, and the nuclear attacks on New York, DC and Los Angeles would certainly qualify all on their own, but the follow on nerve gas attacks that had created millions of homicidal maniacs out of the population was the larger crisis.

Rachel and I hadn't fought our way out of Atlanta, rescuing three downed Air Force personnel in the process, and made it to Arnold Air Force Base in Tennessee just so I could become a cog in the big green machine again. Even if I was a highly trained and very valuable cog that had Delta Force Operator as part of my resume. My priority was to get to Arizona to find my wife Katie. I hadn't talked to her since the day before the attacks, about two weeks ago, and I had no idea if she was even still alive.

"Colonel, that's going to be a real problem for me. I've got a wife in the Phoenix area that I'm trying to get to. I don't know if she's alive, infected..." I trailed off. Rachel, standing beside me, took my hand in hers and gave it a squeeze to let me know she was on board with whatever I needed to do.

Crawford rubbed a big, callused hand across the brush cut hair on top of his head and suddenly looked very tired.

"I understand your predicament, but this isn't optional. Right now we need every experienced man we can get. We're trying to consolidate our resources and be ready to protect the remaining civilian population from the infected, and I can't even go into what's being planned as a response to the Chinese for attacking us."

He let out a long sigh and seemed to be wrestling with a decision. "For the moment, you two get some rest, and I'll see what I can do about helping you find your wife. We'll talk in a few hours."

Crawford ordered the Air Force intel clerk that had run the background checks to get us some chow and some quarters. I was surprised he specified he wanted us in the visiting officers' quarters but didn't question the gift.

If the clerk wasn't happy about taking orders from an Army Colonel he did a good job of hiding it, jumping to his feet and telling us to follow him. We exited the secure intel working area, leaving

Crawford behind, and were escorted out of the building. Dog, a large German Shepherd that had adopted us during our escape from Atlanta, raced ahead and took full advantage of every tree and bush he could find. A short walk later we arrived at another large, brick building.

Opening the door for us, the clerk led the way through a blackout curtain, and we were immediately hit with the wonderful smell of baking bread. We passed a door labeled 'Officers Mess' and stopped at a small reception desk manned by an Air Force Senior Airman. The clerk explained the situation to him and soon we had a key and directions in hand to our room, the clerk wishing us a good evening and heading back to the intel building.

The room was on the second floor, and true to Air Force tradition was every bit as nice as any Hilton I had ever stayed in. It was nicely appointed with a large king sized bed, flat screen TV, and bathroom with oversized tub. Rachel let out a decidedly girlish squeal of delight and dashed to the tub and started it filling with steaming water. I smiled, picked up her pack and weapons where she had just let them fall on the floor and deposited them alongside my pack against the far wall of the room. When I returned to the bathroom door, Rachel had already stripped off her grubby clothes and was brushing her teeth with a toothbrush from the plastic wrapped toiletry kit that had been waiting on the bathroom counter.

"I'm going to get us some food," I said, waiting to make sure she'd heard me. Apparently she did because she waved at me with her free hand and kept powering the brush across her teeth. Dog followed me through the door, and I momentarily thought about making him stay behind since I was going to the mess hall, but decided the hell with it and headed for the stairs at the end of the corridor.

At the bottom of the stairs we stopped at the reception desk, and I asked for clean clothes for Rachel and me, not surprised that the Air Force also had women's underwear available. I took a guess at Rachel's sizes, and the Airman promised he would deliver them to our room within the hour. Thanking him, we walked down the hallway to the mess, Dog's nails clicking loudly on the highly polished linoleum covered floor.

Pushing into the mess hall, I wasn't at all put off when the conversations at three separate tables stopped, and every head in the room turned to stare at me and Dog. I had been fighting in the field for almost three weeks, had been shot and was exhausted from running and fighting. I was also well armed with an M4 rifle, pistol, fighting knife and a tactical vest loaded down with spare magazines and ammunition. Oh, and I was blood-stained, dirty as hell and smelled like an elephant's ass as someone dear to my heart used to say.

Ignoring the stares, I walked up to the serving line and grabbed a large plastic tray. I loaded it down with fresh baked biscuits, mounds of bacon and eggs, fresh fruit, a pile of sausage patties and a stack of pancakes that threatened to topple over every time I slid the tray on the shelf in front of the line. Adding flatware and two big glasses of orange juice, I thanked the civilian food workers and tossed a sausage patty to Dog. He snatched it out of the air and swallowed after only chewing once, if at all, then followed me out of the mess hall with his nose raised close to the tray.

Back in our quarters, I set the heavy platter of food on a small table. Rachel was in the tub, water up to her neck. I portioned food onto one of the plates I'd brought and took it along with one of the OJs into the bathroom, sitting it on the edge of the tub. Rachel thanked me without opening her eyes, and I went back out and devoured every remaining bite of food. Well, not every bite. Dog got his share, too.

Pushing the tray away, I stood up and waddled to the door when there were three sharp knocks. It was the Airman from the reception desk delivering our new clothes. We each got two sets of standard issue Air Force uniform pants and blouses along with three sets of socks and underwear for each of us, including bras for Rachel. Separating the clothing, I delivered hers to the bathroom and told her to get moving. It was my turn. A large splash of water was her answer, Dog getting the worst of it.

Saying the hell with it, I reached into the shower stall, cranked the water on hot, stripped out of my grimy clothes and stepped in. The hot water felt marvelous as it beat down on my head and shoulders. I had to soap and rinse twice to feel clean, shaved my head with a disposable razor that had been provided with the room, rinsed and turned off the water. A towel came flying over the top of the shower door, and I snatched it out of the air and dried off.

Towel wrapped around my waist I exited the shower and shaved my face after wiping the steam off the mirror. Rachel stood next to me, towel wrapped around her torso. She was forcing a comb through her long, wet hair, accompanied by a steady string of curses as the comb worked out tangles.

"So what's the... ouch, shit... plan?" She asked, peering at me through wet hair that covered her face and hadn't been combed out yet.

"I'm deciding," I answered, rinsing the razor and setting it aside for future use. I found a small tube of lotion and rubbed some into my freshly shaved scalp. "Suggestions?"

"I'm with you whatever you decide," she answered, pausing her combing and holding hair out of her eyes to look at me. "You should know that by now. We've been through too much together for me not to help you. If you want to slip out of here and hit the road, I can be dressed in five minutes."

I met her eyes and smiled, knowing she was serious and wouldn't think twice about helping me become a deserter from the Army.

"For now, we both need rest and another good meal, then we'll decide. I'd much rather have the support the Army can provide, but I'm not going to start playing soldier and forget about Katie. And... thanks. I'm glad you're with me." I reached out and squeezed her hand before walking out of the bathroom.

Digging through the clothes we'd been provided I found a pair of clean underwear, pulled them on and climbed between the sheets. Dog jumped up on the foot of the bed and curled up into a big ball of fur. Rachel had taken to sleeping in the same bed with me, chastely, after being abducted and abused by a group of survivors. I wasn't surprised when a few minutes later she crawled into the bed and stole most of the covers.

2

"Twenty-four hours." Colonel Crawford sat across from us in the Officer's Mess. A large, steaming cup of coffee was tightly gripped in his large hands. Rachel and I had just finished a late breakfast when he joined us, scratching Dog between the ears as he sat down at our table.

"What?" I asked, not sure I had heard him right.

"So here's what I can do for you. There's an Air Force C-40 leaving tomorrow morning for DM – Davis Monthan Air Force Base – in Tucson. I can get you on that flight. There's a C-130 departing from DM twenty-four hours after you land in Tucson, heading to New Mexico. There will be a five-man Green Beret A-Team on that plane, and I need you to lead them on a recovery mission to pick up two scientists. I'm told these two specialize in nerve and biological agent weapons. We need them at Fort Campbell. Give me your word that you'll be on that return flight and I'll give you twenty-four hours to find your wife. After that, I need you back in harness and ready to lead a team."

Crawford held my eyes with his, waiting for my answer.

"You have my word," I said, holding my hand out. He shook it, my not so small hand nearly disappearing in his giant paw. "Thank you, Colonel."

"Oh, I almost forgot," he said, sliding a large manila envelope across the table to me. I opened it and dumped a gold oak leaf into my hand. A thick sheaf of papers remained in the envelope. "Your reinstatement papers, which need to be signed and dropped off at the JAG's office here on base. They'll take care of forwarding to BUPERS – Army Bureau of Personnel."

I wasn't interested in the papers. I was wondering what the hell a Major's rank insignia was doing in my hand. Crawford continued, "You were reinstated at your old rank, Master Sergeant, but completion of a college degree qualified you for officer rank and you were bumped to Captain automatically. I exercised a field commander's prerogative in time of war and promoted you to Major. I got the clearance and read most of your file last night. I need your leadership as much as I need your combat skills."

The Colonel reached out, took the insignia out of my hand and pinned it onto my uniform blouse in the center of my chest.

"Now, you need to know the situation on the ground in Arizona as well as the details of the recovery operation," he said. "I've set you up for a briefing with one of the Air Force intel guys at 1300. He'll bring you up to speed on what you need to know, then deliver you to the Quartermaster so you can draw the equipment you need."

He started to stand, but I held up my hand.

"Not that I don't appreciate what you're doing, but I've got to ask. Why?"

Crawford stood the rest of the way with a long sigh and stared down into his coffee cup. After a long, uncomfortable silence he started speaking.

"My wife and two daughters were visiting her sister in Los Angeles when the attacks happened. If I thought there was even the slightest chance that they were alive, I'd be doing what you're going to do. Besides, I need you, and if you're head's not on straight, you won't do me much good."

I stood, moved around the table and held my hand out again. Crawford shook it as I thanked him for everything he was doing. When I moved aside, Rachel stepped in and wrapped him up in a big hug. This took him by surprise and embarrassed him, but she didn't let go until he returned the hug. When she stepped back, he turned and walked quickly away, but not before I saw the moisture in his eyes. We watched him exit the mess area then

Rachel turned to me and smiled as she squeezed my hand.

It was over an hour until the intel briefing started, so I sat back down and pulled the paperwork out of the envelope. I didn't bother to read the reams of legalese. What did it really matter anyway? All of the places for signature were marked with little red stick-on flags, and I quickly signed my life away and tucked the paper back into the envelope.

Finishing our coffee, Rachel and I set out in search of the JAG office. Walking around the busy Air Force base it took me by surprise the first time a group of airmen saluted as they approached. I returned their salutes, but it wasn't as much fun as I had thought it was going to be. Kind of a pain in the ass to tell the truth.

"What's your wife going to say when you show up with me?" Rachel asked as we walked down a long street shaded by massive oak trees.

"There won't be a problem. We've been married a long time, and she knows that I'm too afraid of her to mess around." I answered with a grin. "Besides, you aren't going. You aren't trained for this, and I'm going to have to move fast once I hit the ground in Arizona."

Rachel grabbed my arm and pulled me to a stop, yanking me around to face her.

Crucifixion

"Hey, Asshole! I'm coming with you whether you like it or not. I've saved your ass from infected, patched you up when you got shot... you need me." Rachel's eyes grew damp as she stepped forward and shoved her face into mine. "We've saved each other, and like it or not we kind of belong to each other now. Get it through your head. You're not going anywhere without me."

Sensing the tension, Dog trotted over and pushed between us and sat down. Without thinking, I put my hand on top of his head and started scratching his ears. I wanted to argue with Rachel, but I had gotten to know her well enough to realize that it wouldn't do any good.

I'd have to lock her up to keep her from boarding that plane, and if I were to admit the truth I wanted her along. We had made a good team as we fought our way out of Georgia and I would be lying if I didn't admit how fond and protective of her I had become.

"OK, you win," I said after a few moments of eye contact with her. Damn, she was like Katie in so many ways. Why did I always manage to wind up with such headstrong women?

Rachel looked into my eyes to satisfy herself that I wasn't patronizing her. Happy with what she saw, she wiped her eyes before circling her arm through mine and starting us walking down the street again. She was at least gracious enough to not gloat over her victory. Much.

We found the JAG office after asking for directions and getting lost twice. I dropped off the paperwork, then with Dog and Rachel in tow headed for the intel building we'd been in when we first arrived at Arnold the night before. Every 30 to 40 yards we had to pause so Dog could sniff up and pee on bushes, sign posts, trees, you name it, and it got marked, but we eventually made it to the building.

The two enlisted Security Forces guards at the entrance snapped to attention and saluted when they saw me, opening and holding the door for us. OK, so maybe this officer thing wasn't so bad after all. Inside we made our way to the same door Crawford had led us through the previous night. I knocked, and a moment later an Air Force Master Sergeant opened the door.

"Major. I was expecting you. The lady..." He stopped when I cut him off.

"The lady is with me," I said, pushing through the door.

He stepped back out of our way, looking at me, Rachel then Dog. After a moment, he shrugged and let the spring loaded hinges slam the door shut.

"Yes, Sir. Please follow me."

Crucifixion

He grabbed a flash drive off his desk and led us down a brightly lit hallway to a small conference room. There was a plate on the door that indicated a classified briefing was in progress and before leading us into the room he flipped it over, then locked the door behind us. Rachel and I settled into chairs at the side of the table, Dog choosing to curl up at our feet. He rested his chin on my boot and tail on Rachel's, closed his eyes and promptly went to sleep.

Inserting the flash drive into a PC sitting in the front corner of the room, the Sergeant turned on a ceiling mounted projector and dimmed the lights. The projector warmed up quickly and displayed a map of the continental United States. The east and west coasts were covered in blotches of red as was most of the gulf coast and the upper Midwest. New York, DC and LA also had radiological symbols superimposed over the red. Large circles of red covered most of the major cities across the country.

"Fourteen days ago, beginning at 2333 hours Eastern Time, the United States was attacked by the People's Republic of China, the PRC. We have since determined that the opening attack was the detonation of eight nuclear warheads timed to detonate simultaneously in the New York City area, two warheads in Washington, DC and three warheads in Los Angeles. Our best estimates are that each of these warheads were in the fifty

Kiloton range, and intelligence suggests that they were smuggled into the country and hidden in place well in advance in preparation for the attacks.

"Additionally, nerve gas attacks on multiple cities were carried out by aerosol sprayers flown over by small civilian aircraft. The areas in red on the map behind me represent the known disbursement areas of the nerve agent. There are a handful of large cities where no nerve agent was released, but we don't know why. The best guess at this point is some sort of problem with the Chinese agents assigned to them, but that's just a guess.

"Current casualty estimates are as follows; 18 million dead from the initial nuclear strikes, 5 million dead within the past two weeks from radiation, 175 million infected by the nerve agent, 25 million dead as a result of attacks by those infected."

I was stunned as the Sergeant read the casualty estimates from a small note card he held in his hand. He paused to give the gravity of the death blow dealt to the US a chance to sink in. The numbers he quoted were staggering. So large in fact that I couldn't really grasp the scope.

It's easy to comprehend single deaths or even multiples of ten or twenty, but when the numbers start getting into the millions, it seems abstract. Like a paper statistic and not real life. Tucking the note card away, he continued.

"By Presidential order, our forces have retaliated on the PRC through the launching of both land and submarine-based ICBMs. Casualty estimates to the Chinese are in excess of 300 million dead from the initial strikes or dying from radiation poisoning. The US strikes on China all occurred within the first eight hours of the crisis, and there have not been any additional attacks by either side.

"Aid from the EU is flowing into the continental US via airlift, but the People's Liberation Army Navy (PLAN) has effectively shut down all shipping traffic into the US. Multiple naval battles have occurred between UK and PLAN vessels in the north Atlantic, and the UK has suffered heavy losses.

"Japanese, Korean, French and German naval units are currently assisting the Navy in engaging three PLAN carrier battle groups in the south Pacific. The Navy has intelligence that the PRC is planning to seize the Hawaiian Islands for use as a staging base to move into Alaska and take the oil fields."

"Where's Russia in all this?" I asked.

"Sir, Russia has so far remained neutral. They have condemned the PRC's actions, and their military is on high alert, but they are in a defensive posture only at this time. We had initially thought Russia was also involved. We did launch missiles at them, but they were aborted and brought down over the polar ice when we realized our mistake."

"Any indication of a land invasion by the Chinese?"

"Yes, Sir. The Chinese have occupied Guam and been massing troops. There are twenty-seven very large troop transport ships trailing their carrier groups. Satellite imagery shows another four hundred converted troop transport ships being loaded and preparing to sail from multiple Chinese ports that survived our tactical strikes. Naval experts estimate each ship can carry twenty-five hundred soldiers."

Never good at doing math in my head I was a little behind the curve in figuring out we were looking at a potential invading army of over one million soldiers.

"The President has authorized the use of nuclear weapons by battlefield commanders to stop the PLAN from taking Hawaii or reaching the west coast. The latest reports are that we have exchanged nuclear strikes at sea, but I do not have a battle damage assessment yet."

He paused, apparently waiting for questions but none were forthcoming. I was too stunned. Rachel reached out and took my hand, gripping it tightly as we were told about the death that had been visited on our country.

"To the immediate threat," he continued, clicking his remote and changing the image on the display to another map of the US, this time with large, amorphous blobs of yellow covering massive swaths of the country.

"This is the current assessment of the threat posed by the infected population of the US. The areas in yellow are territory that has completely fallen, or is so infested as to be considered uninhabitable."

Involuntarily I leaned forward in my seat to peer at the map. The entire eastern and southeastern United States was yellow all the way up to the southern border of Tennessee. North of Kentucky the yellow started again and stretched all the way to the Arctic Circle. To the west were large pockets of yellow infection covering nearly all of the major cities.

The west coast was yellow from Mexico to Alaska. The inland west was mostly clear of infection other than Denver and Salt Lake City. Suddenly the casualty numbers from earlier started to sink in.

"Here is what we have learned about the infection. Our resources are limited as both USAMRIID and the CDC were lost in the initial attacks, but we have been able to isolate the agent and are working with the French and the Swiss in an effort to find a cure or a vaccine. This is what we know so far. The nerve agent is called MX-489.

"It was developed during the cold war to destabilize the civilian population of a country as a precursor to invasion. Within minutes of exposure, it causes a chemical change in the brain that results in the hyper aggression state. What had our researchers stumped at first is that MX-489 in its original form was lethal, typically killing an exposed subject after twenty-four to thirty-six hours of extremely aggressive behavior. The human body is unable to handle the massive amounts of adrenaline that are continually released into the system as a result of exposure and will die of either heart attack or stroke.

"Just this morning it was discovered that the Chinese have paired MX-489 with a virus. The effect of this is to significantly strengthen the body's ability to continue to function despite all of the adrenaline. How long this will preserve the infected is unknown, and so far we have had no reports of infected beginning to die off.

"The only good news is that it is the nerve agent that causes the change, and the agent is only persistent for 48 hours post release before degrading in the environment. Also, the virus seems to have no detrimental impact on non-infected people. However, the researchers aren't sure. They don't know what else the virus may do."

"Where did the MX-489 come from?" Rachel asked. The Sergeant shot me a look, and I nodded my head for him to answer.

"It was originally developed by the US Government in the early 1960s. Half the missiles we had pointed at Russia during the cold war were armed with the nerve agent rather than nuclear warheads. During the Cuban Missile crisis, there were four B-52s in the air at all times with tanks full of it, ready to spray the entire island of Cuba."

He shuffled through some more note cards, found the one he was looking for and continued, "The researchers have started calling the Chinese version the V Plague."

The briefing lasted for another hour. The Sergeant expanding on what the researchers had discovered and then covering why the two scientists in New Mexico were so critical to the research efforts. He handed me a packet with large head shot photos of each scientist and a short biography on each. The packet also contained details on their location in New Mexico and how I would find and extract them. I glanced through it then closed the file and gave him my full attention as he talked about the tactical situation in Arizona.

Phoenix and Tucson, the two largest cities in Arizona, had quickly devolved into chaos after the attacks. Thousands had died very early on in rioting and looting as grocery stores were stripped bare within hours of the attacks. Then came the fighting between first neighborhoods, then neighbors, over food, fuel and water. Civilian law enforcement had evaporated, and less than twenty percent of the National Guard had reported when the call-up orders were issued.

The two cities had only Air Force bases in or adjacent to them and both bases were on high alert and locked down with no personnel to spare to try and quell the unrest. The other two large military installations in the state were a Marine Air Station 200 miles to the west of Phoenix in Yuma, and Fort

Huachuca, which was 90 miles to the south of Tucson near the Mexico border. Neither had the manpower to help and were also locked down and using every available resource for their own security.

Reports were filtering out of the state that local gang leaders had set themselves up as warlords, their ranks swelling with people who were hungry and scared and looking for the protection the gangs offered. Battles raged in both Tucson and Phoenix between rival warlords looking to either maintain or seize control of food, water and fuel stocks. There had been a mass exodus of people trying to get to safety in the mountains of eastern and northern Arizona, but many had run out of fuel and were on foot.

Adding to the misery, it was summer, and the temperatures in the Arizona desert were in the triple digits. Satellite imagery and drones flown out of Luke and Davis Monthan Air Force Bases showed thousands of bodies lying in the desert where refugees had succumbed to the heat, collapsed and died. This wasn't going to be a walk in the park.

I asked the Sergeant about the use of a helicopter to get me from Tucson to Phoenix, which is about 110 miles across open desert. He flipped through his notes before telling me that he had no information about availability of rotor wing aircraft, and it would be at the base commander's discretion.

I asked some more questions, as did Rachel, and when they were all answered I thanked him for the briefing. Rachel, Dog and I followed him out of the conference room, and he escorted us across the air base to a massive building where the Quartermaster was located.

We spent close to an hour getting outfitted with food in the form of MREs – Meal Ready to Eat - uniforms, gloves, boots, body armor, new weapons with military grade sound suppressors and tactical vests, ammunition, comm equipment, night vision gear, first aid kits and a medic pack for Rachel, combat packs and even a ballistic vest for Dog. Working military dogs had been a high-value target for snipers in Afghanistan and Iraq and had needed body armor just as much as their handlers.

With everything stowed away I shouldered my pack and slung my weapons and stepped onto the scale sitting by the Quartermaster's desk. 348 pounds. I subtracted my 230-pound body weight and wasn't pleased that I had 118 pounds of gear on my body. I had packed Rachel lighter than myself, but she refused to get on the scale. Women. Like it mattered, if I knew what she weighed.

Taking the pack off her back, I piled it and her weapons on the scale which reported 73 pounds. Lighter than my load, but by no means light when she couldn't have weighed more than 150, despite being nearly six feet tall. After I signed for everything we exited the building into the humid afternoon.

"So what's the plan?" Rachel asked, struggling to adjust her pack to a more comfortable position. I stepped behind her and took the weight in my arms so she could adjust the straps.

"First, I'm taking you to the firing range to spend some time with an instructor, then I'm going by flight operations," I answered, still supporting her pack. "Need to know exactly what time our flight to Arizona leaves tomorrow morning. I also want to check and see if they're running any SAR – Search and Rescue – operations. I can't stop thinking about those kids we left behind in Atlanta."

When Rachel and I were fighting our way out of the Atlanta suburbs, we had encountered three teenagers that were holed up in their house, waiting for their parents to come home. This was a couple of days after the attacks, and we hadn't been able to convince them to come with us.

We'd left them enough food for a week or two if they were careful with it, then when it became clear that we could only get them to come with us by force, we had driven off without them. I wasn't regretting our decision, there was no other option at the time, but if they were still there and alive, I wanted to see if I could get them some help.

Dirk Patton

I didn't know where either the range or flight operations were, but it didn't take long for a Security Forces Humvee to drive by, and I flagged it down. The young Airman driving the vehicle was happy to give us a ride when he saw the oak leaf on my chest. Rachel and Dog piled into the back seat and after dropping my pack in the cargo area, I climbed in next to the driver.   He drove aggressively, probably in a hurry to get an officer out of his vehicle. In only a few minutes we arrived at the base's small arms training facility.

A squat cinder block building fronted the parking lot, several dozen 300-yard shooting lanes carved into the terrain stretching out behind it. Every couple of hundred feet a tall tower looked down on the firing line. These were where the Range Masters observed and controlled all activity on the range.   I told the Airman to wait and motioned for Rachel to follow me.   Dog stayed behind, pushing his head forward to get a neck scratch from the driver.

Inside the building, I quickly found an Air Force Master Sergeant and Chief Master Sergeant in a cramped office. They were sitting with their feet up, cigarettes burning in an ashtray that was made from a cut-down artillery shell. They both stood up quickly when I stepped through the door of the office, the Master Sergeant stubbing out the smokes before coming to attention. I waved them back into their chairs, pulled out my own cigarette, lit up and plopped into the visitor's chair. The two Sergeants grinned and relit their smokes.

They had heard about Rachel and me – any military installation is the biggest gossip exchange you will ever find – and I patiently answered their questions and gave them enough juicy details to make them feel like they were on the inside. Steering the conversation, I explained to them that Rachel and I were hopping a flight into hostile territory in a few hours, and she needed a crash course on the firing range. They took one look at Rachel, who was beautiful even in all her combat gear and eagerly agreed. When I left, Rachel was smiling, flirting and being fawned over by both of them. She certainly knew how to play the game.

Back in the Humvee, I had the Airman drive me over to Flight Operations. When we arrived, I told him to wait and went into the large building that was immediately adjacent to the flight line. On the opposite side of the building, a tall Control Tower soared into the air, commanding a view of the entire runway and taxiway system. The building itself was a hub of activity, Air Force enlisted personnel working on computers and walking from office to office in a quick and efficient manner. It didn't take long for a young female Airman to stop and ask if she could assist me.

I asked to speak with whoever was in charge of flight operations, then followed her down a long hall, up a flight of stairs and into a large room. Three walls of the room were covered with large flat panel displays that appeared to monitor everything from the weather to air traffic as well as several with constantly updating information that was Greek to me. The fourth wall was all windows that looked out onto the flight line. My escort pointed out a small, Asian woman wearing an Air Force uniform with a Major's oak leaf.

I was surprised a Major was running flight operations as I would have expected this to be the job of a Colonel, but I wasn't going to complain. I was a Major, too, and was happy to not have to deal with an Air Force officer that outranked me. Not that this woman couldn't just dismiss me out of hand, but it was less likely for her to ignore a brother officer of the same rank. I walked up and paused a few feet from her while she finished a conversation with one of her staff before introducing myself.

"Oh, yeah. You're the guy that flew in last night, right?" She was tiny compared to me, five feet tall at the most, and had to crank her head way back to look up at me. The name tape on her uniform read Masuka.

"That's me," I answered with a grin.

"What can I do for you?" She asked, picking up a clipboard and scanning through a couple of pages before finding what she was looking for. "Looks like we've got you on a flight to DM tomorrow at 0730."

"You do, and the first thing I need to ask is, are there two seats and room for a dog?" I grinned what I hoped was a charming grin, but either it wasn't, or she didn't care. Brad Pitt, I'm not.

"The aircraft has been reconfigured for this mission. No seats, just web slings." She put the clipboard down and looked back up at me. "Why? Who are you taking with you?"

"The female team member that made it out of Georgia with me, and my K9."

I was stretching the truth here, making it sound more official than it really was. I was hoping she wouldn't ask for specifics about Rachel and Dog and find out neither was military.

"There's room," she answered after a long pause. "I'll note it for the loadmaster. Was there anything else? I'm a bit busy here."

She started to turn away to speak with one of the enlisted staff that was waiting in line for her, but I spoke up before I lost her attention.

"Yes, there is. What's your SAR capability at the moment? I had to leave some civilians behind, north of Atlanta, and I'd like to get them evacuated."

For this request, I figured the whole truth was the best approach. I gave her the story about the three teenagers Rachel and I had encountered, telling her about their refusal to come with us and that we'd left them enough food that they could still be alive if they'd stayed indoors and quiet.

"Show me on the map," she said, stepping over to a computer terminal and clicking a mouse.

I followed her line of sight and watched one of the flat panel displays show an image that at first looked like Google Earth. As she clicked and scrolled, it became obvious we were looking at real time satellite imagery as you never see clouds when using Google. A couple more clicks and a street map was superimposed over the satellite image, and she motioned for me to take control of the mouse.

"It's just like Google," she said. "Use the mouse to scroll around, double left-click to zoom in, double right to zoom out."

Using the mouse, I navigated around the screen, zoomed in a few times then back out when I didn't recognize the area. The third time I zoomed, I was pretty certain I had the right location. As the screen refreshed, I recognized the neighborhood with just the one street that fed in and out.

Clicking to zoom in tighter, I didn't realize at first what I was looking at, then the screen did a final refresh into sharp HD clarity, and I muttered a curse. Several blocks of the neighborhood were packed with infected standing shoulder to shoulder, all of them pushing forward towards a small two-story house.

"That's got to be them," I said, eyes on the screen showing a throng of infected that had to number several thousand.

Major Masuka took control of the computer back from me, clicking and typing faster than I could even think about. After a few moments of furious work, she hit the enter key and looked back up at the screen, arms crossed across her chest. At first, nothing happened, then the screen blinked, and the same shot of the neighborhood was displayed, only this time, there were no infected in the shot.

A date and time stamp in the upper right corner indicated this was forty-eight hours ago. The screen blinked again, and the indicator changed to reflect forty-seven hours ago. This continued to happen, the images progressing forward an hour at a time until we reached thirty-one hours ago. In that image, a few dozen infected surrounded the house, frozen in time with arms raised as they pounded on the siding, doors, and windows. Another blink. Thirty hours ago. There were now hundreds of infected and more could be seen in the surrounding streets and yards as they streamed towards the house. Blink, twenty-nine hours. Thousands and still growing.

Crucifixion

Masuka paused the replay with a click and entered some more commands, hitting the enter key with a flourish. The time stamp rolled back to thirty-two hours, blinked and started progressing forward in one-minute increments. At the thirty-one hour and thirty-eight minute mark, a lone figure was visible moving towards the house and Masuka reached forward and hit a button that changed the replay to normal speed, paused it, rolled it back two minutes, zoomed in a little and let it roll.

Soon the figure appeared in the image about a block away from the house. I recognized Kevin, one of the three siblings I had met. He was running and kept looking over his shoulder. Rounding a house, he nearly ran into the arms of an infected male, stumbled backwards, pulled out a pistol and shot it. I sighed. The sound of the gunshot. That had brought every infected in a large radius down on their heads.

Kevin kept running, and now other figures were entering the frame of the shot. Some of them were shambling males, but there were also females. The females sprinted after Kevin. He was not in good shape, and his run looked like a slow jog compared to the speed of the females. Two of them were only yards behind when he stumbled on the lawn of his house, going to his knees only feet from safety. He was immediately tackled from behind by both females.

The front door of the house opened, and Gwen ran out onto the lawn, pistol held at arm's length, but it didn't look like she fired. Probably afraid of hitting Kevin. As she watched, the females ripped into Kevin, his bloody death displayed in high definition on the flat panel. Gwen slowly lowered the pistol and seemed to be rooted in place until more females appeared. She turned and ran back into the house, slamming the door behind her moments before infected started pounding on it.

"Can you go to real time?" I asked.

Masuka hit a few keys, and the image blinked before sharpening back to clarity. The house was absolutely mobbed with infected trying to force their way in.

"They're still alive in there," I said, eyes glued to the screen. "How soon can you get a rescue bird in the air?"

Masuka puffed out her cheeks then let the air out slowly, "Two days before I have anyone available. Plenty of birds available, but we're low on personnel, and every pilot I have is supporting the build up at the state border to defend against the herd that's moving towards us."

She looked up at me defiantly, expecting an argument. I stared at her for a long moment then turned my eyes back to the scene on the display.

Crucifixion

"What if I can get my own pilot and door gunner?" I asked. "Will you let me have a helicopter that can make the trip?"

"One pilot? No co-pilot? Only one crewman? That's against every policy the Air Force has." She answered, facing me with her arms crossed again.

"What's the Air Force policy on leaving two teenage girls to be torn apart by infected?" I asked in a low voice, leaning towards her.

Part of my strategy was to not make a scene and put her on the defensive in front of her staff, but I also know I can be fairly intimidating when I want to be. With 15 inches of height and probably 130 pounds on her, I hoped my physical presence would help change her mind.

Masuka stared right back at me, head turned up to meet my eyes like a child looking up at her parent. And she never blinked. We stared at each other like that for a bit before she uncrossed her arms and broke eye contact.

"Tell me what you have in mind," she said.

"The pilot that flew me in last night, Lieutenant Anderson. And the Senior Airman that was part of his aircrew. They can't be assigned to anything yet. They fly, I get the kids out of the house, and we bring them back here to safety."

I straightened back up, giving her more space and shut my mouth. If she said no, I'd find Anderson and steal a helicopter if I had to. She looked back at the display, the mass of infected bodies choking the streets and lawns around the house and shook her head.

"How do you think you're going to get them out of that?" She gestured at the satellite feed.

Got her! She was in.

"That's a two story house. I fast rope down to the roof, punch through a window and winch the kids back up. Easy peasy lemon squeezy."

Shaking her head and making a decision she called one of her staff over, a young, gangly kid wearing an Airman's stripe on a uniform that looked almost as new as mine. He dashed across the room and came to attention in front of us. Masuka looked up at me and gestured to the kid.

"Tell him who you need and he'll go get them."

"Lieutenant Anderson, he's probably in the BOQ – Bachelor Officer Quarters – and Senior Airman Mayo. Don't know where Mayo is, but the LT will know."

The kid stood there waiting for something else until Masuka barked at him to get his ass in gear. He turned and ran for the door, and she grabbed another staffer and started issuing orders to get a Pave Hawk fueled and on the flight line, ready to go. Ignoring me, she turned her attention to the line of people that had been waiting to speak to her. I left her to it and went down the stairs and back outside to where the Security Forces Airman was waiting with Dog.

They were outside the Humvee, and Dog had convinced him to throw a stick he'd somehow found. I told him to take Dog back to the firing range and deliver him to Rachel and let her know that I was taking a short trip and would be back in plenty of time for our flight to Arizona. I knew Rachel would be pissed at me, but I didn't really see that she could be anything more than a passenger on this trip, and she needed the time on the range.

The Airman sped off, and I lit a cigarette, enjoying the warm afternoon sun. Behind me, on the flight line, a jet engine throttled up and screamed like a banshee. The smell of jet fuel was heavy in the air. I already missed Rachel and Dog.

Two cigarettes later the gangly Airman wheeled into the parking lot in an Air Force blue pickup truck. Anderson sat in front, and Mayo was sprawled out in the back seat. I walked over to greet them as the driver pulled into a parking space and shut off the engine. When they stepped out of the truck and spotted the rank on my uniform, both of them looked at me with quizzical expressions on their faces.

"Recall by order of the Commander in Chief," I explained, shrugging my shoulders and grinning.

Anderson and Mayo came to attention, but I waved them off, forestalling the salutes that I knew were coming. Motioning for them to follow, I led the way into flight operations, explaining what was going on as we walked. Reaching the large operations room, I introduced Anderson to Major Masuka and faded into the background while they talked. Masuka handed a small flash drive to Anderson and waved me over.

"Major," she said. "I think you're a damn fool for going out there. Pave Hawks need a crew of at least four, preferably six, but I admire you for not just walking away from these kids. But you do need to know that if you run into trouble, I don't have anyone available to come get you. I've told the Lieutenant and Senior Airman that this is voluntary. I won't order them to do this so severely undermanned. You'll be glad to know they've both volunteered. Good luck to you, and I hope I see you in a few hours."

She stuck her hand out, and I took it, thanking her. The same Airman that had retrieved Anderson and Mayo was tasked with getting us to the Pave Hawk that was waiting on the flight line and we followed him out of the building without any further discussion.

The Pave Hawk was waiting for us on the tarmac, two ground crewmen just finishing fueling the external tanks. I didn't know the operational radius of a Pave Hawk, but I was glad to see we would have extra fuel for the flight. Anderson jumped out of the pickup as soon it came to a stop and headed for the helicopter. He was met by a Tech Sergeant, who emerged from a hangar when we pulled up, and the two immediately started walking around the aircraft, checking whatever it is pilots check before takeoff.

Mayo walked over and climbed in the open side door and began checking over the mounted minigun. I smiled when I saw the weapon. Six rotating barrels and electrically operated, it could fire up to 6,000 rounds per minute and would absolutely pulverize anything short of heavy armor. A friend of mine had called it 'the Finger of God' because whatever it reached out and touched just ceased to exist.

I tossed my pack in the helicopter as Anderson climbed into the pilot's seat and hit the starters for the engines. Climbing aboard, I connected to a safety tether that would keep me from falling out of the open door. The engines whined and quickly built to a deafening roar, and I scrambled to get a headset on to protect my ears.

Crucifixion

I watched as Anderson scanned all of the instruments, and apparently satisfied he plugged the flash drive Masuka had given him into a USB port on the navigation console. It took the system a moment to process the data then a screen flashed to life displaying our flight path to the target – rescue location in this case.

Anderson left the radio linked to the intercom, and we could hear him contact flight control, requesting clearance. They held us on the ground for a few minutes then released us and Anderson hit the throttle and pulled on the collective causing the Pave Hawk to leap into the air. He didn't bother to stabilize into a hover, rather immediately banked the big helicopter and put us on a heading to the southeast. On the navigation display, a blinking green symbol in the shape of an 'X' started following the thin green line that represented our flight path.

I busied myself with checking my weapons and making sure all the spare magazines distributed across my tactical vest were fully loaded. Taking the headset off long enough to insert the earpiece for the secure field radio I tested it with Anderson, then put the headset back on over it.

Next, I carefully checked over the rope I would use to get onto the roof of the house. The line is a heavy piece of braided nylon, just under two inches thick and is shackled to the frame of the helicopter. Fast roping out of a hovering helicopter is not one of my favorite things to do as I'm afraid of heights, but you do what you have to do.

Everything as ready as it could be, I sat back and chatted with Anderson and Mayo over the intercom as we flew. They wanted to know where Rachel was, and I filled them in on the fast approaching flight to Arizona and where Rachel was at the moment. They both agreed with me that she was going to be pissed that I'd run off without her. We talked about my recall to the Army and my newly acquired rank, then fell quiet as we all got lost in our own thoughts.

It wasn't a long flight and soon we were over the edge of the suburbs to the north of Atlanta. Out the right side of the aircraft, I could see the lake where we'd all met and shook my head at the thought that it seemed like weeks ago, not just a couple of days. Ahead of us smoke still rose from the ashes that had been downtown Atlanta. Beneath us, the trees thinned as we flew over more established residential areas. I kept my eyes open for other survivors, but all I saw moving were large groups of infected, all heading in a generally northern direction.

"Five minutes," Anderson's voice came over the intercom, giving me a heads up that we were almost to the target. "We've got enough fuel for 15 minutes on target, 20 if I go into the emergency reserves, then we either go, or we're walking part of the way back."

"Understood," I replied, already shifting mental gears as I prepared for the assault.

I triple checked the status and security of my weapons and spare magazines then slipped on a pair of gloves with heavy, leather palms that would protect my hands as I slid down the rope. The rope was coiled neatly on the floor of the helicopter and was ready to be deployed. Mayo and I had already checked the operation of the winch that would be used to get us back up into the helicopter when I had Gwen and Stacy.

"Fuck me, but look at that!"

Mayo's voice over the intercom pulled my attention to the open door. Looking out, I was shocked at the sheer number of infected that had crammed themselves into the neighborhood surrounding the house. Even though I'd seen it on the satellite image, it was still a staggering site in person. Three to four blocks in every direction the ground was not visible due to the tightly jammed mass of bodies.

As we zeroed in on the house, Anderson cut our speed and put the helicopter into a tight orbit so we could get a good view. The sun was setting, and while it wasn't still full daylight, there was plenty of light to see the infected. It seemed as if every face in the crowd of thousands was turned upwards, and for a moment, the infected pressed against the house stopped pounding and clawing on the walls as they looked up at the noisy helicopter.

"You sure you want to do this, Major?" Anderson asked.

"No choice," I replied. "Look at that shit. We're those kid's last chance."

Anderson didn't answer, probably didn't know what to say, and a moment later he pulled out of the orbit and brought the big Pave Hawk into a hover over the roof of our target. The house was a small two story with an attic on top of the second floor. There weren't any balconies or decks off the upper floors, but the infected had piled on top of each other until their hands were banging on the second story windows.

The windows appeared to have been boarded up from the inside, and with the proximity of the infected, I realized that my idea to go in an upper story window wasn't going to work. Oh well, there are other ways to gain entry. I reached into the pack I would be leaving behind in the helicopter and grabbed a zippered nylon bag that I clipped to my vest.

"Ready," Anderson said when he was comfortable the helicopter was in a stable hover.

Crucifixion

I kicked the rope out of the door, and it uncoiled smoothly, hitting the roof of the house, the final few feet slithering across the shingles and falling into the mass of enraged infected. Mayo called out heights and adjustments to Anderson and the helicopter gained a few feet of altitude, and the rope pulled out of the throng, two females hanging on to the end. I leaned out the open door and picked each of them off with my rifle, their bodies crashing down into the waiting arms of the herd.

"Switching to comms," I said, taking off the headset.

Unclipping from the safety tether that had kept me in the helicopter I stepped out the door and onto a small peg, wrapped my hands around the rope, pinched with my feet and dropped away from the aircraft.

Fast roping, while it may look like rappelling is actually nothing like it. You are not using a descender to control your speed, rather you slide down the rope just like a fireman going down the pole in a fire station. Even with the heavy leather palmed gloves my hands heated up, but not so much that I couldn't grip the rope and maintain a reasonable rate of descent.

Very quickly my boots hit the shingles, and I stepped away from the rope, holding it in one hand to keep control, so it didn't whip around and either knock me off the roof or tangle in my legs and drag me with it when the helicopter pulled away. Mayo, leaning out of the door and staring down at me gave me a thumbs up when I was clear of the rope and Anderson moved the Pave Hawk up and away from the house to go back into an orbit to wait for me.

The moans and screams of the infected were loud in my ears once the noise of the helicopter moved away. Below me at the rear wall of the house, they were continuing to pile on top of each other and hands were just a couple of feet from the lip of the roof, well above the second-floor windows. I checked the other three sides, moving carefully as a stumble and fall off the roof would be fatal, and found similar results everywhere I looked. I moved back to the middle of the roof and made a call on the secure comm unit.

"Mayo, I'm about to have company on the roof. Can you do something about these uninvited guests?"

"Fuckin' A, Major. Stand by."

The Pave Hawk stopped orbiting and settled into a stable hover 200 feet in the air. I could see Mayo, tethered in behind the door mounted minigun, calling adjustments to Anderson over the intercom. When the aircraft was where he wanted it, Mayo unleashed hell.

Crucifixion

A minigun doesn't sound like a gun. It sounds like a very loud and very angry swarm of bad ass bees. As I watched, a nearly solid stream of lead tore into the infected piling up against the house, and the bodies just disintegrated, all the blood and other fluids in them forming pinkish-red clouds that quickly settled.

Tearing my eyes away from the show, I zipped open the nylon pouch I had clipped to my vest. Inside was what looked like a thumb thick length of rope, but rope doesn't usually go boom. This was a breaching charge made of a specialized casing that was filled with a small amount of C-4 plastic explosive.

It was very flexible and could be molded to any surface in any shape, and when it was detonated the casing focused the force of the explosion and 'cut' through what it was attached to. I laid out a three by three-foot square, inserted four evenly spaced wireless detonators and moved to the far side of the roof.

Mayo was still firing the minigun, and it almost drowned out the heavy thump when I pushed the button to detonate the C-4. But, the explosion was still audible and rattled the roof underneath the soles of my boots. Stuffing the actuator back into the nylon pouch and zipping it up I trotted across the roof and looked down through the hole I had just made.

"Gwen! Stacy!" I shouted, hoping they were in the attic, and this would be easy. Unfortunately, as an old friend of mine who was a SEAL used to say, the only easy day was yesterday.

Pulling my rifle around I clicked on the rail mounted flashlight and stuck the barrel into the hole I'd just blown in the roof. Dust and small particles of floating debris choked the air, and the powerful beam of light didn't penetrate more than a few feet into the attic space. I crab-walked my way around the opening, shining the flashlight and trying to see any threats, but there was just too much dust in the air.

"Major, the infected are piling up faster than we can keep them knocked down," Anderson's voice came over my ear piece. "You've got maybe two minutes before the roof is compromised."

"Copy," I answered, made my decision and dropped through the hole in the roof.

My boots hit the rafters with my shoulders and head still above the roof line. Squatting, I got my head down into the attic, switched off the flashlight and dropped the NVGs – Night Vision Goggles – over my eyes. The entire space snapped into sharp focus in shades of green and black.

I scanned the attic and spotted two figures huddled together at the far end of the space, one of them holding a pistol aimed in my direction. I also noted the sound of the infected coming through the second-floor ceiling that I was standing on. They were in the house.

"Gwen," I called out, turning off the NVGs and clicking on a handheld flashlight that I aimed at myself so she could see I wasn't an infected. "I'm here to get you out. Come to me. We have to move."

"Who are you?" Her voice was weak and shaky, whether from fear or injury I didn't know.

"Remember a couple of weeks ago a man and woman in a truck gave you some food? That's me. I'm back, we've got a helicopter waiting, and we have to go. The infected are almost on the roof."

As if to emphasize my point Anderson spoke up on the comm channel, "Major, it's getting a little dangerous out here. You'd better get a move on."

"Copy," I answered. "Gwen, we have to go now, or we're going to die in here."

I started moving towards the two girls. Halfway there, one of the rafters I was walking on snapped under me and I crashed through the ceiling and on top of a group of infected that had squeezed into a small bedroom.

The rafter had snapped with no warning. No ominous creaking of wood stressed beyond its limit, no spongy feel beneath my feet, just SNAP! and I was falling. My brain sped up and wasted a blink of time thinking it was either termites or dry rot that had weakened the board, then my feet and legs were thrashing at the infecteds' eye level.

The rafter that had snapped had a couple of exposed nail heads, and my rifle's sling had caught on one of them. It had arrested my fall as the sling tightened around my chest and left shoulder, pinning the rifle tight to my body. Hands immediately started grabbing at my feet and legs, pulling hard. I started kicking, swinging from the single point where I was hanging from the nail, and I must have looked like a big, delicious piñata to the infected.

I grabbed an adjacent rafter and tried to pull myself back into the attic, but every time I gained a few inches an infected got a good purchase on one of my boots and pulled me back down. Rifle uselessly stuck against my body, I drew my pistol and started firing into the faces looking up at me.

I burned through 16 quick rounds, and the bodies were piling up, but that just gave a boost to the infected that were flooding into the room. They were climbing on top of the ones I had killed. Hands were now up to mid-thigh, and I could feel hungry mouths biting into my heavy combat boots. The thought of hands reaching higher and finding my balls caused a shiver to start at the base of my spine and go all the way up.

Still kicking and trying to swap magazines in my pistol one handed, I almost freaked out when hands grabbed me under my arms and started pulling. I looked up and met Gwen's eyes as she pulled for all she was worth. Flailing my feet, I felt heads bouncing off my kicks, had an idea and stopped kicking.

When I felt hands and mouths on my boots again, I pulled my legs up and stepped on the top of several heads and pushed off just as Gwen gave a big tug. I came far enough up into the attic to grab the rafter Gwen was sitting on, frantically pulling myself the rest of the way and quickly moving away from the hole in the ceiling.

"Major, infected on the roof!" Anderson's voice in my earpiece again.

Shit. So much for a quick and easy extraction. I crouched with my weight spread across two rafters and told Gwen and Stacy what was going on, instructing them to stay behind me. Daylight was fading quickly, and the attic was close to pitch black.

Foregoing the flashlight, I lowered my NVGs just in time to see a female infected drop through the hole I'd blown in the roof. I brought the rifle up and fired in the same motion, the high-velocity round nearly decapitating the woman. Two more dropped through the opening, and I shot them just as quickly then started duck walking towards the opening yelling for Gwen and Stacy to follow me.

I killed two more as they came in through the hole and spun when Gwen fired several shots from her pistol right behind me. The infected were piling up in the bedroom, and a female had started to climb through the breach in the ceiling.

Making it to the hole in the roof, I looked up as a female infected leaned over and screamed at me, maybe a couple of feet from my face. The rifle was up and at the ready, and I blew a hole through her throat, stood up and shoved the body away as I came back into open air. It was twilight, still too light for the NVGs, and I raised them off my eyes and scanned the roof.

The house was built on a slope, the upslope edge of the roof not as high off the ground, and this was where the infected were coming over the top. The big rotor of the Pave Hawk pounded the air above, and Mayo was still firing the minigun. He had four walls to keep clear and could only target two without having to have Anderson change the position of the helicopter. They were just repositioning over the shortest wall as I stepped onto the roof and shot two females that were charging towards me.

"Ready for extraction," I shouted over the rotor noise, knowing the small throat mic strapped to my neck didn't need me to raise my voice to be heard.

"Working on it," Anderson's voice came through my earpiece a moment later. "Mayo's trying to figure out how to control the winch and still keep the infected knocked back."

"Lower the goddamn line," I ordered. "I'll take care of the infected."

I was already running towards the edge of the roof as I spoke and was gratified to hear the minigun fall silent. Pulling two fragmentation grenades out of my vest, I stepped to the edge of the roof as Anderson brought the Pave Hawk into a low hover and nearly blew me over the side with the rotor wash. I looked over, bracing myself against the wind, and was astonished to see the seething mass of infected clawing their way over each other to get to the roof.

I kicked a couple of females in the face as they reached the edge of the roof, watching them tumble to the bottom of the pile, then pulled both grenade pins. Letting the spoons fly I dropped the grenades over the edge, aiming for a spot a few feet up from the bottom. Five seconds later both detonated within a fraction of a second of each other. I felt the concussion in my chest and was rewarded with the pile of infected collapsing into the void created by the falling bodies that were destroyed.

I turned and ran back to Gwen and Stacy, grabbing the braided steel cable with a canvas harness on the end as it dropped to roof level from the winch arm that extended out from the side of the hovering helicopter. There wasn't time for niceties, so I grabbed Stacy and slipped the harness over her head and shoulders, positioning the cable centered on the front of her body. Grabbing her hands, I wrapped them around the cable and raised my arm in the air and twirled my hand.

Mayo was on the ball, and her feet immediately left the roof as he winched her up. A quick scan of the roof and I spotted two different locations where hands were grasping the edge, and I readied my rifle in time to shoot the first female that climbed up onto the shingles. The body flipped over backwards and disappeared over the edge. More quickly followed and by the time the harness was on its way back down I'd already gone through a magazine and a half of ammunition.

Gwen was pressed against my back, and I could feel her shivering in fright as the volume of infected females reaching the roof increased. I was firing as fast as I could acquire targets, and the only good thing about the situation was the range was so short I was making every shot count.

Another magazine change and I had to shoot down two females that had reached the roof and covered half the distance to me in the time it took to make the swap. Damn, they were fast. I risked a glance behind and saw the harness dangling a foot off the roof and shouted for Gwen to get into it.

"How?" She yelled back.

"Just like I put it on Stacy. Get it over your shoulders and in your armpits and hang on to the cable."

I kept up my rate of fire while I yelled the instructions to her and was now having to defend three edges from infected. Fire, turn and acquire, fire, turn and acquire, fire. As fast as I could. I glanced behind me, and Gwen and the harness were gone. I didn't have time to look up to make sure she was OK.

The infected were coming onto the roof now in numbers that were greater than I could keep knocked down, and I had less than a minute before I would be overwhelmed. I was OK with that as the harness should be heading back down any moment and I'd be plucked to safety in plenty of time. That is if my rifle didn't jam, which it did the same instant the thought went through my head.

Fuck me if I didn't just jinx myself. No time to clear the misfire, I let the rifle drop and hang on its sling, whipped out my pistol and pulled the trigger on an empty chamber. Shit! I hadn't been able to load a new magazine when I was stuck in the attic and had committed the cardinal sin of carrying a weapon that was not ready to go.

I was out of time. Five females were on the roof, climbing and leaping over the bodies of the ones I'd shot as they charged my position and I was down to two edged weapons. I had a Ka-Bar fighting knife with an eight-inch blade and a Ka-Bar Kukri machete with a wicked twelve-inch curved blade.

One weapon in each hand, I met the first female as she charged, side stepping and slicing deep enough into her neck with the Kukri to sever her spinal cord. Kicking the body aside, I spun and buried the knife into the chest of the next, slicing into her heart and dropping her on the spot. I kept fighting. Slicing, stabbing, kicking and even punching. They were fast and strong, but they were still just enraged humans. None of them were large enough to present an individual threat, but if I went down they'd all be on me in a flash, and that would be the end of it.

Consumed by the fight, I had lost track of time and hadn't thought to look for the harness. Suddenly the whole roof and half a dozen females in front of me started disintegrating. I backpedaled and looked up to see Mayo manning the minigun again and Gwen leaning out of the open side door of the helicopter waving at me like a maniac. The line extended down from the winch and the harness lay on the roof ten feet away.

Diving for it as Mayo adjusted fire, I slipped it over my head and slashed open the throat of an attacking female as the winch took up the slack and began pulling me up. I was only a few feet up in the air when another female sprang onto the roof, saw me dangling there and leapt forward with a great bound. She launched herself off the body of the female I had just killed, screaming as she zeroed in on her prey.

Trying to make her miss, I pulled my legs up and twisted away, but she slammed into my lower body and wrapped her arms around me with an iron grip. Immediately she attacked, biting my upper thighs through the heavy fabric of the uniform pants. Fortunately, humans don't have sharp teeth and serious bite pressure like a dog, so she couldn't actually bite through my clothing, but she was able to get a mouthful of flesh in her jaws and son of a bitch if it didn't hurt.

Bare skin would have torn open, but the heavy fabric protected me to a degree. Grunting in pain, I pounded on the top of her head with the hilt of the Kukri, but she was like a Pit Bull and wasn't letting go other than to bite down on a new chunk of flesh on my inner thigh. Damn that hurt, and it was way too close to a really sensitive area.

We were now winched all the way up to the helicopter and hung suspended in the air just in front of the open side door. Mayo had stopped firing and sat three feet away staring at me with his mouth hanging open. The bitch bit down again, even higher this time and I roared in pain and pounded even harder on her head. It still did no good, her grip not loosening in the least.

Now pain has a way of distracting you, and the pain from the bites had distracted me from what I was holding in my hands. Instead of pounding on her head, I should be stabbing or slicing. Reversing the knife in my grip, I stabbed into the side of her neck, ramming it in to the hilt and sawed away from my body, feeling the blade bite into her spine. Her grip instantly loosened and she fell away, Ka-Bar still stuck in her neck.

Mayo snapped back into action and reached out for my now empty hand. I grabbed his wrist, and he let out slack on the winch as he pulled me into the helicopter where I collapsed on the vibrating deck. He pulled the harness off over my head, snapped a safety tether to my vest and left me alone as I rolled into a ball with my hands tucked protectively between my legs, pressing on the spots that hurt the worst.

The deck of the helicopter was hard with an anti-skid coating sprayed on it. I noted this as my face rested on the rough, textured surface and I pressed on the tender areas where the infected female had clamped down on me. She had managed to get her teeth on the very upper portion of my inner thighs, and only good luck had kept her from getting a mouth full of balls, or worse.

The pain was intense, but not as intense as it could have been. We were in flight and since I wasn't a pilot, and not needed at the moment, I was happy to stay right where I was. Curled in the fetal position and feeling sorry for myself.

"Stacy! What's wrong?"

It was the tone of Gwen's voice that made the small hairs on my arms stand up. Shoving the pain aside, I sat up and looked around to where the two girls had been huddling at the back of the helicopter. Gwen was kneeling over her sister who was laying on the deck and convulsing violently.

Mayo and I both moved at the same time. I pushed Gwen aside as Mayo grabbed a first aid kit that was mounted to a bulkhead, ripped it open and kneeled next to me with a Syrette of Morphine. I was cradling Stacy's head in my lap to keep her from fracturing her skull on the hard deck. Trying to restrain her enough to prevent injury, I jerked back when she suddenly let out with an ear piercing scream, then went perfectly still, staring up into my eyes.

"What's wrong with her? Help her?" Gwen screamed and tried to push in to reach her sister, but I held her back.

Mayo had the Morphine Syrette poised in mid-air, looking to me for instructions. That was when it happened. Stacy's eyes bulged nearly out of their sockets, for all the world looking like a cartoon character who's eyes pop out of their head in exaggerated surprise. When I thought they could grow no larger, the whites were flooded with red as every capillary in her eyes burst, then they receded back to their normal position.

"Back!" I shouted, scrambling away and letting Stacy's head fall to the deck with a solid thud.

Mayo and I put as much distance between us and Stacy as we could. I cast around, looking for the Kukri I had dropped on the deck when I made it into the helicopter. Spotting it a few feet away, I dove for it as Stacy leapt to her feet with a scream, looked around and launched herself at Mayo. I'll never know why she ignored Gwen, who was right next to her. Perhaps even infected she recognized her sister or more likely Mayo was just the first person she saw, but she tackled him to the deck.

They rolled over twice, getting tangled in his safety tether which effectively tied their legs together. He wound up on his back trying to hold her snapping teeth away from his flesh. Kukri in hand, I stepped behind Stacy, grabbed a fistful of hair, yanked to raise her head and swung the machete.

"Nooooooo!"

Gwen's scream of agony was loud even over the roar of the Pave Hawk as her sister's head was sliced from her body and left swinging by the hair balled into my fist. Bright red blood poured out of the cut and began covering the deck. I hadn't intended to behead the poor girl, my only thought being to save Mayo. Shit.

I looked around the bloody compartment. Mayo stared at me from the deck, covered in blood with a shocked look on his face. Gwen stared at me from the rear of the compartment. More accurately she stared at her little sister's head that was still swinging in my fist from the motion of the helicopter. A low moan came from her, rising in pitch to become a keening wail as she sank to her knees and buried her face in her hands.

I stood there for a long moment, head dangling from my hand and blood continuing to drip onto the deck. Mayo was still frozen in place, breathing hard. Gwen had rolled onto her side, her whole body shaking as she sobbed. Not knowing what else to do I tossed the severed head out of the open door.

Kneeling down, I helped Mayo untangle from the tether that held the body pressed on top of him. Freeing him, I lifted Stacy's body, and it followed her head through the open door. I watched it pinwheel through the air as it fell until it disappeared in the thick forest several hundred feet below us.

Mayo retrieved the headset that had been knocked off in the scuffle, and I could see him talking into it, filling in Anderson up in the cockpit. The noise of the helicopter in flight was too loud for me to hear what he was saying, but I had my own concerns. What the hell had just happened?

The nerve agent was only supposed to be effective for a maximum of 48 hours. Stacy had been fine two weeks ago when I'd first met her and was fine when we winched her up into the aircraft. The only thing that made sense was the briefing I had received earlier in the day was wrong. How many of us were about to become infected?

I watched Gwen closely, but she just lay in a ball on the deck sobbing. Mayo, who had had lots of contact with Stacy and was covered in her blood, looked completely freaked out but otherwise seemed fine. I looked down at my blood stained hands, and a little thrill of fear ran through me.

Something about bio-weapons has always terrified me. Probably because it's not something I can see and fight. Putting aside fears that I couldn't do anything about, I grabbed one of the headsets and slipped it on my head. As soon as the noise canceling kicked in I could hear Mayo and Anderson speaking. Not waiting to find out what they were discussing I cut in on the conversation.

"Anderson, can you get me on the radio with flight ops at Arnold?" I asked, lowering myself into a web sling seat and keeping my distance from Gwen.

"Can do, Major. Stand by."

The headset went silent for a few moments then Anderson's voice came back, "Major, go ahead for Arnold flight operations."

"Arnold, Major Chase here. I need to speak to Major Masuka. Immediately."

"Wait one, Sir."

It was actually more than one, more like five before I heard Masuka's voice in the headset.

"Major, I'm pretty busy right now. Can't this wait until you're back?"

"Are we on private comms?" I asked.

There was silence for a moment, then a hum and click. "We're private. What do you need?"

"We rescued two teenage girls. Both were healthy when we got them into the aircraft, but one of them just turned right in front of me. The intelligence that the nerve agent is no longer a threat seems to be flawed."

I kept an eye on Gwen and Mayo both while I spoke. One surprise for the day was enough.

"Repeat that," she requested.

From the tone of her voice I could tell she had heard me just fine but wasn't processing the bad news, so I repeated myself. After a few moments of silence, she acknowledged she understood.

"Find an Army Colonel named Crawford," I said. "He's either still at Arnold or has recently left for Fort Campbell. He needs to know about this ASAP. And I would suggest you get some armed MPs into flight ops right away."

"Understood," was her only reply, then another click and she was gone.

"How long to Arnold?" I asked Anderson over the intercom.

"Uh... twenty minutes, Major. You want me to step it up?"

I didn't even hesitate, "Yes. Get us on the ground as fast as you can."

The noise and vibration increased as Anderson pushed the Pave Hawk to its top speed. Gwen still hadn't moved. Mayo had found a blood borne pathogen response kit in a storage compartment and was washing as much of the blood off his skin as he could with a large squeeze bottle of Hydrogen Peroxide. He held it out towards me, and I gratefully extended my hands.

The liquid bubbled when it hit the blood on my hands, and I rubbed them together, scrubbing as well as I could. When we were as clean as could be for the moment, he used the rest of the bottle to hose down the blood that was congealing on the deck, but nothing short of a fire hose was going to get this helicopter clean.

Twelve minutes later I felt our speed and altitude change and looked out the door. We were over the outer perimeter of Arnold AFB, and Anderson was taking us straight into the flight line we had departed from. A couple of minutes later he flared only a dozen feet above the pavement and set us on the ground with a barely perceptible thump, executing a textbook perfect dust out or combat landing.

I've flown with a lot of Viet Nam era pilots that perfected the dust out landing, and Anderson did it as well as any seasoned vet. Moving to the back of the space, I bent down and touched Gwen's shoulder, pulling my hand back when she jerked away and swung at me. She looked at me with eyes swollen and red from crying, and I could see the hate burning in them.

"Go ahead, Major. I've got this," Mayo said softly as he secured the minigun.

I nodded my thanks to him and looked Gwen back in the eye.

"I'm sorry," I said.

I knew I didn't have any choice once Stacy turned, but that didn't mean I didn't feel like shit about what I'd had to do. Turning away, I stepped to the door and jumped the few feet down to the pavement. Just as my boots hit the ground, gunfire erupted from the direction of the flight operations building. Leaning back in the door, I yelled at Anderson to get the helicopter refueled and stay with it, grabbed my pack and took off at a fast run towards flight ops as the sound of a rifle on full auto reached my ears.

Flight operations was a couple of hundred yards from the flight line, and as I ran an additional rifle on full auto sounded. Damn it. Didn't the Air Force train their personnel not to waste ammo?

Regardless of popular conception based on movies, full auto is almost never the way to go. The rifle is hard as hell to hold on your target, and you will wind up spraying bullets uselessly all over the place, hitting nothing. These guys needed to be using semi-auto or burst mode and picking their targets.

Pounding across the pavement, I angled towards a steel access door set in the wall facing me, bringing my rifle to the ready position as I closed inside 50 yards. As I approached the door, it slammed open, and two figures tumbled through and fell to the ground. They were both dressed in Air Force uniforms, and I had to close within a few feet before I could tell which was the infected and which wasn't.

They rolled over and the infected wound up on top, grasping its victim and struggling to reach his throat. I stepped in and kicked the infected in the side of the head. I was wearing steel toed combat boots, and if I had been an NFL kicker would have just made a field goal from the 50-yard line.

The infected's head caved in, and the body went limp. I reached down and grabbed the back of its belt and hauled the dead body off the struggling man. Tossing the infected aside, I reached a hand down and was surprised when I pulled Captain Roach to his feet.

Roach was in the Air Force Security Forces – the Air Force version of an MP – and I'd had a run-in with the officious little prick when we had landed the previous night. I'd won the battle and we'd not parted as friends. Fortunately, my newly minted oak leaf carried more authority than his Captain's bars, so it looked like I had won the war as well.

"You're on me," I told him, yanked the door to flight ops open and stepped inside.

I found myself in a lighted hallway lined with offices. The sounds of a firefight were louder and coming from the far end of the building. Rifle at my shoulder I started advancing down the hall, not waiting to see if Roach was following.

I bypassed closed doors. I had yet to encounter an infected that could work a door knob. Open doors, however, slowed me down as I had to clear each room before proceeding, not willing to risk leaving an infected to my rear. I thought about just closing the doors and moving on, but opted for clearing each unsecured room as I went. The first two rooms I cleared were empty of personnel, but the third was occupied.

A female clerk huddled behind an overturned conference table as an infected male officer leaned over the edge and tried to reach her. He was snarling and waving his arms in frustration but didn't have enough mental faculties remaining to just pull the table out of his way. Conserving ammo, I drew the Kukri and buried half the blade in the back of his neck, severing his spinal column.

He dropped without a sound and I motioned the girl, an Air Force Airman, to stay put. Exiting the office, I closed the door behind me to keep her safe and was pleasantly surprised to see Roach standing in the hall with his pistol in hand at low ready, scanning back and forth for any threats. He was still a prick.

Moving on down the hall, I cleared two more rooms, both empty, and started up the stairs to the second floor where the large flight operations center was located. The firing had stopped, and that was either a good thing – all of the infected had been put down, or a bad thing – the infected had won the battle. The stairs were two half flights with a landing in the middle that forced an 180-degree turn to continue up.

Rifle raised to engage any targets on the stairs above, I stepped onto the landing and swiveled to cover the upper flight of stairs. An infected female screamed and launched herself down the stairs when she saw me. I pulled the trigger, and the rifle spat out a three round burst that stitched across her chest and head. All animation left the body, and its momentum carried it down the stairs to crash into the wall next to me.

Stepping over the body, I slowly climbed the upper flight and paused at the top. Hundreds of spent shell casings lay on the shiny floor, the walls and ceiling ripped apart by the inaccurate, full auto firing I had heard. Three dead infected lay in the hall, pools of blood looking even redder against the polished linoleum.

The double doors that led into the operations center were closed and also showed damage from multiple bullet strikes. Moving to the left side of the double doors, I motioned Roach to take up position on the right. I listened for a moment and could hear movement from inside the ops center, but couldn't tell if it was survivors or infected.

Meeting Roach's eyes with mine, I gave hand signals to indicate I heard movement and was going to open the door. He pushed his shoulder into the wall, adjusted his grip on his pistol and nodded. Using the barrel of my rifle, I gently pushed on the door, and it started to swing in. Immediately, full auto fire blasted through the wood, showering the hall as well as Roach and me with splinters.

"Cease fire! Friendlies coming in," I shouted.

Roach started to step in front of the door, but I stopped him. Just because I had yelled out didn't mean whoever was firing that rifle wasn't still so freaked out, they wouldn't open up on anything that moved. After a moment a female voice I recognized as Major Masuka called out for us to come ahead. Stepping in front of the door, I pushed it open with my left elbow as I kept my rifle up and ready. The rifle's muzzle was the first thing to enter the room then I pushed the door all the way open and stepped fully into the opening.

Bodies were everywhere in the room, and it stank of blood, bowels, and gun powder. Most of the flat panel displays that were mounted on the walls were shattered, and the entire bank of windows that faced the flight line had been blown out by gunfire. I just had time to take this all in before my legs were nearly taken out from under me.

Dog, frantically happy to see me, forgot that he weighed over 100 pounds and wouldn't stop jumping against me until I leaned over, hugged him with one arm and scratched his belly with my free hand. Straightening up, I came face to face with

Rachel, who wrapped her arms around me for a quick hug then stepped back and punched my chest. Hard.

"That's for going off without us," she said and went back across the room where she had been giving first aid to the injured.

I heard a snort from Roach behind me, and I thought about turning around and breaking his nose for him. Fortunately, for him, Masuka walked over to me just then.

"Your heads up saved a lot of people," she said, holding a compress to her arm.

"What happened to you?" I asked, gesturing at the bandage.

"Stray round," she replied. "It happens."

She tried to shrug it off. I looked around the room and spotted two Airmen in full battle rattle, rifles held across their chests, standing at the far end of the room.

"Yours?" I asked, turning to Roach.

He nodded his head. Turning to the two MPs, I whistled to get their attention and waved them over to where I was standing. They glanced at each other then walked timidly across the room, stepping over bodies, and came to attention in front of me. I told them to stand at ease.

Crucifixion

"Were you two the ones doing all the firing on full auto?" I asked.

The Senior Airman, senior of the two, swallowed audibly before answering, "Yes, Sir."

"Good work keeping these people safe," I said. "But, I want you to put those rifles in semi mode and practice some fire discipline. If you get caught out in the open and go rock 'n roll, you'll burn through your ammo too fast and wind up somebody's lunch. Understand?"

They both acknowledged and stepped away when Captain Roach motioned them to follow him out to the hall. When they moved away, I went over to Masuka.

"Did you get word to Colonel Crawford?" I asked.

"Yes. A Black Hawk out of Fort Campbell picked him up a while ago, and I got word to him over the radio."

"Did he make it to Fort Campbell?"

"Don't know, and haven't had time to check. We've got two Globemasters orbiting while we dealt with this, whatever the hell this is, and..."

A massive explosion from the far end of the flight line cut off whatever it was she was about to say.

The night lit up as a giant ball of flame engulfed two hangars and several parked fighter jets. With the heavy glass windows that faced the flight line blown out, there was nothing to shield us from the shockwave that slammed into the room seconds later. What few shards of glass had remained in the window frames became shrapnel as the wave of air blasted through, and more bodies hit the floor, several of them screaming in pain. When my hearing returned a few heartbeats later, I could hear sirens sounding the alarm.

The explosion and fireball had been large and intense enough to create a small mushroom cloud, just like a miniature nuclear weapon. As the flames fed the superheated air, the cloud was lit from within and looked like a gate to hell had opened up. I spun at the sound of a scream from across the room that was uniquely different from those of the wounded.

A female infected wearing an Air Force enlisted uniform leapt up onto a console and screamed again at a group of co-workers that were huddling behind another console. I snapped my rifle up, flipping the selector to semi-auto as I brought it to my shoulder then squeezed the trigger. The infected's head snapped to the side then her body fell limp to the floor. What the fuck was going on?

I swung my rifle around at the sound of running boots behind me, but it was only Roach and the two MPs responding to my firing the rifle. Roach looked in the direction I pointed, saw the dead infected and quickly sent his two men to opposite sides of the room. I was surprised and gratified to hear him repeat my admonishment about keeping their rifles on semi mode. Lowering the rifle, I turned back to find that Rachel had moved up next to me.

"This place is about to completely fall apart," she said in a low voice. "We need to get out of here while we still can."

I nodded. She was right. I didn't know if there had been another release of the nerve agent, or if it had a delayed reaction on some people, but in a group didn't seem like the safest place to be at the moment. I walked over to where Masuka was intently listening on a field radio. She held up a finger in the 'one minute' gesture as I approached.

"Copy that," she said and handed the handset back to a radio operator who was standing at her side.

"Infected attacked a maintenance crew while they were refueling an F-18," she said. "Firearms and jet fuel aren't a good combination."

I started to respond, but movement on the flight line caught my attention. Dozens of figures were silhouetted against the fire, and all were shambling towards us. I pointed, and Masuka turned to look, cursing when she saw the infected. Other people in the room noticed us and looked and a swell of voices raised in panic. It was time for me to take charge. Grabbing Masuka's arm, I pulled her attention away from the infected stumbling across the tarmac outside the windows.

"We need to get these people to a secure area," I said. "I don't know this base. Where do we take them?"

"There's a fallout shelter in the basement of this building," she replied.

"No good," I said. "Fallout shelters have one way in and out and the infected will pile up outside that door and trap us. We'll only survive as long as the food and water lasts. The flight I was supposed to be on tomorrow morning. Is that plane here? Do we have a pilot?"

"It's not here. It's due in from McConnell in a few hours." She was referring to McConnell Air Force Base, which was a couple of hundred miles southwest of Kansas City near the Oklahoma border.

Crucifixion

"OK, what about those Globemasters you said were orbiting? Can we get one on the ground and start evacuating?"

I was getting antsy as I watched the infected move closer to the building we were in. We needed to move, but I wasn't getting much help in coming up with where to go.

Masuka turned to her radio operator and started barking orders. Even before she was through he had the handset to his head and was presumably talking to the pilots. After a few moments, he lowered the handset and looked at Masuka and me.

"Foxtrot one seven is diverting to McConnell. Foxtrot one nine is lining up for a landing and will be on the ground in five minutes."

I didn't wait for Masuka.

"Everyone form up in a group," I raised my voice loud enough to be heard over the moaning of the wounded and the hubbub of frightened conversation in the room. "If you're not armed, help the injured. If you are armed, I want you on the perimeter of the group. We're going to evacuate to the flight line and board a Globemaster that is inbound."

Everyone stared at me, only a couple of older Sergeants starting to move. We didn't have time for this.

"Move now or you're going to die!" I shouted, galvanizing everyone into action.

I turned to Roach and told him he was bringing up the rear. I would take point and lead the group out of the building and out to the flight line. I spent a few seconds checking my weapons and spare magazines, then went over to the body of a fallen MP near the door and collected five full rifle magazines from his harness. Rachel had her pack on, rifle in her hands, and I handed her two of the magazines and kept three for myself. Telling her to stay close I activated my radio to check in on Anderson and Mayo.

"Anderson, you up on the net?" We hadn't been on a planned mission and didn't have designated call signs.

"Go ahead, Major." His reply came back almost instantly.

"What's your status?"

"Fueling complete. Mayo found ammo for the minigun and is loading us up right now. We're ready to go when you are, which had better be soon. There's a lot of infected headed this way."

Crucifixion

"Copy. Moving to the flight line with a group of survivors. Got a big bird inbound and the plan is to evac on it. Get your passenger ready to move and keep an eye on her. People are still turning."

"Copy that," he replied. "We'll be ready."

By now the survivors had formed up into a tight group. Eight unarmed people helped four wounded, and I spent a moment getting us into a movement formation with me at the point and Rachel right on my ass. Roach's two MPs flanked the group, and Roach was at the rear. I bent and retrieved the rifle and three more magazines from the dead MP, handed them to Roach, then moved back to the front of the small group and pulled the doors to the hallway open.

I had to immediately engage two infected males who had been feasting on a body in the hall. Both went down before they could rise and I moved into the hallway, stepping over the bodies. Dog took up position to my right front as we moved, head and tail lowered but ears straight up as he stayed alert for any threat.

The hallway to my left led deeper into the building and was clear. Ahead was the top of the stairs and I moved forward, rifle ready and aiming down the stairwell ahead of my line of sight. Behind me I could hear the group moving, making more noise than I wanted as several feet kicked spent shells sending them tinkling across the hard floor.

Dog trotted down the upper flight of stairs, stopping on the landing. The fur along his back stiffened and went straight on end as he let out a low growl. I moved quickly to stand beside him, swinging the rifle's aim down to the lower stairs. Approaching were three infected males, and I decided to keep us as quiet as I could. I had a sound suppressor for the rifle in my pack, but I didn't have time to dig it out.

Holding up a clenched fist, I signaled for the group behind me to stop as I lowered the rifle. Drawing the Kukri, I descended the lower stairs and moved forward to meet the infected. The first infected I reached was wearing Air Force blue coveralls with Tech Sergeant's stripes and grease stains on the sleeves. He looked like one of the ground crew that had helped with the pre-flight on the Pave Hawk earlier that afternoon. He wasn't that man anymore.

Leading with the tip of the Kukri I rammed it into his throat, then torqued it, so the blade sliced up into his skull as I pushed. The body dropped, and I yanked the machete free and met the next infected who was wearing sweat pants and an Air Force Academy T-Shirt. He was younger and in great physical shape and moved faster than any male I had encountered so far. Not as fast as the females, but fast enough to make me adjust my swing with the Kukri and miss slicing into his neck as the blade cut into his upper arm and got stuck in the bone.

In a flash he was on me, trying to wrap me up as his snapping jaws sought out my face. I had already released the handle of the Kukri and got my arms in front of me. Hands flat on his chest, I shoved with all my strength. He flew backwards, tumbling to the hallway floor, the blade of the machete popping free from his arm when he fell. The momentary distraction with him allowed the third infected to move in and grasp my left arm with an inhumanly strong grip.

Reaching across my body with my right hand, I grabbed his wrist and turned my whole body, breaking his grip and pulling his arm into a cross lock. With a quick jerk I snapped his elbow, but for all his reaction I might as well have hit him with a feather pillow. He kept coming forward, grabbing with his good arm and trying to grab with his broken arm. By now the infected I had knocked to the floor was back on his feet and pressing the attack.

OK, fuck quiet. These weren't normal humans that could be subdued in hand to hand combat. Shoving hard against each of them, I gained a few feet of space, drew my pistol and shot each in the head. Scooping up the Kukri and sheathing it I shouted for the group to start moving again as I brought my rifle back to the ready position. They quickly filed down the stairs and stacked up behind me in the hall.

We moved forward again as a group, several soft gasps sounding from behind me as we passed the bodies on the floor. Reaching the closed door where I had left the young woman earlier, I paused our movement and tapped on the door with the barrel of my rifle. No screaming or pounding from within the room so I turned the knob and cracked the door open, ready to fire if anyone or anything charged at me.

The woman was still huddled behind the overturned table, eyes wide in fear. I motioned her to come to me, but she was frozen in place. Reading the situation, Rachel stepped past me into the room, talking to the frightened woman in a calming voice. A minute later she had her on her feet and rejoined the group, giving the woman an assignment of helping with the wounded. I had maintained watch on the remainder of the hall and the exit ahead while Rachel brought the woman out to the group, and started moving forward again when I felt Rachel's hand on top of my left shoulder.

"Major," Anderson's voice came over my earpiece.

"Go," I replied in a low voice, keeping my focus on the exit door at the end of the hall.

"It's getting damn scary out here. Infected are coming from every direction. Seems like there's a major outbreak, and the explosion and fire are drawing them in."

"What's your status?"

"Aircraft is fueled, re-armed and ready to go, but we're going to have to start burning through ammo real quick. We've got a pretty large group headed our way."

"Copy," I replied. "Get your ass in the air and stay in the area. I'm about to exit flight ops with a group of survivors. That Globemaster should be touching down any minute, and I'll probably need air support to get these people on board."

"Copy that," he replied, and I could already hear the Pave Hawk's engines spooling up over the radio. "We'll be on station when you need us."

10

I pushed out through the metal exit door, and the first thing that hit me was the smell of burning jet fuel from the massive fire at the far end of the flight line. The fire was close to half a mile away, but it was large enough to light up the entire area. Silhouetted between me and the fire were hundreds of infected, some heading in our direction, others apparently mesmerized by the flames and just standing there staring.

Closer to the fire several figures stumbled along as their clothing burned. As I watched, they eventually fell to the ground. There were a couple of dozen infected males within 50 yards of us, and I started firing single head shots, dropping them as we moved forward. Behind and to my left another rifle started firing single shots, and the two of us quickly dispatched all the infected that were too close for comfort. When the last one fell, I glanced around, expecting to see Roach, but Rachel smiled at me and lowered her rifle. I guess the time on the firing range had paid off.

Overhead, I could hear the heavy rotor of the Pave Hawk as Anderson kept it in a tight orbit over the area. Masuka came forward and touched my arm and pointed off to the right, her arm indicating a spot a few degrees above the horizon. I looked and saw an impossibly large jet that appeared to be hanging suspended in the air. The optical illusion was quickly dispelled as it grew larger by the second.

The Globemaster is the heavy lift aircraft for the Air Force. It's almost two hundred feet in length, with a wingspan as wide as the aircraft is long. They are capable of carrying armor and troops anywhere in the world and are one of the largest aircraft in the US Military inventory.

As I watched, the pilot brought the gigantic plane down onto the runway closest to us and the four massive engines roared loud enough to shake the ground when he activated the thrust reversers to slow down. The plane rolled for a long way as speed bled off then the noise reduced as it rolled to a stop and the engines were throttled back to idle. I glanced around in dismay as every infected in sight zeroed in on the new arrival and started towards it.

"OK people, double time. Let's move!" I shouted and started running, leading the way towards the idling jet.

We were several hundred yards from the Globemaster, and I couldn't count the number of infected that were in our way. The only good news here is that the military is predominantly male, so there were very few fast moving females to deal with. A couple of them noticed our small group and broke away from the main body that was collapsing in on the plane and sprinted directly for us. Dropping to a knee, I brought down one of them while she was still over 100 yards out, missed the second one with my follow on shot, then split her head open when I fired again.

The group had stopped behind me when I went to my knee, but they stayed close with me when I rose and started running again. Males were shambling towards us on our flanks and rifle fire started up behind me as we ran. I was glad to hear single shots; not full magazines being emptied in a couple of seconds. I slowed our run to a fast trot to help us aim better and started engaging targets directly to our front as the converging males took notice of us and started turning to attack.

I burned through my first magazine, did a quick change and started firing again. My accuracy was suffering due to running while I was shooting, often taking two or three shots for each infected. Slowing down to a walk was not an attractive option though as time was not on our side. We still had at least three hundred yards to go to reach the plane.

"Anderson," I called on my comm unit.

"Go for Anderson." The response was immediate.

Crucifixion

"We need some air support down here. Too many infected in the way. We're not going to make our ride."

"Stand by, Major." A few seconds later he was back, "Major, turn on your strobe."

I reached up to my shoulder and flipped the switch on a small infrared strobe light attached to my vest. Light in the IR spectrum can't be seen by the human eye but it would be very visible to Mayo through his NVGs and would let him keep us spotted and hopefully not hose us down with the minigun.

"Got you," Mayo's voice came over my earpiece.

A few moments later the Pave Hawk roared into a low hover a hundred feet over our heads and the minigun started chewing up the infected in front of us. A red tracer was placed in the ammo belt at a ratio of one for every 100 rounds, but the rate of fire of the minigun is so high that it looked like a solid stream of red reaching down and destroying the infected to our front.

Mayo used very controlled bursts to both conserve ammo as well as more effectively keep the weapon on target. Quickly, a nice wide path opened up, and I took down the half dozen infected that had been too close to us for Mayo to engage. When the last one in front of me dropped, I noticed there were no sounds of firing behind me. Glancing back, I saw the two MPs just standing there watching the light show from the minigun. Infected were closing on our flanks, and they weren't paying any attention.

Spinning, I fired twice at the right flank, each round finding its target and dropping an approaching male. Rachel turned with me, saw the danger and started firing at the left flank, killing an infected, moments before it would have wrapped up the MP on that side in a deathly bear hug. I ran back to the left flank and slapped the MP hard on the side of his helmet before getting in his face.

"You dumb motherfucker," I shouted, my nose an inch from his. "If you want to die, let me know, and I'll drop you myself. You will pay attention, and you will keep these people safe. Am I fucking clear?!"

"Yes, Sir!" he shouted back, eyes wide with fear.

I held his eyes for half a second, looked over at the other MP to make sure he'd gotten the message then glanced back at Roach, who wasn't there. Shit. I scanned the tarmac behind us but couldn't tell which of the multiple bodies might be his. Grabbing the MP, I'd just dressed down, I shoved him to the rear of the group and told him he was on rear guard. Running to the front, I sent

Rachel to the left flank, told Dog to go with her, and started running towards the plane again.

The path that Mayo had cleared was already collapsing as more infected pushed into the area and I yelled for the group behind me to move faster. Rifles started firing behind me, and I was burning through a lot of ammunition to keep the path open. I was about to call Mayo on the comm unit when the Pave Hawk roared back into a hover, and the minigun opened up again. Bodies started disintegrating from the heavy slugs which continued on through them to also shred the pavement.

We ran through the aftermath of this, the air thick with a fog of pulverized asphalt mixed with body fluids from the devastated flesh of the infected. Sure wish I had a mask on. We still had a good distance to go when the minigun fire ceased, infected quickly moving into the open space it had carved.

"Minigun is jammed," Mayo's voice told me over my ear piece.

Not bothering to acknowledge, I changed rifle magazines again and slowed so I could maintain a level of accurate fire, but there were so many infected the herd was closing in faster than I could shoot them. Even though the three rifles behind me were firing single shots, they were all firing as fast as their triggers could be pulled. I was worried that nerves were getting the best of Rachel and the two MPs, and they weren't hitting anything, but I couldn't spare a moment to check. Three females were pushing through the lumbering males, and one of them had just broken free of the press of bodies and was sprinting directly at me.

I had her head lined up for a shot when a body slammed into me from the side, very nearly knocking me to the ground. Reflexively my finger pulled the trigger and the round punched into the female's body instead of her head. She stumbled for a step, then resumed her sprint.

I glanced to the side and saw Major Masuka on the ground wrestling with an infected female that had apparently sprinted into the flank and tackled her. The two of them had then slammed into me. Taking care of the more immediate threat first, I pulled my pistol to engage the sprinting female to my front who was now almost close enough to touch. Whipping the pistol up, I fired just as she launched herself into the air. The heavy bullet destroyed her face and punched out the back of her skull, but the corpse was already in motion and slammed into me, knocking me back onto my ass.

Kicking the body away, I scrambled back to my feet, grabbed the long hair of the infected that was on top of Masuka and yanked the female into the air. A badly bleeding Masuka scrambled to her feet as I tossed the infected a yard in front of me. A male tripped over the female and fell on top of her, giving me a moment to holster my pistol and bring my rifle to bear.

Two fast shots dispatched each of them then I raised my aim, searching for the two other females. They were less than 10-yards away, and I snapped off two more quick shots to put them down. More males pushed in as they fell and there was nearly a 50-yard deep wall of flesh between us and the plane.

"Get that goddamn minigun going!" I shouted into the comm unit.

Blasting through the remainder of the magazine, I put in a fresh one but instead of starting to fire I grabbed a grenade off my vest, yanked the pin with my teeth – always wanted to do that and it only took the apocalypse to make it happen – counted to three and tossed it deep into the mass of bodies in front of me. A heartbeat later it detonated and cleared a small area. I repeated the process with five more grenades until I was out, then brought the rifle up and started dropping infected again.

The firing behind me was still at a furious pace, and I could hear three distinct rifles, so I was reasonably confident our rear and flanks were still intact. Males kept pressing in all around us, and I was about ready to go full auto just to keep them out of grabbing range when a machine gun started hammering away from the side, cutting a swath through the infected.

I didn't have time to look and see who had joined the fight, rather maintained my rate of fire to keep a couple of yards of clear space in front of me. We were no longer moving, having bogged down completely in the crush of bodies, but after a minute of well-placed machine gun fire I was able to start slowly moving forward, shouting for the group to stay tight on my back. I kept firing, the rifles behind me still in action and the machine gun hammered away and bit by bit we began moving faster despite having to continually step over infected bodies that littered the ground.

Finally reaching the far side of the herd of infected I sped up to a fast jog, looking around to make sure the group was staying with me. It looked like everyone was there except for Roach. Major Masuka was starting to lag behind, her uniform blouse soaked in blood from the nasty looking bite marks on her arms and face. I could only see three infected still between us and the plane and I slowed but shouted at the group to keep running.

Taking careful aim, I dropped the three in front of us then turned to the rear as the last of the group passed me. A solid wall of infected stared back at me as they shambled forward, arms raised as they sought out their prey. I did a quick scan and didn't see or hear any females, turned and trotted after the group.

Looking around as I ran I spotted our saviors. An up-armored Humvee with a pintle mounted machine gun was sitting 50 yards to our right, a carpet of dead infected surrounding it. I didn't recognize the driver or gunner, but couldn't have been happier to see them. I waved, and the gunner waved back as the driver pulled forward and positioned the vehicle between my group and the pursuing infected. The gunner opened up and knocked the first few ranks of bodies down, the driver turning and following us to serve as rear guard.

Ahead I saw Masuka stumble and go down to her knees. I ran forward and waved the MP on that flank away as I scooped her up and over my shoulder. Burden secured, I ran to catch the group. Behind me the machine gun sounded occasionally, keeping the infecteds' advance to a minimum. There was a scream from a female and another burst from the machine gun silenced the bitch.

Overhead, the Pave Hawk returned to hover, and I stopped and turned to watch. The minigun started firing, and Mayo walked it down the whole front rank of the herd, then reversed direction and adjusted fire into the main mass. Bodies either fell or just disintegrated, depending on how many of the high-velocity slugs struck them. The effect was absolute hell on earth.

No mortal army could endure that kind of punishment and not break and run for cover. But the infected weren't like any mortal army on Earth. They showed no fear. No awareness that what was happening to the ones in front of them was about to happen to them. They kept coming, stumbling over the body parts on the ground in their path, not deterred in the least.

"Save your ammo," I called over the comm unit.

We were clear to the plane, and there wasn't a tactical reason to keep expending ammo. A moment later the minigun fell silent, and the Pave Hawk moved off, going back into a tight orbit around the airfield. The Humvee pulled up behind me to guard my back. I waved my thanks to the driver and turned and ran for the Globemaster.

Ahead, the group was getting close to the plane and the rear ramp was descending to accept them. I could see Rachel had moved into the front, Dog staying at her side, leading the group. The back of the ramp touched the tarmac just as she arrived and stepped aside to wave the group into the cavernous opening.

Crucifixion

She didn't see the female infected running at her from the far side of the plane, but Dog did. He leapt at the same time as the infected, meeting her in the air and crashing to the ground with his jaws locked on her throat. A moment later he raised his head, blood dripping from his muzzle. The female infected lay still.

11

The small group climbed the ramp and disappeared into the plane as I approached, Humvee still guarding my back with its machine gun hammering away. Reaching the ramp, I climbed aboard, Rachel and Dog falling in behind me, and handed Masuka off to waiting hands. From outside the plane, the machine gun continued firing. A grizzled man wearing an Air Force jumpsuit with Master Sergeant stripes, the Loadmaster, ran up to me and shoved a wireless headset for communicating on the jet's intercom into my hands.

"Major, the pilot needs to speak with you."

He turned away and started shouting at the new arrivals, getting them organized and seated on canvas slings that lined the walls of the giant cargo area. Three well used Bradley fighting vehicles filled most of the interior with room for passengers on the web seats.

"Major Chase up on intercom," I announced my presence and moved back onto the ramp to keep an eye out for any infected that slipped past our rear guard.

"Captain Trask, Sir." The pilot answered quickly. "We need some help. There's too many infected on the runway for me to taxi and take off."

Crucifixion

While he was talking, I raised my rifle and dispatched two females that were sprinting in on the blind side of the Humvee.

"Copy, Captain. I'll see what I can do about that." I ripped the headset off and tossed it to the Loadmaster and exited the aircraft onto the tarmac.

Rachel and Dog stayed on my heels, Rachel firing on another female that came around from the far side of the plane. Running to the Humvee, I yanked the door open and leaned in to speak with the driver.

"You're a goddamn sight for sore eyes," I yelled to the Sergeant in the driver's seat over the nearly constant hammering of the machine gun. He grinned back and stuck his hand out.

"Glad to be of service, Major. We about ready to get the hell out of here?"

"Got a small problem. Too many infected on the runway. The pilot can't taxi or takeoff. I'm going to do what I can to thin them out. You and your gunner un-ass this vehicle and get on that plane."

My plan was for Rachel to take over driving and I would man the gun. Along with support from the Pave Hawk's minigun we'd clear enough of the runway for the Globemaster to get off the ground, then Anderson could pick us up.

Dirk Patton

"If it's all the same Major, I'm not too partial to running from a fight." He grinned what I'm sure women found a charming grin.

"No discussion, Sergeant. Move your ass. I've got a ride to pick me up as soon as the jet's in the air."

"Yes, Sir," he answered, still grinning. Turning, he smacked the gunner on the leg and yelled at him to evacuate the vehicle. They gathered their gear, clambered out of the vehicle and ran for the Globemaster's waiting ramp.

I waved Rachel and Dog into the vehicle, sending Rachel to the driver's seat while I multi-tasked and inventoried the ammo reserves on board, shrugged out of my pack and called Anderson on my comm unit.

"Go ahead, Major."

"The pilot can't get this big bitch in the air with all the infected on the runway. What does it look like from up there?"

"Wait one," he answered, and I finished up my quick survey. Happily, there were close to five thousand rounds of ammo for the machine gun stored in the vehicle, which was an extraordinarily large amount, but it was time we had a break.

Crucifixion

"Major, we're going to need to clear out about five hundred infected to your west so the jet can taxi and turn into the wind for takeoff. Is the bird loaded or empty?"

"Loaded," I answered. "Three Bradleys on board."

The radio was quiet for a moment then Anderson came back on, "OK, he'll need about 7,500 feet of runway to get in the air. There's infected thick on the ground for about three hundred feet to your east then there's just an occasional straggler."

"Copy. I'm in the Humvee. I'll start clearing room for taxi and turn, you get started on the east side. And we're going to need a ride when they get in the air."

"Copy that," he answered, and a moment later I heard the pitch of the Pave Hawk's rotor change as it came to a hover over the side of the runway, then the minigun started mowing down bodies like the Grim Reaper's scythe.

I shouted instructions to Rachel, and she hit the throttle and steered us to the front of the giant plane. I absently noticed that the fire ahead of us at the end of the flight line was growing and spreading, but didn't have time to do anything other than bring the heavy machine gun into action. It started hammering, and I used the tracer rounds to direct and concentrate my fire into the mass of infected lumbering towards us.

They began falling, and I kept up the fire, feathering the trigger as I swung through an arc large enough for the plane to pass through. Every few seconds I let off the trigger to give the barrel a moment to cool down, but also to scan around me for females. I was standing with the top half of my body above the roof line of the vehicle, and if a female got close, they were certainly agile enough to leap up and attack me.

Rachel was letting the Humvee proceed at an idle, and after we had cleared and progressed a hundred feet or so I heard the massive jet engines behind us throttle up as the pilot started following. If not for the noise from the machine gun and the screaming jet engines, I suppose there would have been the sickening crunches as bodies lying on the tarmac were pulverized under the oversized landing gear. I shook my head as I scanned again for females, wondering why I even had random thoughts like that, then had to swing the machine gun around and cut down two females running in from our right, rear quarter.

"Major, we're pretty clear back here," Anderson called over the radio at the same time I heard the jet engines throttle down.

Crucifixion

Looking behind me, I saw the Globemaster pivoting around, looking impossibly large and ungainly on the ground. I shouted directions to Rachel, and she whipped a U-Turn and raced around the plane so we could assist in making sure the runway was clear. The pilot wasn't worried about bodies lying on the runway.

The heavy landing gear would roll right over them and probably no one on the plane would even feel a bump. The concern was an infected getting sucked into an engine. Birds are always a concern for pilots as they can damage a jet engine if they are sucked in. The difference in size and hardness of bones between a bird and a human is huge, and I didn't blame the pilot for being cautious.

I kept firing, cutting down any infected that was still standing after the minigun's aerial barrage. The aftermath of the minigun, no matter how many times I've witnessed it, always amazes me. The runway was literally carpeted with a thick mass of bodies and body parts. Hundreds of infected had been blown apart by the ferocious rate of fire and only a few still moved, somehow having been missed as Mayo worked the weapon.

The last one standing fell to a short burst from my machine gun as the jet completed its turn and the pilot wasted no time in shoving the four throttles to the firewall. The noise instantly rose to an ear shattering bellow, and I slapped Rachel on the shoulder and pointed for her to drive away from the runway so we wouldn't get blown over by the jet blast as the Globemaster passed us.

While she was getting us a safe distance away, I checked on the location of the Pave Hawk and saw it hovering 100 feet off to the side of the runway just over a mile away. Turning to look back to the west I grinned as infected were scattered like leaves in a hurricane as the jet blast hit them. My grin faded as they started climbing back to their feet after having been blown tumbling a hundred yards down the pavement. Damn but these things were tough.

The Globemaster roared past us, picking up speed as it rolled. The blast from the four huge engines blew the bodies and body parts off the runway after the jet rolled over them, creating a bloody fog in the air that I didn't want anything to do with. Diving down into the Humvee I shut the access panel in the roof with a slam and settled into the passenger seat to watch the takeoff. Dog had squeezed his way into the front of the vehicle and sat with his head resting on my left leg.

The big jet kept picking up speed, and I noticed Anderson slip the Pave Hawk a little farther away from the runway as it approached. I could see Mayo still firing the occasional burst from the minigun as infected wandered too close to the runway, but it looked like the takeoff was going to be a success.

That was until two female infected darted out of a hangar and behind the hovering helicopter. They were on the opposite side of the aircraft from Mayo as they sprinted onto the runway.

"Infected at your six, on the runway!" I shouted into the comm unit.

Anderson responded almost immediately, spinning the helicopter around and Mayo traversed the minigun. But they were too late and stopped firing as the females ran farther onto the runway. The Globemaster was fast approaching, probably close to take-off speed and getting very close to the end of the runway.

I could see the control surfaces on the wings move to full deflection as the pilot recognized the threat and tried to get the heavy jet in the air, but he just didn't have enough speed built up, and the landing gear stayed firmly on the ground. The scene went into slow motion as first one; then both infected were sucked into the engine farthest out on the right-hand wing.

There was an immediate gout of flame that shot out of the back of the engine, moments later the engine exploding. Half of the wing shredded when the engine exploded and the impossibly massive jet began to twist sideways to its right as both good engines on the left wing were still at full throttle and were no longer being balanced by equal thrust from the right.

Shrapnel blew outward from the destroyed engine, some chunks appearing to be as large as the Humvee I was sitting in. Anderson responded and turned the Pave Hawk away from the disintegrating Globemaster, but not soon enough. A chunk of engine, the size of a small car, rocketed through the air, trailing smoke and flames, and slammed into the Pave Hawk's rotor.

In almost a coordinated ballet the Globemaster continued its spin to the right as the Pave Hawk tilted first to the side then nose down as the rotor blades sheared off. The Pave Hawk crashed nose first into a parking lot adjacent to a hangar, exploding into a large fireball on impact. Seconds later the Globemaster's landing gear, not designed for the lateral stress it was experiencing as the plane skidded sideways, collapsed. The belly of the plane smashed into the pavement and skidded in a shower of sparks.

Moments later the already compromised right wing snapped off and spilled hundreds of gallons of jet fuel that was instantly ignited by the sparks from the skid. The Globemaster exploded in a tremendous fireball, the shockwave from the concussion rocking the Humvee on its suspension.

12

A wave of emotions washed over me as Rachel and I sat in the Humvee and watched the two aircraft crash and explode into flames. Even though I knew it wasn't my fault, a wave of guilt hit me at the thought of the survivors I had put on the Globemaster as well as the loss of Anderson, Mayo, and Gwen in the helicopter.

Sensing our distress, Dog whined and pushed his head all the way into my lap. I absently rubbed his head as the flames consumed the remains of the crash and quickly spread to the adjacent hangars and parked fighter jets, setting off additional explosions. The Humvee rocked again from another shockwave, then there was a solid thump on my door as a female infected crashed into the vehicle and began beating on the ballistic glass.

"We need to move," I said to Rachel, who looked as distraught as I felt.

She didn't respond, just sat behind the wheel watching the growing conflagration at the far end of the runway.

"Rachel, can you drive?" I raised my voice and put my hand on her shoulder. Shaking off her torpor, she nodded and looked around.

"Where?"

Good question. I checked my vest and found I was down to one full magazine and one partial for the rifle. Checking Rachel's didn't produce dramatically better results. Climbing over the seat into the back of the vehicle, I found only ammo for the machine gun. We had plenty of that but were dangerously low on rifle and pistol ammo.

"We need to find the armory and resupply our ammo, then we need to get the hell out of here."

Back in the front seat I looked out my side window and met the eyes of the infected female that was pounding on the glass. Rage and hunger stared back at me.

"OK. Got any idea where that is?" Rachel shifted into reverse, backed up a few yards, shifted back into drive, jammed the throttle and ran down the female without so much as batting an eye.

"First, get us away from the flight line, then head towards the firing range. It should be fairly close if the Air Force does anything like the Army does."

Nodding, Rachel stepped on the throttle, and we bounced over several dead infected, hopped a curb into the parking lot for the flight operations building and headed north on a narrow road that looked familiar from earlier in the day. Rachel drove fast but well, not bothering to slow when another female infected charged us head on. The heavy front bumper smashed the body and sent it sailing through the air to land in a roadside ditch.

The road widened and forked, Rachel slowing as she looked for landmarks before taking the fork to the left. Ahead I could see a single weak light at the squat cinderblock building in front of the firing range. Rachel slowed and swung into the gravel parking lot, the headlights shining brightly on the closed steel access door. When she shut off the lights, I engaged the NVGs. I didn't see any infected in the area, told Rachel to stay behind the wheel, popped the door open and stepped out with rifle at the ready and Dog on my heels.

The idling diesel in the Humvee was loud, and I motioned for Rachel to shut it off, the engine going quiet a moment later. I stood still for a minute, scanning the area, then checked on Dog who was alert but calm. Reaching back into the vehicle, I found the sound suppressor for my rifle still tucked safely away in my pack. Removing the M4's flash hider, I screwed the suppressor into place and closed the Humvee door softly.

Walking slowly across the gravel I reached out and tried the doorknob, but it was locked. I thought for a second and decided to try knocking before forcing my way in. There was an answering thump to my knock on the door, and I could hear snarling coming from inside the building. Dog let out a low growl then went quiet, eyes focused on the door.

After another quick check of the area, I lowered my rifle and opened the pack clipped to my vest that held the breaching charges. Using the Kukri, I cut off six inches of rope and molded it around the knob and deadbolt, inserted and activated a detonator and stepped behind the Humvee. When Dog was at my side and safely shielded I pressed the remote and the C-4 detonated with a dull bang.

Moving back toward the door, I was satisfied with the results. The explosion had cut through the steel surrounding both the knob and deadbolt and released the door which was swinging out as an infected male pushed through. It was one of the Sergeants I'd met earlier that had worked with Rachel on the firing range. I dropped him with a shot to the head, the rifle nice and quiet with the addition of the suppressor. I waited a few more moments to see if there were any more infected that were going to come to the party, but apparently he'd been alone.

Swinging the door fully open, I scanned the interior through my NVGs and saw no threat. Dog at my side I moved into the building, scanning and ready with the rifle, but it was still clear. Stepping back to the doorway, I gave Rachel a thumbs up, pulled the damaged door closed and flipped on the lights as I pushed the NVGs up off my eyes.

The room was much as I remembered it other than several items the infected had knocked off desks as he stumbled around the space. Starting a quick search, I checked the two large metal cabinets first and didn't find ammo but did find tools and chemicals for cleaning firearms. Grabbing an ammo can stuffed with cleaning supplies I set it by the front door and kept searching.

The third storage room I came to was the only one with a lock on the door. Expecting I'd found what I was looking for, I quickly gained access by blowing the lock off the door with some more C-4 and was rewarded for my efforts. Inside were wooden cases of fully loaded thirty round magazines. At least that's one thing the Air Force did the same way as the Army.

Time at the range was too valuable to waste on the trainees sitting there loading magazines a round at a time. The Army would pick a couple of Privates and detail them to load magazines in advance, so all the trainees had to do was grab a couple and start shooting. Each crate held thirty magazines, and there were twenty crates sitting there for a total of 18,000 rounds ready to go. There was no way the Humvee could hold all of them, but I was going to take as many as I could stuff into the vehicle. I let the rifle hang on its sling and grabbed the first one and headed for the door.

Rachel saw me coming and got out and popped open the rear of the vehicle and I loaded the crate in. Four more crates and we were full with 4,500 rounds. I tossed in the cleaning kit and back inside loaded my vest from one of the crates I was leaving behind. I took a few more minutes and dug through the crates and boxes in the room and almost overlooked a single wooden crate in the back corner. It was stenciled with black paint that had faded, and all I could see was two numbers, 67.

Moving some boxes out of the way I saw the full stencil, M67, Grenade, Fragmentation. That's more like it! After opening the crate to make sure it really contained grenades, I carried it out and placed it on the back seat. One more trip to get enough magazines to fully restock Rachel's vest and we were ready to go.

Humvee loaded, and our vests restocked we stood by the front of the vehicle looking at each other. The fires at the flight line were very visible over the tree tops, and occasionally another explosion would rock the night. I felt we were OK for a few minutes. I had scanned the entire area with the NVGs and hadn't spotted any infected. They were all probably heading for the commotion at the runway as fast as they could.

"What the hell is happening?" I asked Rachel, looking over as Dog trotted to a lone tree at the edge of the parking area.

Rachel thought for a minute before answering.

"All I can come up with is it has to do with the viral component of the nerve gas release. The briefer did tell us that our researchers haven't identified everything the virus can or will do. Either that or they were grossly wrong about how long the nerve agent remains viable once it's released into the environment, but I doubt they're wrong about that."

"Why are we OK? Or are we?"

"I don't know. Maybe we're immune; maybe we just haven't turned yet. It's all maybes at this point." Rachel let out a sigh and turned to watch the fires. "So what do we do now?"

"That's what I'm trying to decide. If this is happening here, I think it's a safe bet it's happening everywhere. We've got a very sturdy and well-armed vehicle so we can pretty much get to wherever we decide to go as long as we can find fuel."

That thought prompted me to walk around to the back of the Humvee and check for extra fuel. Four, five-gallon metal jerry cans were strapped down to a platform attached to the back, but they were all empty. Not surprising since they would normally only be filled in preparation for going into the field for an extended time.

Another thought crossed my mind, and I dug out the main controller for my comm gear. I was pleased to find it was an upgraded unit with the capability of changing frequencies. This was a relatively low powered device and would have no chance of reaching a ground-based radio more than a couple of miles away, but that range was greatly extended if I could reach an aircraft. Not expecting there to be any civilian air traffic I changed the radio to the Military Guard Channel – reserved for aircraft emergencies – and started transmitting.

"American ground forces transmitting on Guard. Any station receiving, please respond." I listened for a few but heard nothing and repeated my transmission.

"Station transmitting this is Royal Air Force Angel Flight. Please identify yourself." The signal was weak and static filled, but the voice was distinctly British.

"Angel Flight, Major John Chase, US Army at Arnold Air Force Base in Tennessee. Arnold has fallen to infected. I need to know status of other US installations. Is Fort Campbell still operational?"

Crucifixion

"Stand by, Major. We're a little concerned ourselves up here. Nashville went radio silent half an hour ago." The signal was clearer. I suspected this was one of the UK aid flights that was inbound to Nashville.

After what seemed like an eternity the UK pilot came back on the radio, the signal now perfectly clear. For the hell of it, I looked up and scanned the sky but couldn't spot the aircraft.

"Major, we are still not getting a response from Nashville, and Fort Campbell is not responding either. There is some faint radio traffic we are picking up that indicates some major battles are underway, but we cannot tell where they are coming from."

By the time the pilot finished speaking the signal was already growing weaker as the plane was apparently now moving away from us. I thanked him for the information and thought he wished me good luck, but it was hard to tell over the growing static.

"That's not good," I said to Rachel, shutting the unit off to save the battery before stowing it in my pack.

A couple of screams sounded much too close, and we quickly piled back into the Humvee, me behind the wheel while Rachel and Dog had a brief skirmish over the passenger seat. Starting the vehicle, I spun around in the parking lot as two infected females raced around the corner of the building and charged towards us. Spraying gravel, I accelerated out of the lot and onto the asphalt, quickly outdistancing them.

"So what are we doing?" Rachel asked, leaning forward to peer at the females in the side mirror.

"Unless you've got a better suggestion we're heading west again. I don't feel like fighting our way to Fort Campbell to just find that it has fallen too."

Rachel thought about that for a few minutes as I drove across the Air Force Base. The fires at the flight line were burning brighter than ever, and there was still the occasional explosion as either an aircraft or vehicle's fuel tank detonated.

"I think that's probably our best bet," she finally answered, turning to look at me and rubbing Dog's head which was firmly planted in her lap.

"OK, then," I said. "We've got to avoid Memphis. It was one of the cities that was on the original list of nerve gas attacks. There's also still the herd moving up from the gulf. I'm going to take us north. Move up into Kentucky, then across the Mississippi river into Missouri, but stay well south of St. Louis. We'll worry about finding a safe bridge crossing when we get there."

Crucifixion

Once again I found myself without a map but was willing to start the journey without one and hope to loot a convenience store or truck stop along the way. We slowly worked our way across the base. Infected were everywhere. It seemed as if almost everyone that had been fine when we arrived was now infected. I started to speculate on what could have happened but shut down that line of thinking. I needed to focus on the task at hand, not worry about something over which I had no control.

On a fairly regular basis, we were running down infected males, females charging us from out of the dark and slamming into the fenders or doors of the Humvee. Once we saw a lone survivor, but he was too far away and fell under a pack of females that tore him to ribbons before we could get close enough to help. Poor bastard.

After several dead ends that forced us to backtrack, we finally found a gate that would allow us to exit the base. The gate was a rolling section of chain link fencing about 12 feet high, and there were probably close to 100 infected pushing up against it. None were in military clothing, so I suspected they were civilians from the small town next to the base. There was a good mix of males and females, and as we approached the gate, they all went in to a frenzy, fighting with each other to get closer to the gate.

"Now that's new," I commented, watching a large male club smaller infected out of his way so he could press up against the chain link.

"I wish they'd just fight each other and leave us the hell alone," Rachel said.

"Yeah, well, I wish I was hung like John Holmes, but I don't think either of us are going to get our wish."

I put the Humvee into park as Rachel laughed. It was the first spark of life out of her since the Globemaster and Pave Hawk had crashed at the flight line. Glancing around to make sure we were in the clear I climbed into the back of the vehicle, Dog protesting my invasion of his space with a series of grunts, and told Rachel to join me. After a moment, she climbed into the back too. Standing up, I unlocked and pushed open the hatch in the roof that allowed a gunner access to the machine gun.

"You need to learn how to use this," I said, gesturing for Rachel to stand up in the gunner's position.

When she was in place, I opened the rear door and stood on the edge of the vehicle floor to be up at her height. I gave her a quick tutorial on how to load and change ammo belts and charge the weapon. After she had removed the belt and reloaded the weapon a few times, I felt she had that part of it down.

"The most important thing, other than not shooting me, is to not melt your barrel," I said. Rachel looked at me like I was speaking Martian. "Machine guns get very hot, very quickly, and under continuous firing, the barrel will overheat and warp. If that happens, you might as well throw the gun at them for all the good it will do you."

"So how do I keep that from happening?" She asked with a note of trepidation in her voice.

"Short, controlled bursts. Don't fire continuously for more than five seconds. This weapon fires nine hundred rounds a minute. That's fifteen rounds per second, so in a five-second burst, you've gone through seventy-five rounds. Get in your mind that you will fire for five seconds, not fire for three seconds, then fire for up to five more.

"There's a red tracer every tenth round so you'll see one tracer a second to help you direct your fire. A green tracer is at the mid-point of the belt and again three rounds from the end of the belt with two reds together as the last two rounds to let you know you're out. The mount will absorb and control the recoil, but the gun will hammer your arms."

Rachel was looking at me like I was crazy to be trusting her with this, but she was also paying attention.

"OK, ready?" I asked.

"For what?"

"Clear those infected out so we can open the gate and get out of here," I replied, pointing at the mass of bodies fifty yards to our front.

Stepping back down into the Humvee I closed the door and sat in the rear seat next to Rachel's right leg. After a moment I heard her click the safety off then the gun hammered out a short two-second burst.

Watching out of the windshield, I saw a few infected drop then the second tracer round flew over their heads as Rachel let the gun climb off target. A couple of seconds later the hammering started again, lasting almost five full seconds and mowing down a dozen infected before a tracer flew high. Three seconds later she cut loose again, this time keeping all the rounds on target, shredding infected and also doing a number on the gate.

Soon she was controlling the weapon and walking the stream of bullets across the ranks of bodies which were rapidly thinning. Two more bursts and there was only half a dozen infected still standing. I tapped Rachel's leg to let her know I would clean up the rest with my rifle.

Checking the area, I saw a large group of infected males approaching from the rear, most certainly attracted by the horrendous noise the machine gun makes. I pointed them out to Rachel, and she swung the gun around and cut them down with two quick bursts. Damn, she caught on quick. Popping the door open, I walked to the gate raising my rifle, and in short order dispatched the remaining infected with head shots.

The stench of unwashed bodies, blood, bowels and bladders was almost overpowering and even though it was night, flies were already descending on the nauseating banquet. Breathing through my mouth, I found the latch for the gate near the guard shack, released it and forced the gate open on its track.

Back in the Humvee, I checked to make sure Rachel had locked the access hatch to the roof, shifted into drive and slowly made our crunching and squishing way over the shattered bodies. Rachel held her hand over her nose and mouth when the smell hit her, trying to roll down her window when we were clear. She quickly discovered the tradeoff for having an up-armored vehicle with ballistic glass. The windows are fixed in place and don't roll down. She settled for cracking the door open a few inches and holding it there while we drove, the smell quickly venting out of the vehicle.

The small town outside the gate, I never learned its name, wasn't much more than one long street that looked like streets near every military base I've ever been on. Bars, tattoo parlors, liquor stores, strip clubs and a couple of low-rent motels that advertised hourly rates. Brought back memories.

The power was still on, and every building had some sort of gaudy neon sign, almost all of them in red that washed the whole street with light that made the place look like one of Dante's levels of hell. More infected were moving, coming out of the businesses, out of alleys and side streets, all drawn by the machine gun fire and the sound of the Humvee.

Crucifixion

Accelerating slightly, I pushed our speed to over thirty. The long street resembled a gauntlet and the infected were quickly spilling onto the asphalt and closing ranks ahead of us. Moments later I slowed back to twenty as we started smashing through the bodies. The herd thickened, and I slowed to just over ten MPH for fear of damaging the vehicle – you can only ram hundred and fifty to two hundred pound bodies for so long before something gives – but we finally reached the far end of the street which was clear of infected. Ahead the road disappeared around a curve as the heavy forest in the area closed in.

Rounding the curve found us in a dark tunnel, trees pressing right to the edge of the pavement on both sides as their upper branches tried to meet in the middle. The Humvee's headlights were not very bright, but it had been outfitted with a set of high intensity off road lights that I switched on after groping around the dash for the switch. The night turned to day inside the tree canopy, but we couldn't see anything to the side beyond the first row of trees. I momentarily thought about cutting all the lights and using the NVGs but discarded the idea. Infected would find us from sound, not light, so we really had little to gain by running dark.

"Do you know where we're going?" Rachel asked.

"That way," I answered, pointing at the windshield.

"Funny. I'm serious. What are we heading into?"

"Right now the idea is to get north into Kentucky a ways, then cut to the west. I want to stay well clear of any population centers. Whatever is going on with more people suddenly becoming infected can't be isolated."

Rachel fell silent, not particularly satisfied with my answer, but it was the best I could do at the moment. We had a very capable vehicle, were well armed and reasonably well provisioned with a week's worth of MREs in our packs. Things could be worse.

We both fell silent as I drove, the hum of the hard rubber all terrain tires on the pavement almost hypnotizing. I kept our speed down, never getting over 45. Too many times I had seen infected suddenly lurch in front of us. I wanted to be going slow enough to not damage the Humvee in a collision, or worse, try to avoid the collision and wind up crashing. The vehicle was our lifeboat, and I didn't want to have to find out how long we'd last without it.

After an hour, we rounded a curve, and I slowed to a stop as we reached an intersection. This was the first real side road we had encountered since leaving Arnold. There had been several muddy tracks cut into the forest, but even though this road wasn't marked it headed west and would hopefully stay south of Nashville. There were no other signs, and I had no idea what or where the next town was going to be. Tossing a mental coin, I decided to take the new road and start heading west, turning the wheel and slowly accelerating.

Rachel had fallen asleep in the dark and Dog was snoring like a saw mill in the back seat. I was tired, reminding myself that I had already flown to Atlanta, fought infected, flown back to Arnold and fought some more since the last time I slept. We were in the middle of nowhere, or at least seemed to be, and I was considering pulling into the next muddy track I saw and getting some sleep myself when I saw the first stake. Gawking at it as we drove past, I took my foot off the accelerator and let the vehicle slow as several more came into view.

The stakes were thick wooden poles driven into the ground and atop each one a severed human head had been impaled, facing the direction we were coming from. Idling past I could see a small forest of them in the reach of the lights before the road disappeared over a small rise. I couldn't tell if the heads had come from infected or survivors when they were driven onto the stakes. It didn't matter.

Someone was one sick fucking puppy and was using them to warn away travelers, or mark their territory, or something else I couldn't even comprehend. It didn't matter; I wasn't about to go any farther and find out what the deal was. Reaching over, I shook Rachel awake as I braked the Humvee to a stop on the top of the rise.

"Oh, fucking hell," she said, waking up and looking out the windshield at the couple of dozen staked heads I pointed to in front of us.

"Fucking hell is right," I said, shifting into reverse and turning us sideways in the road to turn and head back where we'd come from.

I hadn't completed the turn when bright lights from my left, the direction we had come from, suddenly lit up the night and pinned us like a spotlighted coyote. Shit, shit, shit. The good news was we were in a military vehicle that could withstand any civilian weapons they might have. The bad news came a second later when more light came on to my right, neatly boxing us in. We'd driven right into a trap.

"Get ready to drive," I barked, scrambling over the seat and unlatching the gunner's port in the roof.

Standing up in the position, I swung the machine gun to my left and didn't hesitate to open fire, walking the bullets across the spotlights and knocking all of them out. I could hear shouts from the men who had been behind the lights, but I ignored them and swung to my right, pumping a few hundred rounds into the lights and vehicles they were mounted on. More shouts, then bullets started pinging off the armored side of the Humvee.

"Drive!" I shouted at Rachel as I swung the gun back to the group I'd fired on first. Bracing against the motion as she floored the vehicle I lined up as best I could and started hammering away.

I thought we'd make it. Felt confident that with the armored Humvee and machine gun we could fight our way clear of the ambush. And we might have if not for their sniper. I saw the muzzle flash before I heard the boom and half a second later the Humvee's diesel engine went quiet, and we rolled to a stop. The report of the rifle was distinctive, and I knew someone had a .50 caliber sniper rifle, probably with API - armor piercing incendiary - ammo since they had disabled our engine with one shot.

The .50 cal rifle fires one hell of a slug, about the size of your thumb, and it fires it with tremendous velocity. I've personally seen experienced snipers take out targets at 1,500 yards with a .50. I've read of accounts of targets being effectively engaged as far out as nearly two miles. At one hundred yards that slug penetrated our armored grill and shattered the engine block without much effort.

The only mistake the sniper had made was firing from somewhere that allowed me to see the muzzle flash. Swinging the machine gun to that point, I opened up and hammered out burst after burst until I had run through the belt. No more .50 caliber fire came our way, no fire at all from the direction I had targeted, but high-velocity rounds from what were probably deer rifles were slamming into the back of the vehicle. Slapping a new belt in and swiveling around I walked fire across the vehicles blocking the road in that direction. The firing stopped but started up from the area where I had taken out the sniper.

"Get your pack on," I shouted down into the vehicle to Rachel. "Grab two of those empty canvas bags and fill one up with grenades and the other with rifle magazines. Let me know when you're ready."

Not waiting for an answer I pulled the trigger on the machine gun again, walking fire alternately across both road blocks. To discourage anybody that was showing some initiative, I swept bursts across the forest to each side of us, then went back to hosing down our attacker's vehicles. I had to stop firing to load in a new belt and had an idea.

Crucifixion

"Rachel!"

"What?" She yelled back, not stopping filling the bag with grenades.

"Open up several ammo cans for the machine gun. I want you to link all the belts together. You'll see how to do it when you get them open. Then find the duct tape in my pack and tear me off an eight-inch strip."

I had said all this during pauses in firing, not wanting to give the assholes that had ambushed us a break. Less than a minute later I felt Rachel smack me on the leg, and I glanced down to see her handing me the strip of tape. In her other hand was the end of an ammo belt and I could see half a dozen ammo cans sitting in a row, lids open and belts connecting the contents to each other. Taking the tape from her, I leaned into the opening and also grabbed the end of the ammo belt she held.

"Out the door and straight into the woods," I told her. "Take Dog with you. Keep going when you get into the bush. I'll catch up."

I ducked as a rifle round pinged off the armor right next to my head, swung to the direction the shot had come from and sent a hundred rounds downrange.

"We'll wait for..."

"Goddamn it," I cut her off. "Move your ass now! I'll be right behind you."

Not waiting to see if she was doing what I told her I kept the firing going until the gun ran dry, then inserted the end of the very long belt that Rachel had clipped together for me. Most of the rifle fire was coming from my front so I sent a couple of bursts their way then dove into the Humvee to shrug into my pack. The ten-second lull in firing gave them a chance to bring more rifles to bear and rounds were splattering off the Humvee's armor fairly rapidly when I poked my body back through the roof.

I fired a couple of long bursts which stopped the rifle fire, locked the machine gun into place on its mount, threaded the duct tape through the trigger guard and used it to pull and hold the trigger. The machine gun started firing, held tightly on target by its mount, and I wrapped the tape around the back of the guard to hold the trigger down and dropped into the Humvee.

The machine gun was still firing and would continue to fire until it either ran out of ammo or overheated and malfunctioned. I hoped for the former as there were 2,500 rounds linked together, enough to last for three minutes if the gun didn't melt. Grabbing another canvas bag, I spent fifteen precious seconds filling it with grenades before bailing out of the side of the vehicle.

Crucifixion

I had kept two grenades in my hand and pulled the first pin and threw it hard in the direction the machine gun was still firing. Turning, I pulled the second pin and threw that one then ran into the forest, lowering my NVGs into place. Seconds later the two explosions sounded, but I was already ten yards into the heavy brush and moving as fast as I could.

Ahead of me, I could see Rachel and Dog moving through the forest. It wasn't like seeing them in the daytime, I couldn't recognize them, but in the green and black world of the NVGs, I could see a human and K9 figure. Not imagining there was anyone else out walking their dog I adjusted my direction to follow them, slowing to reduce the noise I was making.

Behind me, the machine gun had stopped firing. Glancing back, I was dismayed to see several figures following. I checked front to see several more angling in towards Rachel and Dog. Fuckers had to have night vision too.

The suppressor was still attached to my rifle, and I pulled up to a stop to make use of it. Raising the NVGs, I activated the night vision feature of the mil-spec scope, raised the rifle to my shoulder and took aim on the figures pursuing Rachel and Dog. Taking my time, I sighted and fired and the first one dropped, the others freezing in place.

That told me these weren't combat veterans. When you see someone in your group fall, the last thing you want to do is stand there and let the shooter pick you off, but that's exactly what they did. There were three more of them, all motionless, and I had dropped two of them before the last guy figured it out and dove to the forest floor.

Ignoring him for the moment, I checked behind me and counted five men approaching, all nicely bunched together and about 40 yards away. Slipping behind the thick trunk of a tree, I pulled a grenade from the canvas bag, pulled the pin which sent the spoon flying and started counting.

Grenades are supposed to have a five-second fuse, and I was doing what is known as "cooking off" the grenade, or using up some of that fuse time before throwing it. Done right, this results in a grenade exploding almost simultaneously with its arrival on target. Done wrong... well, I think you get the idea. As I reached the count of three in my head, I leaned around the tree and tossed the grenade into the middle of the group, ducking back behind the trunk as the explosion shattered the night.

Peeking back around I was satisfied to see all five figures laying on the ground, two of them thrashing in pain from their wounds while the other three didn't move. Next lesson – don't bunch up.

Turning back to the front, I spotted Rachel and Dog, but they were almost at the limit of the NVGs ability to see. The figure that had gone to ground was apparently still eating dirt because I couldn't see him, so I stepped off as quietly as I could, moving towards his last position. A few steps later and a better angle and I could see him crawling on the ground back the way he'd come from. Raising the rifle, I put three rounds into him, and he lay still. It's never a good idea to leave a healthy enemy behind if you have the choice.

Resuming my path behind Rachel and Dog, I had only gone a few yards when my NVGs suddenly blinked out. Damn it! Reaching up, I flipped the power switch off then back on with no luck. Slapping them didn't produce favorable results either. It wasn't the battery. I would have gotten a low battery alert in my field of vision well before they died if that was the problem. I tried the switch once more with the same negative results, gave up and pushed them up and off my face.

I still had the night vision scope on the rifle but didn't want to try and navigate through the forest with a rifle scope held to one eye. Moving over to the bodies of the group I had shot I found that only one of them had night vision, but it was a cheap civilian set that had probably been purchased at Walmart. It relied on infrared bulbs to provide up to maybe 30 feet of light that could be seen by the goggles.

I've done a lot of night work and decided they would be more of a hindrance than a help so left them on the body. Raising the rifle, I looked through the scope and could no longer see Rachel or Dog, but I knew their direction of travel and didn't expect to have any problems tracking them.

My eyes quickly adjusted to the lack of the NVGs – I've always had very good natural night vision – and the moonlight that was making it through the trees provided all the light I needed to pick my way through the forest. Occasionally I could make out a scuff mark in the carpet of dead leaves and moss on the forest floor where Rachel had dragged a foot. Less frequently, I came across branches that were bent or snapped off by her passing.

I took the time to mask these signs and set up some false trails in case our attackers had someone who knew how to track. I was hearing sounds of pursuit from behind, but they weren't close enough yet to cause me concern.

The ground was rising, and ahead I could see a crest in the terrain and dropped to my stomach to crawl the last few yards. Reaching the crest, I popped my head up for a look. Below was a large valley. On the valley floor and at least a mile to my left were numerous camp fires burning like beacons in the night. Taking a look through the rifle scope, I spotted Rachel and Dog again.

They were a hundred yards in front of me on the slope down into the valley and were stationary, Rachel appearing to be kneeling with Dog at her side. I scanned with the rifle and saw her hesitation. Below her position were a couple of dozen shambling figures, all moving in the direction of the camp fires.

After another scan of the area I slithered over the crest – try slithering sometime with one hundred plus pounds on your back – and climbed back to my feet when I was far enough below the edge to not show myself to any pursuers. A gentle breeze was blowing in my face so I knew Dog wouldn't scent me as I approached. Moving cautiously and quietly, I stopped ten yards from them and stepped behind a tree in case I startled Rachel enough to make her trigger happy.

Peering around the tree, I whistled low and soft, hoping I sounded as much like a night bird as I was trying to. Dog shifted and looked straight at me. Rachel didn't hear me but snapped her head around and raised her rifle when Dog shifted his attention.

"Dog, come here," I called, just loud enough for him to hear.

He got up and trotted to me, tail wagging, and I could see Rachel relax and lower the rifle. Scratching Dog's head, I walked to Rachel and kneeled down next to her.

"How the hell did you get so close without either of us knowing?" She asked in a quiet whisper.

"I used the Force," was my flippant answer. Rachel just looked at me. "Really? That does it. Next town we come to I'm finding a copy of Star Wars and making you watch it."

Rachel looked at me for a few moments, let out a quiet sigh and shook her head.

"There's infected moving through the forest toward that camp," Rachel said, pointing down the valley.

"I saw them. There's also some of the guys from the ambush coming up behind us. I think we need to avoid everyone; camp, infected and ambushers."

Rachel shook her head and looked me in the eye, "What if that camp is just some innocent survivors? It's too out of the way to belong to the guys that blocked the road, and they may not be ready for the infected. I think we should try to help them."

"Not our fight," I said, shaking my head. "We're running for our lives. We don't have the luxury of riding in to save the day."

"Listen," Rachel said, reaching out and grasping my arm. "I've followed your lead without question, but you're wrong here. There could be children in that camp."

"And there could be a bunch of assholes like the ones that captured you," I answered.

"True," she answered after thinking about it for a minute. "But we need to find out."

We sat that way for a few heartbeats, staring at each other. The thing was she was probably right, and if my wife Katie was here, she'd be telling me the same thing. Shit!

"OK," I answered with more enthusiasm than I felt.

Raising the rifle, I looked through the scope and tracked the slow, shambling path of the infected. All males. At least that was a little bit of good news. Turning, I checked the ridge line behind us and saw a couple of figures silhouetted against the sky. As I watched, two more joined them, and the four of them lined up nice and straight for me. If we were going to try and help the people in the camp, first things first.

Sighting in on the figure farthest to the right, I fired and immediately adjusted to the next in line. I fired before the first body had even hit the ground. Two more shots and all four were down, one of them falling forward over the crest and tumbling down into the valley.

The body made a lot of noise crashing through the brush, and I spun to see if the infected had heard, but they were apparently far enough away that neither the sound of my suppressed rifle nor the body falling down the slope caught their attention. I held the rifle pointed at the crest for five minutes to see if any heads were going to pop up but none did, and I finally stood up, slung the rifle and helped Rachel to her feet.

"Stay behind me and stay quiet," I told her.

Stepping forward, I moved farther down into the valley. A few minutes later we passed a rocky outcropping with a shallow cave, and I stopped. Shedding my pack, I stuffed it into the cave, feeling every ounce of the weight that had just come off my back. Helping Rachel out of hers, I stashed it with mine, took a look around to imprint the location in my mind and started moving again. Without the packs, we moved much faster and within a few minutes had caught up with the rear stragglers of the small herd of infected.

Two males shambled through the forest, side by side, just a dozen yards ahead of us. Both appeared to have leg injuries that were slowing them down, but they kept pushing on, continually stumbling on the uneven terrain but managing to stay on their feet. Wanting to save my ammo I drew the Kukri and moved up behind them with short, quick and silent steps.

I dropped the first one by severing the spinal column in the back of his neck. Wrenching the blade free, I turned to meet the other who had stopped when his traveling buddy went down. An upward thrust buried the steel all the way into his brain, and he too dropped to the forest floor and lay still. Wiping the blade clean I waited for Rachel and Dog to move forward, then we continued our pursuit of the infected.

The next group we caught up to was five males, and they pretty much seemed to represent a good cross-section of America. A teenager was the furthest back, his progress hindered by the baggy jeans he wore that had fallen to his ankles and limited him to a slow shuffle. It would have been funny if he wasn't one of the infected.

I came up behind him and took him out with a quick thrust of the blade into his back, piercing his heart. The next infected was dressed like a used car salesman, polyester pants included and was grossly obese. Not wanting to tangle with that much mass I raised the rifle and took a moment to scan the area.

There were the four remaining infected right in front of me, oblivious to my presence, then another small group about seventy-five yards farther ahead. Swinging back to the fat man, I shot him in the head, adjusted aim and brought down what looked like a farmer wearing overalls. The remaining two, one wearing surgical scrubs and one in a three-piece suit heard the rifle and turned, snarling, but I quickly zeroed on their heads and put them down as well.

I re-scanned 360-degrees, but there were no immediate threats. Waving to Rachel we moved out again, continuing our pursuit. After a few minutes, I paused and scanned 180-degrees to our front, spying eleven more infected with the scope. They were bunched tightly and moving at a decent clip, and I could make out another seven farther in front of them. That was all I could see, but the two groups were a little too large and bunched together too tightly for me to want to go charging in with the Kukri.

I wasn't happy with my firing lanes so changed direction and started angling to the left of the two groups, moving fast enough to pass them. My intent was to get to their front and set up so I could fire down the slope of the side of the valley. Fifteen quiet minutes later we were in place amongst an outcropping of rocks. I settled in behind a large boulder on my knees, rifle resting on my left arm along the top of the boulder, and sighted on the lead group through the scope.

I had 18 targets to take out. Suicide, most likely, if these had been soldiers who could respond, move and shoot back in a coordinated effort. But being infected, I knew they would just keep shambling along, ignoring the deaths of the ones around them. The biggest risk was the noise I was going to make with the rifle. Yes, it was equipped with a sound suppressor, but that doesn't mean it's silent, regardless of portrayals on TV and in movies.

A suppressor will significantly reduce the sound that comes out of the muzzle of a firearm, but it doesn't eliminate it. It doesn't make the weapon sound like a blow gun. It helps, a lot, but the weapon is still loud enough to be identified and located within about 50 yards. I also worried about infected or ambushers stumbling up on our backs, and I set Rachel up to watch behind us so I could focus on my targets.

Calming my breathing I sighted on the target farthest to the front and squeezed the trigger, a blink later watching the body fall in the scope. Methodically I started working my way back into the group, a body falling every time I pulled the trigger. Nine infected were lying dead on the ground when my rifle misfired. I could tell by the sound of the bolt cycling that it didn't fully load a new round after I shot the ninth target. Reaching down in the dark I could feel the bolt being held open by a round that was sticking out of the ejection port.

Crucifixion

Going through the progression for clearing a miss-feed, I first slapped the bottom of the magazine to make sure it was seated properly, then pulled on the charging handle to hopefully cause the round to eject so a new one could feed in. The handle pulled back, but the round was stuck. Taking a second, I scanned with the scope and saw that the infected had heard the rifle and were shambling up the slope towards us. The closest one was about forty yards away, but his lack of coordination and the slope he was climbing meant I had lots of time before he arrived.

I fought with the stuck round for what seemed forever, finally prying it free and tossing it away. Pulling the charging handle I was happy to hear the bolt cycle completely, brought the rifle back up, sighted on the approaching infected and pulled the trigger. Nothing. Damn it! Grabbing the charging handle, I pulled it, heard the ejected round hit the ground, let it go, and it slammed home. Sighted again on the infected that was getting a little too close, pulled the trigger and... nothing.

The infected was now less than twenty yards away, and the rest of the small herd was right on his heels. I thought about going to my pistol, but I was hesitant to fire a weapon that wasn't suppressed. I didn't know how many more infected might be in the area that would zero in on the noise, let alone whether or not there were females roaming the woods. I also had to think about the ambushers as well as the people in the camp we were trying to protect. I didn't have time to reflect on the irony of trying to protect people that might want to try and capture or kill me.

Placing the malfunctioning rifle on the ground I stood, drew the Kukri, and stepped around the rock to meet the approaching infected. Dog moved up beside me, head down and hackles raised as he growled and showed his teeth. Advancing, I swung the Kukri and nearly decapitated the infected closest to me, stepping to the side as the body hit the forest floor. Dog bounded past me and slammed into the chest of a large male, carrying him to the ground where he started ripping into its throat.

I was in a frenzy, slashing and stabbing infected as I moved farther down the slope. Dog took another male to the ground, rolling in its embrace before locking his jaws on its throat. Hands brushed me and once a hand got a grip on my left sleeve and started pulling, but I slashed with the blade and severed the arm of the attacking infected at the elbow, reversed the Kukri and buried the point in his head. Then there were no more infected.

Looking around, I counted nine bodies on the ground. Dog had killed three, and I had hacked and slashed my way through the other six. During the battle, I had wound up moving almost fifty yards down slope, and slowly I climbed back to where Rachel was waiting. Dog bounded past me, his four long legs eating up the ground. I had just made it back to the rocks where I had initiated the battle when a blinding spotlight lit up the area.

15

Sometimes you get caught so unprepared that there's not a damn thing you can do about it. The spotlight was from up the slope and slightly to the side, in the area Rachel was supposed to be watching, but far enough off to the side that if she wasn't scanning through 180 degrees continuously, she would have missed them. I should have been clearer in my instructions when I put her on rear guard.

I had a bloody Kukri in my right hand, my incapacitated rifle was laying on the ground where I'd left it, and the spotlight was far enough away and bright enough that I couldn't tell if there was one man or one hundred in the darkness behind it. Dog growled and started to move towards the light, but I stopped him with a firm hand on his back. Rachel looked over her shoulder at me, the panic on her face plain to see.

I didn't have a move at the moment and decided to play it cool and bide my time. Bending slowly, I wiped the Kukri blade clean on the carpet of leaves, sheathed it and stood back up with my hands held out at my sides and faced the light.

"That was an impressive display," a voice called out from behind the light, and I couldn't have been more surprised to hear a woman's voice. I stood mute and noticed Rachel stand up in my peripheral vision.

"Honey, you don't need that rifle. If we wanted to hurt you, we'd have already done that."

Rachel looked over at me, and I nodded for her to keep the rifle pointed at the ground. Apparently satisfied with the situation the speaker stepped into the light and came down the slope to stand in front of us. She was not what I expected.

The woman was at least in her mid-fifties and despite being dressed for the forest, she didn't look like she had spent a lot of time outdoors. Middle aged spread had definitely set in, her ass was as wide as my shoulders, and grey hair framed a face set off by gold-rimmed glasses. Bright blue eyes studied me in the light. For all the world she looked like what I remembered my third-grade teacher looking like.

"If there's more infected around, that light is going to draw them in," I said, keeping my hands in plain sight.

I didn't know if she had rifles behind the light pointed at us and wasn't ready to find out the hard way.

"That's what you call them? Hmmm. Fits, I suppose. Are you really Army?" She asked as she studied my clothing and the oak leaf on my chest.

"Yes, ma'am. I am. Major John Chase," I introduced myself, figuring a little good old fashioned courtesy couldn't hurt.

"And who's she?" She asked, looking over at Rachel.

"She is his traveling companion, and her name is Rachel," Rachel answered, apparently not appreciating being talked about like she wasn't there.

The woman turned and stared at her, seemingly assessing her character just by looking at her. After almost a minute she made a 'humphing' sound in her throat, turned her head and called over her shoulder.

"Turn off the light."

A long moment later it shut off, and I was as blind as a bat, night vision completely destroyed by several minutes of the light shining in my eyes.

"Thank you," I said. "Who are you, and what are you doing out here?"

"I think the more pressing question is what are you doing out here?"

I couldn't see her face, but I knew she was still intently watching me. Trusting my gut instincts about this woman I told her an abbreviated version of the truth, starting with the night of the attacks when I was in Atlanta. I debated holding back the part about the ambushers that had forced us into the forest, but if she was mixed up with that group, we would likely have already been shot.

"OK, now you know who we are. What about you?"

She started to answer but was cut off before she could speak a word by the scream of a female infected that sounded way too close. My night vision was coming back, and I saw the flash of fear wash across her face before she turned and motioned towards where the light had been. Grabbing my rifle off the ground I watched as half a dozen teenagers, two boys and four girls, dashed forward and huddled around her. They were armed with sticks, rocks, a couple of pocket knives and a big ass battery powered spotlight.

Rachel had already raised her rifle. Dropping the magazine from mine, I cycled the bolt and ejected the round that had failed to fire. Skills from a day gone by guided my fingers as I quickly separated the lower and upper sections of the rifle, extracted the bolt and checked it by feel. Everything felt as it should.

Next, I stuck a finger into the chamber and could feel part of a shell casing jammed in there. Apparently the last successfully fired round had come from a shell that was weak and had separated, leaving part of the brass casing stuck in the chamber. It took some force, but I got it out, reassembled the rifle and loaded up with a fresh magazine.

All of this had taken less than a minute. Again, I was thankful for the instructors that had beaten lessons into us, sometimes literally. I had been taught to field strip and assemble rifles while wearing a blindfold. Once I could do that the instructors had added blows to the head, neck and back from a baton during the process. If it took longer than a minute to complete, they would start hitting below the waist. It didn't take long to learn to do it in less than a minute.

Rifle ready, I raised it and sighted through the scope, scanning the surrounding terrain. Sprinting along the valley floor and quickly closing on us were three females. They were moving fast, even for the females, and as I watched they hurtled and dodged obstacles like NFL running backs. As I was tracking them, another scream sounded from behind us, much too close, and I heard Dog growl and scramble up the slope to meet the infected.

"Rachel?" I asked.

"Got it," she said, and I kept my attention on the three fast approaching threats.

Behind me there was another scream, immediately drowned out by Dog's snarling and the sound of bodies hitting the ground in a struggle. Dog's snarling rose in pitch then it was quiet, a moment later his furry head back by my side.

"Good boy," I muttered, then pulled the trigger and dropped one of the females.

The other two kept coming, not slowing or showing any indication that they cared their sister had just gone down. Tracking, I shot the second one as she leapt over a fallen tree, her body going limp in the air and crashing to the forest floor in a tangle of limbs and coming to rest against the trunk of a massive oak tree.

The last female was the fastest and was weaving her way through the trees, now no more than fifty yards away. I waited a moment until she started up the slope to where I was standing then pulled the trigger twice. One round to the heart, one to the head. The body slammed to the ground and lay still.

Raising the rifle back up, I scanned left, right, left quickly, didn't see any threats, and then did a slower scan to make sure I wasn't missing something. Satisfied for the moment, I spun and checked behind me, glad to see Rachel scanning through a full 180 degrees with her scoped rifle, but double checked her. Again, all clear.

Letting out a big breath, I let the rifle hang on its sling and turned back to the old woman and kids. The kids looked terrified, the boys trying to look tough through their fear. The woman looked like this was something she saw every day. Perhaps she did.

"I'm going to guess the camp down the valley with all the camp fires is yours," I said.

"Yes, that's us," she answered, some of the certainty in her bearing that had been there earlier was now gone.

"Those fires are attracting the infected, and they're also going to bring in the guys that ambushed us earlier." I didn't like what I was thinking but didn't have much choice.

"Rachel, you and Dog get them to their camp and get those damn fires put out. I'm going for our packs and will meet you there."

I waited for Rachel to nod, then took off at a run, back in the direction we had come from. I didn't like the idea of sending them off alone, but I really didn't like the idea of losing the extra ammo, food, medical supplies and all the other equipment that was in our packs.

Settling into a fast trot, I moved through the forest and for a moment flashed back to running through a dark Central American jungle with Soviet military advisors – read Spetsnaz – in hot pursuit.

Forcing my attention back to the present, I touch checked the readiness of my rifle as I ran.

I was making a little noise, but less than most people would have and was able to hear the shambling feet dragging along through dead leaves before I could see the infected. Raising the rifle, I spotted the target and shot it without breaking stride, dodging around the body and quickly leaving it behind.

Earlier we had been moving slowly as we tracked the herd and even though we'd spent a lot of time walking we hadn't gone very far. In less than fifteen minutes, I was at the shallow cave and hoisting my pack onto my back. With it in place, I lifted Rachel's and put it on backwards so that it was resting on my chest. Between the two packs, I now had almost 180 pounds hanging on my upper body, and I had also blocked my access to spare magazines. Oh well, I'd just better be careful.

Taking a moment to scan the surrounding forest, I didn't see any threats but thought I could hear voices in the distance. Standing perfectly still and calming my breathing I listened intently and was sure I could hear something back in the direction of the ambush, but couldn't tell what I was hearing. Whatever it was almost sounded like chanting, but it was still a long way off, and I didn't have time to worry about it until it became a threat. Turning back towards the direction of the camp I started a slow jog which was all I could manage with this much weight.

Half an hour later I was approaching where I knew the camp had to be. I had killed three more infected males with the Kukri as I jogged down the valley and I was thankful that I hadn't run into any more females. Coming to a stop, I raised the rifle and scanned, finding no threats. Keeping the rifle up across my chest, I proceeded, now at a walking pace.

After another hundred yards, I stopped and scanned again, spotting two more infected males off to my right. They hadn't detected me, and I didn't want to leave them loose behind me. I moved their way, used a tree to lean on to steady my aim and dropped them both with two quick shots. Another scan and back to a fast walk.

Five minutes later I started smelling a recently extinguished fire and knew I was close to the camp. Slowing, I moved into some deeper brush and scanned the forest again. Ahead, probably about fifty yards, a small group of figures huddled in the dark. A dog sat to the side of the group looking off to his side into the forest. Dog smelled me about the same time I spotted him, and he came running, tail wagging.

Rachel had the old woman, and the kids huddled with their backs against a sheer rock face that soared up into the night. There were two more boys and a girl that hadn't been with the group when we'd encountered them earlier. Not comfortable staying in the area where the camp had been so visible, I told the woman we were moving farther down the valley. Two of the girls started to complain, but she shushed them and got everyone on their feet. Putting Rachel and Dog at the back of the group I took point and we moved a slow mile.

I had started us off at a good pace, but the kids made so much noise in the forest that I had to slow our pace. Towards the front of the group two of the boys were talking to each other and after the first time, I gestured for them to be quiet I had to call a halt and get in their faces to get the message across.

Finally reaching a smaller valley that branched off to the north and had a small stream trickling through it, we followed the water until finding a wide, flat spot on the valley floor that was heavily forested. Moving the group into the thick brush, I settled them down with warnings to stay quiet and went to find out their story from the woman.

16

Betty Jasinski snapped awake instantly when she heard the first screams outside her motel room. A mother and grandmother, she was conditioned to responding to any noise that sounded like a child in distress, and when a second scream reached her ears, she threw the covers off and started dressing quickly.

Betty was a bus driver for the Nashville School District and currently had a charge of two teachers, two parent chaperones, and twenty-seven ninth graders on a field trip to Six Flags amusement park north of Atlanta. It had been a good trip, the kids as well-behaved as you could expect for their ages. They were spending their last night in a budget motel with plans to make the six-hour drive home the next morning.

Betty pulled her shoes on, stood up, glancing at the clock which read 4:03 AM, and went to the window. Parting the heavy curtains, she failed to suppress a sneeze when a cloud of dust came out of the fabric. Wiping her nose and eyes, she looked out the window from her second floor room. Below, the parking lot looked empty, and she automatically sought out the big yellow bus with her eyes to make sure it was where she had left it. The bus looked fine.

Crucifixion

Betty's attention was drawn to two figures at the edge of the parking lot, what looked like a man lying on the ground with a woman straddling him and moving about vigorously. Betty's first thought was the couple was drunk and had decided to have sex in the parking lot, but that idea was dispelled when she saw the woman lean into the man's throat and appear to tear it open with her teeth.

In shock, Betty kept watching as the woman continued to rip chunks of flesh off the body. Another scream to her left shifted her attention as a second woman raced across the parking lot and joined the first in attacking the man.

A knock on the motel room door immediately to her left caused Betty to jump back from the window with a small gasp of fright. The knocking continued, and a woman's voice started calling out her name. Gathering herself after she recognized Miss Welch's voice, she unhooked the safety chain and yanked the door open.

Miss Welch was the youngest teacher in the school. To Betty, she seemed hardly older than the kids she was responsible for educating. She rushed into the room, eyes wide with fright and her whole body shaking.

"What's happening?" She cried, grabbing onto Betty the way a child would her mother.

"Easy, child," Betty said, sounding much more reassuring than she felt. "Something bad is happening, and I think we need to get these young people on the bus and head home."

"But there's women out there EATING someone!" Tears were flowing now.

"That's what it looks like, but we don't know what's going on. Right now it's our job to make sure these children are safe. Can you help me do that?"

Betty grasped the younger woman's shoulders in her hands and looked into her eyes. Miss Welch nodded her head and wiped at the tears running down her cheeks.

"Now, do you have your key?"

Betty was referring to the master key the motel manager had given to each teacher that would allow them access to all of the rooms the kids were in. Miss Welch nodded her head.

"Good. Now what you're going to do is wake up Mrs. Hatfield, Mrs. Wilson, and Mr. Jackson and get them to help you round up all the kids and get them on the bus. Can you do that?" Miss Welch sniffed back tears and nodded her head again. "Honey, I want to hear you say it."

"Y – y – yes. I can do that."

"Good, now get busy. No time to tarry."

Betty gave a gentle push towards the open door. Miss Welch turned and dashed out, Betty following after pausing long enough to grab her purse and the bus keys off the small table in front of the window. Everything else she had in the room was just clothing and toiletries that could easily be replaced.

Outside, she turned and headed down the second-floor walkway towards the stairs at the end of the building, keeping her eyes on the two women at the far edge of the parking lot. They were still engrossed with the man lying on the ground and weren't paying any attention to her. Reaching the top of the stairs she turned to start down them and froze in her tracks. To the south a massive fire burned, bright enough to light up the entire horizon.

"Good Jesus, help us tonight," she muttered as she started down the stairs.

Betty hadn't reached the bottom step when a scream from above froze her in her tracks. Looking up she watched as Mr. Jackson appeared to be hugging Miss Welch in the door to his room, then they fell back into the dark interior, and she lost sight of them. She hesitated a moment, wanting to get the bus started and ready to go, but afraid something was terribly wrong with Mr. Jackson and Miss Welch.

Reversing direction, she climbed back up the stairs as fast as she could, hurrying to the door where she had last seen them. Arriving at the door, she stopped and tried to peer inside, but the room was completely dark.

She could hear a wet, slurping sound intermingled with guttural snarls and involuntarily took a step back. Forcing herself forward, she stepped back to the doorway and reached inside, feeling on the wall for the light switch. Finding it, she flipped it up, and dim lights came on inside the room.

Mr. Jackson was on top of Miss Welch, tearing at her throat with his teeth. The horrible sounds were coming from him as he ripped into her. She lay on her back, legs twisted under her, arms splayed out to the side, and her face was turned to the door. Her dead eyes stared up at Betty.

Betty remained rooted in place, her mind refusing to process what her eyes were seeing. She had forgotten to breathe and finally the need overcame her terror, and she drew a sharp breath. Mr. Jackson's head instantly snapped up in her direction, and she gasped. His eyes were as red as the blood that coated his face and ran down onto his chest.

With a gurgling snarl, he lurched to his feet, never taking his focus off the doorway where Betty stood. Reaching his feet, he took a step forward and growled. Betty snapped out of her shock, reached forward and pulled the door shut as she stumbled back. Her foot struck something that clattered metallically on the concrete balcony, and she looked down to see the master key. Miss Welch must have dropped it when Mr. Jackson grabbed her.

Scooping up the key, Betty started dashing down the line of rooms, unlocking doors and screaming for people to get up. The third door she opened was a room shared by four of the girls and one of them screamed and leapt at her as soon as the door moved. Betty's hand was still on the knob, and she jerked backwards away from the attack and pulled the door shut in her panic. Hard thumps immediately started from inside the room as the girl pounded on the door in a rage.

Trying to shake off her terror, Betty continued down the row, but now she banged on each door with her fists before opening it. Several times there was an answering scream or snarl and banging from inside the room, and Betty left those doors closed.

Less than five minutes later Betty had roused all of the kids that were in rooms without one of the monsters and had them standing on the balcony. Mrs. Hatfield, the other parent, and Mrs. Wilson, the other teacher were both missing. When Betty had knocked on their doors, there had been screams and loud thumps as a response. The same had happened at several of the kids' rooms.

As the group stood there, screams and pounding coming from the rooms at their backs, Betty took a quick head count. Nineteen. That's all that was remaining from the twenty-seven she'd brought from Nashville. Betty had no idea what was going on, but she knew she had to get these kids to the safety of the bus and get away from Atlanta.

Quickly she herded the kids into a group, trying to be compassionate for the ones who stood there crying, but the need to move faster prompted her to start pushing and grabbing arms to get control. A minute later she led the group to the stairs, and they started down. The kids were completely terrified and bunched tightly together and against her back as they moved. Halfway down the stairs the sound of shattering glass caused them to pause and look up. Mrs. Wilson pushed through her room's broken window and screamed when she saw them on the stairs.

Crucifixion

"Run!" Betty cried, rushing down the stairs and urging the kids to move.

Mrs. Wilson was a young woman, a former alternate for the US Gymnastics Olympic team. She showed her athleticism by vaulting over the second-floor balcony railing and landing on the roof of a parked car, shattering all of its windows as the roof caved in under the impact of her feet. She leapt to the ground without even a pause and rushed at the group.

Her step-daughter, Riann, froze and stared, still standing there when Mrs. Wilson launched herself into the air and tackled the young girl to the ground. Riann screamed, but it was cut off as her step-mother ripped into her throat. Another window on the second-floor shattered and Betty ran as fast as her aging, out of shape body could go, fumbling the bus keys in her hand so she would be prepared to unlock the doors as soon as she reached them.

Another window on the second-floor shattered, but Betty didn't take the time to look and see who it was. The bus was now only thirty yards away, and most of the kids had run ahead of her and were just reaching it, yelling for her to hurry. Out of the dark from the far side of the bus two men lumbered into sight, each grabbing a kid and pulling them to the ground.

Dirk Patton

A female dashed in from the other direction and tore open one girl's throat with a slash of her nails before falling onto another girl and savaging her face and neck. Betty charged up, huffing like a steam engine, and tried to still her shaking hands so she could get the keys in the lock for the bus doors. While she did this, two more females charged the group, each taking a boy to the ground with screams of rage.

Finally getting the keys in the lock, Betty opened the doors and stepped aside to hurry the kids onto the bus. They jammed up at the doors, too many bodies trying to get through at the same time. While she wasted precious seconds sorting them out, another woman and two more men showed up, and each took another kid. The terror of seeing his classmates being torn apart and eaten was too much for one young boy.

Turning away from the crush of students trying to get onto the bus he started walking out into the parking lot, a vacant look on his face as tears and snot flowed. A few moments later he was descended on by three women who tore into him with a savagery that shocked and terrified Betty.

Kids finally on the bus, she quickly stepped up and leaned her weight into the lever that operated the doors, slamming them a second before a screaming woman crashed into them. The glass cracked in a spider web pattern, and the woman

170

started beating on it with her fists and continued to scream her rage. Betty slipped behind the wheel and started the bus.

Not waiting for it to warm up, she shifted into drive and hit the throttle. The big diesel engine clattered and roared, and the bus slowly started moving. Betty stayed on the throttle as the front bumper crashed into a sedan, shoving it out of the way with a screech of metal as more women ran screaming at the bus and slammed into the sides. The kids screamed with every impact, and Betty fought the wheel to straighten the bus out and head north on the highway that would take them to Tennessee.

"How did you wind up here?" I asked in a quiet voice.

Rachel was seated on the other side of Betty listening to the story. The kids had formed up into a tight group and huddled a few feet away from us. Dog had found nine new friends and was soaking up the petting and attention he was getting from them. Watching them, I was reminded of a news story I had once read about pets being used to help kids deal with post-traumatic shock. It certainly looked like Dog was a welcome addition.

"We drove for a few hours. Those crazy women just kept attacking the bus and the men just stood in the road. I had to run so many of them over because they won't move. I tried to get to the interstate, but we got trapped in a gridlock of wrecked and abandoned cars. We waited for two days for the police or the Army, or anyone, to come help us.

"When no one showed up, and there weren't any of those things prowling around we finally left the bus and started walking. My family is from around here, and when we came to Wallace Creek I knew where we were, and we left the road and started cutting through the country."

"You and these kids have been on foot for two weeks?" Rachel asked in surprise.

"That's right, sweetie." Betty looked at her and smiled. "Like I said, my family is from around here, and I know the area, but I also grew up a tomboy, and I know how to live in the woods. This is Tennessee after all, not Atlanta."

"But what have you been eating?" Rachel was amazed.

I was kind of proud of the old woman. Again, I was reminded never to judge a book by its cover.

"Darling, if you know where to look there's plenty of food in these woods. Maybe not McDonalds, but a body can do just fine on roots and berries, and trapping squirrel and rabbit sure ain't rocket science. Kind of good for me, actually. I think I've lost some weight." Betty said the last with a chuckle as she patted her ample hips.

"What were you doing away from your camp when you found us?" I asked, taking a moment to raise the rifle and scan the woods.

"We heard the gunfire, must have been you being ambushed, and thought maybe it was the police or the Army. Well, I guess it was the Army since it was you we heard." It was too dark to see, but I imagined there was a twinkle in her eye when she said this. "Gotta be careful. Letting an old woman and a bunch of kids get the drop on you like that."

I grinned, both in embarrassment and agreement.

"One thing about that," I said, my tone gentle. "You're very fortunate my rifle was out of commission. If it had been in my hands, I would likely have opened up on that spotlight."

"Don't you think I knew that, young man?" Betty softened the rebuke by reaching out and patting my forearm.

Properly chastised, I sat back and thought about our next move. Now that I had gotten involved I couldn't just walk away from Betty and her kids, but at the same time, I was really feeling the internal pressure to get to Arizona and find Katie. It would be nice if I could get them to Nashville and be on my way, but after the recent additional outbreaks, I didn't know if Nashville was still a safe place.

There was also the massive herd of infected moving towards the area that Max had talked about on the radio, and I no longer had much confidence that the Army was in any shape to hold them at the border. The other option, dragging them along with me all the way to Arizona, was not one I was willing to entertain.

Crucifixion

"Betty, how far are we from Nashville?" I asked, raising the rifle and scanning the surrounding woods again.

She thought for a minute before answering, "If we follow the creek north it will take us up to Murfreesboro; then it's just a few miles up 24 to get into Nashville. What are you thinking?"

"Here's the thing," I said. "I'm trying like hell to get to Arizona to find my wife, but I'm also not going to go off and leave you and these kids to fend for yourselves. I want to see all of you to safety, and getting you out of these woods and at least as far as Murfreesboro is what I need to do."

"Young man, we've survived for two weeks in 'these woods' and have been just fine. We don't need your help."

I could tell by the tone of her voice that I had offended her. Time for some stark reality and a little diplomacy.

"Betty, no offense, but how many infected have you had to fight off? What about other survivors? There's been a second outbreak, and things are pretty bad and headed to worse. You've done an absolutely amazing job of keeping these kids safe up to now, but things are getting worse and like it or not, if you want to continue keeping these kids safe you need my, our, help."

Betty was quiet for a long time, digesting my words. "We haven't had to fight any of the infected, and you're the first survivors that we've come across."

Rachel reached out and took Betty's hand in hers and started talking, relaying first the story of the men who had tried to ambush us at the outfitter store we'd raided in Atlanta, then moving on to her abduction aboard the cabin cruiser. While Rachel talked, I stood and moved a few yards out into the brush to do another check of the area.

I was on my second slow scan when movement caught my attention. Focusing on the area, I was able to see what looked to be at least 20 figures moving up the smaller valley, following our path. There was one figure out in front, the remainder bunched up together behind it, and they only moved when it moved. These weren't infected. These were men following a tracker who was on our trail. Holy hell couldn't we catch a break?

I moved quickly and quietly back to the area where everyone was sitting and called Dog to me with a soft pat on my leg. He jumped to his feet and trotted over, staying at my side as I moved. Betty was hugging Rachel when I walked up to them, but I didn't have time to be sensitive to the moment.

Crucifixion

"We've got trouble," I said, interrupting them. Rachel wiped her eyes and got on her feet, then helped Betty rise as well.

"We've got about twenty men coming up the valley, following our trail. I suspect they're part of the group that ambushed Rachel and me, looking for some payback. Betty, get the kids on their feet and make sure they are absolutely quiet. No talking. Rachel, stay with them and get them moving farther up the valley. I'm going to set up some surprises for our guests then I'll catch up."

Each of the women nodded, and I shouldered my pack and trotted off towards the approaching group, Dog on my heels. I stopped and told him to stay with Rachel, pointing back the way we had come from. If he was human, he would have complained as he turned around and ran off to find her.

I did a quick check through the rifle scope and saw that the group had covered very little ground and estimated I still had almost ten minutes before they reached me. Moving farther towards them, I was careful to control my noise. Fifty yards closer to them I stopped, knelt and dug through my pack. Supplies in hand I left the pack on the ground and started working quickly.

Less than five minutes later I was done, grabbed the pack and moved into the brush and climbed the slope away from the valley floor. Finding a spot I was happy with, I placed the pack on the ground and lay on my belly, using the pack as a rifle rest. I sighted in on the area of the valley floor where I had set up a little surprise for our pursuers. Taking advantage of their lack of tactical knowledge, which was evident by the way they bunched up when they moved, I had picked two trees on either side of the trail, about twenty feet apart and fairly well obscured by vines.

On the side of each trunk facing the trail, I had duct taped three fragmentation grenades about four feet up from the ground. Straightening out each grenade's pin so it would pull easily, I had linked all of the pins together with a thin, black nylon cord. The cord stretched around a couple of anchoring sticks I had jammed into the ground and was taut across the path at about six inches of height and thirty feet farther down the path from where the grenades were waiting.

My plan was that as the tracker moved down the path, he would walk into the trip wire which would then pull all six pins. With the bulk of the group nicely bunched up about thirty to forty feet behind him, the grenades should do some nasty damage.

Grenades were not ideal for this type of trap. Once the pins pulled, there was a five-second fuse before they detonated. Five seconds doesn't sound like a long time, but if the tracker realizes what he just walked into when he trips the wire and warns the group, it's enough time for many of them to get to a safe distance.

I'd have seriously considered giving up my left nut for a couple of Claymore mines to use in my trap. A Claymore is packed with C4 and seven hundred steel ball bearings that will absolutely shred anything in the blast zone of fifty meters. And Claymores don't have time delay fuses. Oh well. Once again I reminded myself of the old adage that you fight with what you have.

I was settled into the rifle stock and watching through the scope when the tracker approached the trip wire I had set up. Behind him about twenty-five feet were nineteen men, all armed. Even though they were bunched up, the narrow path forced them into a formation only two bodies wide, so they were stretched back another twenty feet. Perfect, as long as the tracker didn't warn them in time for them to scatter to safety. Slowly the tracker advanced, walking with his head down, occasionally pausing to reach down and touch the path.

How was he seeing the ground well enough to track us? That thought hadn't even gone through my head until now, and as I peered through the scope, I could make out the IR flashlight and goggles he was using. Shit! Would he spot the black cord before tripping it with his feet? I now regretted having set up a trip wire rather than running a line up to my location so I could pull the pins at precisely the right moment.

Scanning the group, I was glad to see that all of their attention was on the tracker. They weren't paying any attention to the environment around them, and I could probably have been standing on the edge of the trail, and they wouldn't have noticed me if the tracker didn't point me out. That was fine. I shifted my aim back to the tracker and saw him pause by the two trees where I had taped the grenades.

I had intentionally not pushed into the brush at those points, not wanting to leave a trace that could be detected, but something had caught his attention at the edge of the path. Bending down he touched the ground, looked off to the side directly at one of the grenade clusters for a moment, but apparently didn't spot them as he finally resumed moving forward. I let out a long breath that I hadn't realized I was holding.

A long minute later he was at the point where I'd strung the trip wire across the path. I quickly checked, and the group following him was nicely centered on the two trees. Back to the tracker, I watched him stop and hold up a fist. The group stopped, but not after bunching up a little tighter. I felt a small thrill of exhilaration. It looked like my trap was going to work.

A moment later I was dismayed to see the tracker drop to one knee and closely examine the trip wire, then turn his head first to the right then left to see where it went. Making a snap decision, I sighted on his head, exhaled and pulled the trigger. He was on his knees and leaning forward over the line to look at it, and my bullet struck his left temple and blew out the right side of his head, the plume of blood and brains visible in the night vision scope.

The body collapsed instantly, falling onto the trip wire. I couldn't tell if the pressure on the line that pushed it down six inches to the ground was enough to pull the grenade pins. I'd find out in five seconds.

Moving my aim back to the group, I saw them tense up, and all start trying to move at the same time as they reacted to their tracker going down. Fortunately for me, they were standing so close together that all they initially succeeded in doing was to bump into each other as there was no coordinated direction of movement. One guy at the very back had the right idea and turned to run, but I dropped him in his tracks with a well-placed shot.

Quickly shifting back to the front of the group, I shot the lead man, then pulled the trigger on another as my mental count reached five. A heartbeat later a ripple of explosions tore through the forest where they were still standing, and I lost sight of all of them from the dust and debris that six grenades blasted into the air. Both trees were blown in half at the point where the grenades had been attached and toppled to the forest floor, throwing more dust and debris into the air.

Before the dust cleared, I started hearing the screams of the wounded. I've known guys that couldn't handle hearing those screams, finally opting out of the military to get away from them, but they were music to my ears. Hearing the screams of your enemy means you're still alive and have inflicted more damage than you've taken. Hopefully. Unless you're hurt too bad to scream.

I kept watching through the scope, but there was no breeze in the valley, and it was taking a long time for the dust to settle. Movement at the back of the dust cloud drew my attention as two men supporting each other made a break back down the path. I shot both of them before they made it ten yards.

Finally, the dust thinned and I was able to make out the carnage I had wrought. Bodies and parts of bodies were scattered along the path. In one of those scenes from battle that will always stick with you as clear as the moment you saw it, I spotted a human arm dangling from a shattered tree branch, swinging slightly like it was waving at me.

Not letting myself get distracted I kept scanning and started counting bodies, running out of corpses when I reached 17. Three unaccounted for. I took a moment to scan and count a second time, but the number didn't change. Leaving the pack where it was, I moved laterally then descended towards the path, keeping to the heaviest brush. I heard number 18 before I saw him.

He was sobbing and moaning and when I angled around a large tree that had blocked my view of him I could see him sitting on the ground with his back against the trunk. His hands were clasped across his belly in a futile attempt to hold in the intestines that had spilled out when the blast had ripped him open. I showed him the only mercy I was in the mood for by shooting him in the head.

Moving closer to the trail, I kept a constant scan going for 19 and 20, finally spotting movement back down the path as a figure broke from the trees and started running. I was a blink away from pulling the trigger on him when a body crashed into my left side, knocking the rifle off aim and me to the ground. Grunting with the impact of the body and the ground I rolled to get my hands up and between us, but this guy had been in a few tussles and knew what I was trying to do.

When we had landed, he came down on top of me and was using his not inconsiderable body weight to pin my legs as he controlled my upper body with a hand locked into my vest while he pounded my head with his fist. Feeling his weight shift I knew what was coming and got my hips turned just in time to take the knee that was intended for my balls on the side of my thigh. It still hurt like hell, but at least wasn't incapacitating like a shot to the boys would have been.

I stopped trying to fight against his pressure and instead rolled on the ground in the direction he was pushing. This caught him by surprise and with his arm pinned against my chest he had to roll with me. We wound up on our backs with me on top. He tried to wrap me in a bear hug, but I broke the embrace and started rocketing elbows behind me into his ribs. The second elbow I threw, hit perfectly, and I felt at least two of his ribs snap.

One more elbow in the same spot brought a grunt of pain from him then I raised my head and smashed it back into his face as hard as I could. For a moment, his grip on me went slack, and I rolled off and leapt to my feet five feet away, drawing the Kukri as I rose into a crouch. He started to fumble for a holstered pistol, and I lunged in and buried all twelve inches of the blade in his guts and cut upwards until the blade stopped against his breastbone.

Yanking the blade free of the corpse, I looked in the direction the last pursuer had run, but couldn't see him in the dark. Moving on autopilot I started running after him, Kukri held in my right hand, blood running off it and spattering onto the forest path as I ran. I covered ground quickly, keeping my steps light and as quiet as possible.

There was a little moonlight, and I was able to see and avoid sticks on the ground and branches in my path. After five minutes of running, I made it to the larger valley where Betty and the kids had been camped and paused to check the ground to make sure I was still following the man. Before I could spot anything in the jumble of footprints from the passage of two large groups I heard him crashing through the bush to my right, back towards the site of the ambush on the road.

Turning, I broke into a fast lope, now tracking him by sound as he continued to step on a stick or run into a bush every few seconds. Several minutes later I crested a small rise and saw him a hundred yards in front of me. The man was struggling through the dark forest.

He was overweight and out of shape and even from this distance I could hear his ragged breathing. His run wasn't much faster than a very slow jog, and I came to a stop when I heard voices ahead in the forest.

Did I let him escape and tell a terrifying story to his friends? The idea had merit. A frightened enemy is a significantly lesser threat than a mad enemy, and finding all their friends dead would frighten them, but would also make them mad.

However, a lone survivor running out of the woods and telling a terrifying story of how his entire group was wiped out in the blink of an eye could better serve my purpose. Decision made, I turned and started running back down the valley.

Approaching my ambush site, I slowed when I heard what sounded like wild animals fighting. Raising the rifle and looking through the night vision scope I was momentarily disgusted by the site of a small pack of infected feasting on the bodies.

There were four males and two females, and the females would feed on a corpse for a few minutes then move to another. If another infected happened to also be feeding on the new corpse, the female would attack it and force it to back off.

This was another new behavior I hadn't seen before and didn't quite know what to make of. Shooting the first female as she thrust her hands into the body cavity of one of the corpses, I quickly acquired and fired at the second female but missed.

As soon as my suppressed shot had sounded, she had moved, dashing into the surrounding trees. What the hell was that?

Feeling less confident about being able to easily clear them out, I quickly sighted in on and shot all the males, but the female I had missed hadn't reappeared and wasn't making any noise. Not good. Carefully scanning the dark woods, I couldn't spot her. I was almost certain she was still in the area and was stalking me. Lowering the rifle, I drew the Kukri and stepped off the path into thicker brush and started silently circling around the carnage.

I took my time, lowering the toe of each boot gently onto the ground and testing the spot before I transferred my weight. This is a slow way to move, but when stealth is more important than speed, it's the only way to move. Eventually, I had circled the area and was slightly upslope, only a few yards from where I had left my pack.

I started to move towards the pack, then stopped and froze in place. If I was lying in wait for someone and there was something I knew they'd come back for, like my pack, I'd set up on it and wait for them to come to me and attack when they were vulnerable. For five minutes I stood perfectly still, controlling my breathing, the only movement my head turning slowly as I scanned the area repeatedly. Even though I wasn't detecting a threat didn't mean it wasn't there.

Was I giving too much credit to the female? Up until now I hadn't seen any indication that the infected were able to reason or problem solve, rather had watched them repeatedly behave in only a mindless pursuit of any prey that was in front of them. Was that changing? Were they learning? Was this a product of the viral component that the scientists hadn't been able to identify, or had I just happened to encounter a gifted one?

Never one to believe in coincidence, I filed away this one's behavior and refocused on the task at hand. My pack lay on the ground five yards ahead of me on a clear patch of ground that was only a couple of yards across. Heavy brush surrounded the clearing except at the rocky edge where it looked down on my ambush site.

If she was waiting for me, it would be in the brush at the back or on the far side of the clearing. Moving a millimeter at a time, I sheathed the Kukri and raised the rifle. Placing my eye up to the scope it only took me seconds to find the female hiding in the brush on the far side of the clearing.

She was squatted a couple of feet from the edge of the clearing and was sitting perfectly still; her head turned to watch the path below where the corpses lay. She hadn't seen or smelled me.

Crucifixion

The forest was very quiet as if even the trees and rocks were holding their breath, and my current problem was that the rifle was on safe, and it would make a small degree of noise when I moved the selector to fire. Whether or not she would hear it was the question, but I had already seen that these things seemed to have enhanced senses, and I prepared myself to enable the rifle and get a shot off as quickly as possible. Target sighted I exhaled silently, clicked the safety lever with my thumb and fired. Miss again.

She had moved the instant the rifle had clicked off safe. Damn, that was some reaction time. There was no way any normal human could have avoided my shot. She had dropped lower to the ground and moved to the side and now burst into the clearing, charging directly at me on all fours at a surprising speed. I snapped off another shot that missed her head but impacted at the base of her neck, most likely shattering her collarbone as she lost control of one of her arms and crashed to the ground.

Faster than should have been possible she rolled and leapt to her feet and launched herself into the brush to the side. She was breaking off the attack? That was definitely new. Up to now an infected that spotted prey maintained pursuit of that prey until it either escaped or the infected was killed. Self-preservation had not been a part of the equation.

Dirk Patton

Still tracking the female with the night scope, I saw her running down the slope towards the path and I stepped forward into the clearing, waited a moment then snapped off another shot that blew out a chunk of her skull and dropped the body into the dust. I didn't have time to celebrate my small victory as I was tackled from behind and slammed to the ground on my face.

Another female that I hadn't seen or heard was on my back and ripping at me with her hands as she leaned in and tried to bite me. All that saved me was the high collar of the tactical vest and the shemagh I had wrapped around my neck. I could feel the pressure from her bites, but her teeth weren't able to get through the layers of tough fabric. More than a little freaked out I got my hands under me and shoved, pushing both of us off the ground where I was able to twist my body to come back down on top of the infected.

But she wasn't there, and I landed on the ground, hard, flat on my back. She had leapt off me when I had pushed off the ground, and now the bitch straddled me like a lover and lunged her head forward with teeth bared in an attempt at my throat. Her hands were on my upper arms, trying to control them, and while she was much stronger than a normal woman her size she was still no match for a man more than a hundred pounds heavier that could bench press more than his own body weight.

190

Crucifixion

Forcing my arms up and together in front of my chest I was able to get my right hand wrapped around her throat. Pushing harder, I levered her up until my arms were almost fully extended and hit her hard in the face with my left. No effect. Damn these things were tough. Holding her by the throat at arm's length she couldn't reach my face, throat or chest, but she started trying to rip open my arms with her ragged nails.

Again, the heavy, military issue fabric did its job and protected me. Still struggling with her I rolled and got her on her back on the ground. Pinning her lower body with my weight, I leaned into the grip on her throat and squeezed for all I was worth. She thrashed and struggled, a couple of times nearly bucking me off but I held on, and almost two full minutes later she lay still.

Not a trusting soul, I maintained the pressure for another thirty seconds, staring down at the woman and blinking sweat out of my eyes. She had been young and pretty, once. She was slender with long, red hair and had the kind of features that would have made men remember her. Now she was filthy and bloody with matted hair, and she was dead.

Releasing my grip, I flexed my hand a couple of times, drew the Kukri and rammed the blade into her brain. No reason to take any chances. Wiping the blade on her tattered shirt, I sheathed it and stood up. A scan of the area with the scope didn't reveal any more threats, so I grabbed my pack off the ground, shouldered it and set off down the slope to catch up with Rachel, Dog and our new friends.

As I ran to catch up with my group I had to force myself to not think about what had just happened. Dwelling on it would be a distraction that I couldn't afford as I moved through the dark woods. It didn't take long for me to pick up their trail and I stopped for a moment with the intent to disguise it to throw off any more trackers, but there was just too much disturbance to hide.

The kids, like so many teenagers seemed to do, dragged their heels on the ground every step forward they took, and this was leaving a trail that Helen Keller could have followed. Making a mental note to spend a little time instructing them how to walk in the forest I set back off at a fast jog, heavy pack bouncing on my back.

A few minutes later I rounded a curve in the terrain which opened up in front of me. What had been a fairly narrow valley now widened dramatically, the floor spreading out to be almost a quarter of a mile wide. The small creek, Wallace Creek I believe Betty had called it, joined with a much larger creek and formed a small river. The sides of the valley were still manageable if we had to climb, but they were much steeper than they had been and more heavily forested.

I could hear a low roar from ahead that I couldn't identify, but as I moved farther into this new valley I recognized the sound as a waterfall. Pausing where I was, I brought the rifle up, scanned ahead and cursed. Five infected were moving down through the trees ahead of me, apparently tracking the group.

Turning, I checked my rear and was relieved to not see any threats. Back to the front I sighted in on each of the infected and identified all of them as females. Oh shit!

Were they going to be the more dangerous variety I had just encountered? Obviously, I'd just fought two females that were able to think well enough to set up and execute an ambush. I had gotten used to the predictability of the infected. If they saw you, they were attacking and were coming straight at you.

They didn't try to hide and surprise you, and they didn't work together. If this was happening with all of the females, the level of danger they presented had just increased exponentially. Putting my musing aside, I stepped off and started stalking the hunters.

Dropping the pack again, I quickly exchanged the empty magazines in my vest for loaded ones, then left the pack in the brush near the river. Moving deeper into the valley, I started following two of the females who appeared to be moving together. They were walking quietly through the forest, only the occasional tick to their movements giving away the fact they were infected.

If I hadn't seen a few thousand of them before, I probably wouldn't have realized, they were infected until I was right in front of them. Males are easy to spot as they move like someone who's just left the bar after about ten too many drinks, but the females were even more agile once infected than they had been before.

Ten yards behind the two females, I stopped and checked on the other three through the scope. One was thirty yards farther down the valley and a hundred yards to my right. The remaining two were on the other side of the river, several hundred yards away. Back to the two I was stalking, I moved closer, careful to keep my steps either on soft dirt or rocky outcroppings so I wouldn't make any noise and alert them to my presence.

They were close together as they moved, close enough to touch each other if they wanted. I decided to take them out as quietly as possible. Lowering the rifle, I drew the blade, gripped it tightly and leaned forward as I burst into a sprint.

I was a yard behind them when they heard me. Both spun at the same time, the one on the right opening her mouth to scream but the scream never left her throat because I covered that yard in one fast step and sliced through her neck, nearly cutting her head off her body. The Kukri lodged in her vertebrae, and I didn't waste time trying to pull it free, rather released it to remain stuck in the female's neck as she crumpled dead to the ground.

I was in a full sprint and used my momentum to my advantage, lowering my shoulder and ramming into the chest of the female on my left. I heard the breath whoosh out of her lungs from the impact, and she flew backwards, landing on her back in the dirt. Following through I fell on top of her, bringing my knee down with all my weight into her stomach and locking my left hand on her throat.

Even with the wind knocked out of her and a 230-pound pile driver to the stomach, she was still able to fight and started twisting her body and slashing with her hands to try and throw me off. I kept the pressure on and leaned my weight into her throat with my right hand on the ground for balance.

When I touched the ground, my hand was on top of a softball sized stone, nicely rounded by eons of river water flooding through the valley. Grasping the stone, I raised it in the air and brought it down on the infected's forehead, both hearing and feeling her skull crack and cave in. She instantly went still, and the animal light in her eyes blinked out.

Crucifixion

Standing up, I slipped the stone into my pocket before bending and retrieving the Kukri where it had lodged in the other female's neck. Blade sheathed, I brought the rifle around and checked the other three. The one closest had stopped and was looking around like she may have heard something, but the two on the far side of the river were still moving forward and were now angling slightly toward the water.

Trusting there was enough distance to safely use the suppressed rifle, I sighted in on the closest female and dropped her with a shot to the head, then quickly looked for the two across the river. Both were still moving at the same pace and hadn't heard anything. Taking a moment to check my rear again, which was still clear, I ran forward and angled towards the river.

I knew my group was on this side of the valley, and the two females would have to cross the river to get to them. What I didn't know was if the river was shallow and slow enough for the females to be able to ford it. I hoped it was over their heads and running swiftly as it came up to the waterfall, but I couldn't count on it.

My plan at the moment was to keep them in sight and when and if they tried to cross over they would be easy targets. No reason to make it more difficult than it had to be.

Another couple of hundred yards and the females were stalking along the far side of the river which was now close to forty feet wide. The waterfall sounds were masking all other noises in the environment, and I knew it couldn't be far away. Taking a few moments, I scanned behind me, all clear, then ahead of me looking for my group but I still couldn't see them.

That didn't concern me because I was still finding signs of their passing. I was close enough that the footprints they were leaving in the moist soil of the valley floor hadn't even had time to fill up with water. They weren't more than five minutes ahead of me.

The two females came all the way to the water's edge and stopped, looking across the river at an angle that was ahead of my position. I was reasonably sure they were looking at my group. Watching them, I was tempted to take the shots, but the reaction time of the female earlier concerned me.

I didn't want to shoot and get one of them and leave one running around that was alerted to my presence. I'd much rather be the one doing the stalking than the one being stalked. The females didn't stand still for long before they continued down the river bank. I started moving with them, keeping them in sight.

Crucifixion

A few minutes later I could tell we were just upstream from the waterfall. Mist created by the water dropping into the pool at the bottom hung in the air. The foliage, heavy and green from the extra water, was the thickest I had encountered so far. It was so thick I was having trouble pushing through to the edge of the river to maintain my watch on the females.

When I finally got there, I could see them crouched on the far bank. The river had narrowed as it reached the falls and where it spilled over it was no more than twenty feet across. Large rocks thrust up out of the water and dotted the surface, the river swirling around them as it picked up speed to rush over the edge.

I had no idea what time it was, other than probably early morning, but the moon had finally made it directly overhead. It was only a half moon, but there was plenty of light to see, and I didn't like what I saw. There were six large boulders in the swirling river, and while they weren't lined up, they still created a path across the twenty feet of water that could be used if one could jump from boulder to boulder. I knew from experience that infected females were very good jumpers.

I was hearing sounds from my side of the river that were mostly masked by the roar of the waterfall but sounded like screams. The group was in trouble, and my first instinct was to charge in to help, but I had no doubt these two females were about to cross the water, and I didn't like the idea of them coming in behind me.

Even as these thoughts went through my head, one of the females sprang from a crouched position onto the rock closest to her side of the river. A moment later she leapt to the next rock, slipping slightly on the wet surface but regained her balance and quickly leapt to the next one. Now the second one jumped and landed on all fours on the first rock, using her hands to control her landing and grip much like a monkey.

Raising the rifle, I sighted on the one in the rear hoping the other wouldn't notice when she went down. The female was just preparing to jump to the second rock when my bullet blasted through her head. The body tumbled off the rock and was quickly carried over the top of the falls by the river. I shifted aim to the first female and gladly noted she hadn't seen or heard anything. She was leaping to another rock, and as she landed and caught her balance, I shot her.

Just like the other she slipped off the rock into the swirling water and half a second later was gone over the edge. Slinging the rifle, I drew the Kukri to help me move through the heavy brush faster, slashing vines and young trees to open enough of a path to push through. I wasn't being quiet, but I was still hearing screams and was more worried about speed than stealth at the moment.

Hacking and slashing through the brush, I arrived at the point where the group's trail had come up to a sharp drop off that formed the waterfall. They had angled towards the valley wall on that side and made their way down in a zig-zag pattern. The waterfall only dropped about fifty feet and at the edge of the drop off I could see down to the flat valley floor below. The group was huddled tightly, backs against the large pool the waterfall spilled into. Rachel, Dog and Betty stood at the front edge of the group, protecting the kids from a large pack of infected males.

Dropping to my stomach, I looked through the rifle scope. 14 males were shambling towards the group. Six infected bodies lay on the ground, apparently having been shot by Rachel. As I watched, I saw her struggling with the rifle and realized she had experienced a malfunction of some kind.

The kids were screaming and pushing away from the infected, the back rank of the group standing in water up to their knees. The infected were about a hundred and fifty yards away from my position. Not a terribly difficult shot, but not a slam dunk either, especially at night. Taking a deep breath, I slowly exhaled and calmed my body as I sighted on the male closest to the group.

I fired, and his head exploded as the body dropped to the wet ground. Finding my next target, I fired, then kept finding targets and firing as soon as I saw the result of my shot in the scope. When I ran out of targets, I was surprised, which is a good thing. I had been 'in the zone' and so focused on finding and eliminating targets that I wasn't thinking about counting how many I had dropped. Fourteen infected down with fourteen shots, a hundred and fifty yards downhill at night. Not too shabby.

Moving the rifle, I looked at Rachel and the group through the night vision. They were all looking in my direction, but I knew they couldn't see me. Standing up, I waved and started following their path down the steep drop. Dog met me half way down the incline, happy to see me. I couldn't progress until I stopped and scratched his head, then he was content to lead me the rest of the way down to the valley floor.

Walking up to the group, Rachel greeted me with a smile and an extended rifle. I took it, turned sideways so she could observe and quickly cleared the misfire. A round had failed to seat fully and wouldn't let the rifle cycle as it was just far enough out of position that the extractor couldn't grab it when Rachel pulled the charging handle.

I showed her the forward assist knob and gave her a fifteen second tutorial on how to clear the weapon. I didn't ask but guessed that her training on the firing range back at Arnold had been limited to marksmanship, and they hadn't had a chance to go over the nuances of the design of the M4.

I spent another few minutes getting the group rallied and held a brief discussion and tutorial with the kids about dragging their feet. A couple of them got it, but most just looked at me like I was from Mars. Finally, in exasperation, I had them stand in a large circle and watch me walk across it. When I reached the far side, I had them try to find my footprints.

Then I had them get back in the circle and picked one of the sullener kids, a slightly overweight boy who was always the last to start moving and first to sit down and had him walk the same path. As I knew he would, he didn't pick his feet up and left a mark on the ground with each step he took. When I had the kids move in and look, I saw the light come on for most of them. That was when I noticed there were only eight.

"You lost one?" I asked Betty in a low voice the kids couldn't hear.

She nodded. "Jessica Hunt. She went into the bushes to pee when we stopped, and that group of infected took her before we even knew they were there." She gestured at the bodies littering the ground.

I looked around at all the bodies, shaking my head. Then I relayed to Rachel and Betty what I had encountered with the females. Betty absorbed it but hadn't fought the infected like Rachel and I had so it didn't register with her how much this might change the game.

"All of them?" Rachel asked, worry creasing her forehead.

"Don't know," I said. "Two, for sure. The five that were tracking you above the waterfall, I just can't say. I didn't really see any sign of it, but then I never gave any of them an opportunity, so I don't know."

"We're fucked," she said.

"We've been fucked for a while now," I responded with a grin, not wanting her to go into a funk. Depression was the last thing we could afford at the moment. I got a half-assed grin in return.

"Betty, where does this valley go?" I asked.

"This is the Little Chambers River," she replied. "It ends up winding around and emptying into the Cumberland just south of Nashville. But if we follow this valley for a few more miles we'll come to a little county road we can follow into Murfreesboro."

"OK," I said after a moment. "You two get these kids moving again. I had to leave my pack behind, again, and I'm going to go back and check our rear and get my pack. I'll catch up."

Betty reached out and placed her hand on my arm. "Young man, is that the best idea? If you hadn't been here, that group would have finished us off."

I looked at her for a moment, then Rachel and finally at the group of kids sitting huddled by the water. "That pack has ammunition, food and medical supplies we need," I said. "And if I hadn't been behind you there would have been five females attacking from one side while we fought off the males. We need our rear checked and we need the supplies. I'll be back as fast as I can. Keep the kids quiet, remind them to pick up their damn feet and I'll see you before you know it."

Betty kept her hand on my arm for another moment then finally nodded her head and walked away. Rachel reached out and placed her hand on my chest for a brief time then followed Betty to get the kids up and on the move. Dog stood beside me with an expectant look on his face, but Rachel and the group needed him more than I did. I kneeled next to him and wrapped my arm around his thick neck and scratched his chest.

I was rewarded with a tail wag and a big wet lick across the face. The tail stopped wagging when I told him to stay with Rachel. With a wave, I headed back up the valley, quickly climbing the steep slope to the top of the waterfall where I stopped and scanned ahead of me. All clear at the moment.

I had dropped my pack when I'd started tracking the infected females, and it was just up at the head of the valley I was in. Moving quietly through the forest, I was close in about twenty minutes. I didn't go right up to the pack, rather moved up the valley wall on my right and set up in a stand of young trees. My pack was forty yards below me in the brush at the edge of the trail, and I carefully scanned the area around it. Nothing waiting for me.

I scanned again with the same results, then expanded the area I was checking and saw movement across the valley floor at the river, but it was only a couple of deer dipping their heads for a drink. Continuing to scan, I looked up into the narrower valley we had come down earlier and saw more movement. This time, it was of the two-legged variety.

Watching for a minute, I was confident these were not infected. They moved like normal human males that know how to move in the woods at night. There were five of them, and they were spread out across the valley floor. And they were tracking us. Shit! More guys from the ambush? What the hell? Why were they so persistent? What the hell had Rachel and I stumbled into? These had to be locals, up to something.

The guys I'd ambushed with the grenades were definitely locals and were certainly not trained for combat. I didn't get it. They'd gotten their asses seriously kicked. Twice. What was pushing them to keep coming after us? Pride only goes so far. This was something else.

The closest of the five men was over two hundred yards out, and while they weren't moving slow, they were moving cautiously. Breaking cover, I dashed down to where my pack was, did a quick inspection to make sure it hadn't been messed with before touching it, then shouldered it and started back towards my group at a fast run. I wanted to set up a couple of surprises for these guys and needed to get to the top of the drop off by the falls with enough time to get it done. I didn't really expect to encounter any more infected along this stretch of the valley but ran with the Kukri gripped in my hand just in case.

Crucifixion

Ten minutes later I reached the thicker foliage at the top of the drop-off and dropped my pack. Taking a quick look over the edge I was glad to see Rachel and the group had moved on, so I got to work. One thing about having come into the Army while there was still a large amount of Vietnam combat vets serving was the knowledge.

Vietnam had been a very nasty guerrilla war, and the Viet Cong and North Vietnamese Army – NVA – had been masters of booby traps using whatever the forest had to offer. Many of these tricks had been taught to me by an instructor at Fort Bragg, who had been a Special Forces team leader for two tours in Vietnam in the late 60s. He was one tough son of a bitch, and he'd learned a lot from his enemy. When I left the Army, I never thought any of those lessons would be needed. Boy, was I wrong.

I worked for almost twenty minutes and using young, flexible but strong trees I had set up a whip trap that would slash across the path when tripped. The tree trunk that was bent back like a spring and waiting to be released was lined with a dozen sharpened sticks that were each two feet long. Anyone on the path when it tripped would get impaled with at least two of the stakes attached to the tree as it whipped into them at waist height. A secondary trap of the same design was set to trip to the side of the path to catch anyone trying to go around.

The trip wires were the same thin, black nylon line I'd used for the grenade trap; only it was stretched across the forest floor with a scattering of leaves hiding it. The wire was stretched so tight to the stick holding the trap in place that simply stepping on it would trigger the release. Moving down the slope, I set up one more of the same trap.

A little farther down I made the third trap, a loop of line hidden in leaves and attached to a tall tree that I had forced into an arc and set up with another trip wire. Step in it and the tree would release, close the noose around your leg and yank you through the air where you'd slam into the trunk of the tree. For good measure, another half a dozen sharpened stakes protruded from the tree at the same height a body would slam into it. Satisfied with my preparations I shouldered the pack and made my way to the valley floor.

The Reverend pulled a sweat stained bandana out of his back pocket and wiped the sweat off his forehead. He stood just off the pavement in the edge of the forest and watched as his disciples fought with the Pagans occupying the military vehicle they had ambushed. The Pagans were fighting back, and when they opened up with the machine gun the Reverend momentarily feared for his own safety, but the tree he sheltered behind was over three feet thick and no machine gun bullet could penetrate.

As he watched, one of his favorite disciples aimed the large sniper rifle the Chosen had liberated from the National Guard armory and fired at the vehicle, knocking the engine out of commission. Unfortunately, the machine gunner returned fire and shredded the Reverend's followers that were clustered around the rifle, including the sniper.

James Earl Boone said a silent prayer for the fallen disciples and pulled out a small pad to make a note for himself to be sure and praise them during his next sermon. He wrote in a cramped hand, the letters poorly formed and most words misspelled. Jimmy, as he had been called before taking the title of The Reverend, had almost no formal education. The son of a whore that worked the Nashville truck stops along I-40, and an unknown father, he had stopped going to school in the third grade.

Despite a lack of education, The Reverend was a very intelligent man and instinctively knew how to influence and control others as if it was the most natural thing in the world for him. With a formal education, he would have perhaps been a successful politician or even a CEO of a large company, but the voices in his head would have talked to him no matter what he did.

A large man at nearly six and a half feet tall and three hundred pounds, he had worked as a hand on the barges that plied the Mississippi River, bounced drunks out of bars and brothels from St. Louis to New Orleans and had broken legs for Cletus Harmon, the most vicious loan shark in Middle Tennessee. Time spent in prisons in Louisiana, Mississippi and Arkansas had packed muscle onto his frame and refined his fighting skills, but at heart, he was still a coward which he masked by being a bully.

A few years ago Jimmy's voices had told him it was time to spread the word of God and gather a flock of disciples. He had attended adult literacy classes to learn to read and had devoured the Bible, Torah, Koran and the Book of Mormon.

From each of these, he had drawn the beliefs he preached, picking and choosing the parts that spoke to him, but he absolutely preferred the wrathful God of the Old Testament. Many times he had the thought that what the world needed was another vengeful and wrathful God, and in his mind, that was what he was becoming.

The heads of his enemies, who were simply people who had refused to follow him, decorated tall stakes that his disciples had driven into the ground along the highway that passed by their compound. He had thought about also using the heads of the demons that had appeared in the world, but decided they were better used for sport to amuse his flock and routinely pitted his best fighters against them. Knowing that a leader needed to lead, he also occasionally entered the pit with the demons, but only after making sure his most trusted disciples had weakened them in advance by cutting and bleeding them.

Now he watched as the firefight raged on and dozens of his disciples fell to the Pagan in the Humvee. The machine gun finally fell silent, the barrel so hot it glowed cherry red in the darkness and appeared to physically droop towards the roof of the vehicle to which it was mounted. His men started coming out from behind their bullet-riddled vehicles and advancing on the Humvee with rifles at the ready.

Seeing the opportunity, The Reverend moved out from behind the tree and quickly crossed the pavement, arriving at the abandoned Humvee ahead of his disciples. To them, it looked like he was responsible for stopping the machine gun, and as they approached each of them briefly bowed their head to him in a sign of submission and respect.

"The Pagans have fled our might!" He raised his voice loud enough for all to hear, even those who still huddled behind their vehicles. "Brother Chris, take some men and go after them. They must be punished for resisting us. Bring me their heads!"

A small man with a face like a ferret stepped forward bowed his head briefly then pointed to eight other men and told them to follow him. They disappeared into the woods at a trot at the only place the occupants of the Humvee could have gone.

The Reverend spent a few minutes walking around the ambush site and rallying his disciples with words of encouragement. He came across a young boy, no more than seventeen, huddling in terror behind the wheel of a large pickup that had been devastated by the machine gun.

"Rise and fear not the Pagans, young Brother Joseph," The Reverend said, standing over him.

The boy sniffed and shook, his fear still paralyzing him. The Reverend frowned, bent and gathered the front of the boy's shirt in a giant hand and lifted him up with one arm to stand on his toes.

Crucifixion

The smell of urine and voided bowels caused The Reverend's frown to deepen and he released the shirt and took a step back, the boy sinking to his knees in the road and shaking with renewed fear.

The Reverend looked around to make sure his disciples were paying attention and drew a heavy blade from the sheath that hung along his right leg. Grasping a handful of the boy's hair he raised the blade high in the air and slashed with all of his strength. The head separated from the body, and as The Reverend raised his left hand high in the air, it swung slowly back and forth like a pendulum. Looking around the assembled group of disciples, The Reverend again raised his voice.

"Young Brother Joseph was not worthy. Fear became his master. Your only master is the almighty God, and he has chosen me to lead you. I cannot lead you if you accept any master other than God!" His voice boomed across the forest, and spittle flew from his lips. "There is nothing to fear as long as you stay strong in your faith and obedience to me and to God!"

"Praise God! Praise The Reverend!" Jeremiah, his most loyal disciple, started the chant and soon the entire group was chanting their praises at the top of their lungs.

The Reverend looked around, beaming with pride, the severed head still dangling by its hair from his massive hand. The chant was interrupted by a loud explosion that sounded from deep in the forest. The Reverend looked in the direction of the noise as if he could see the battle that was being fought.

The chant died out as the men turned and looked in the same direction. Several shuffled their feet in fear, but no one would dare express any doubt or concern. Fear was a mortal sin in The Reverend's church.

"Brother Jeremiah, who knows these woods the best?" The Reverend asked, tossing the head to one of the men closest to him who fumbled it before quickly pulling it to his body and securing it. He had seen other men hacked to pieces for allowing one of The Reverend's heads to touch the ground.

"Brother Dale, Reverend. He grew up here and has been hunting in this forest for thirty years."

"Good. Send him and a group into the forest. I fear Brother Chris may have failed me."

The Reverend turned and stalked to the edge of the road where he stared at the dark trees and began praying that God would rain his wrath down on the Pagans.

The Reverend stood there for a long time, as still as the trees he stared at and praying to God in a loud voice. His disciples stripped anything useful from the Humvee then pushed it off the road into a shallow drainage ditch. They then set about checking their vehicles, pushing the ones with too much damage into the same ditch and changing tires on others.

Sometime later they rushed to cluster around The Reverend, rifles at the ready, when they heard the sound of something stumbling through the underbrush. Several flashlights clicked on, aimed at the forest, and a few moments later one of Brother Dale's group emerged from the brush and stumbled to his knees in front of the Reverend. The man was gasping for air and soaked with sweat, wattles of fat around his neck quivering.

"What news?" The Reverend asked, wanting to refer to the man by name, but he was a new disciple, and The Reverend didn't know who he was.

In a shaking voice, the frightened and exhausted man relayed the story of tracking the Pagans through the forest with Brother Dale. How they had found the bodies of Brother Chris's group as well as numerous demons that had also been slain. He told of the group following Brother Dale along a narrow path and how Brother Dale had fallen as if shot even though he hadn't heard a shot fired.

Embellishing his role, he described how he had helped fight off the Pagans before escaping back into the trees, the sole survivor of the group. The Reverend stood ramrod straight, bending his head down to glare at the man as he talked.

"Which way are they going?" He asked after a long silence.

"North, Reverend," the man stammered. "They're following the Little Chambers River and should be close to the falls by now."

"Thank you, Brother." The Reverend said, reached out and placed his hand on top of the man's head.

A moment later he grabbed the hair, raising the head up and swinging the blade in a blur, then tossed the severed head to one of the men behind him.

"Brother Jeremiah, I believe we have some former military men that are part of the Chosen?" He asked, still staring at the trees.

"Yes, Reverend. Some former Marines and one Navy SEAL."

"Very good. Would you ask them to make use of their skills and go bring me this Pagan's head?"

"Yes, Reverend."

Crucifixion

The Reverend stayed where he was while Jeremiah organized the next party, then turned and stalked to a muddy Chevy SUV that had been shielded from the machine gun fire by the other vehicles. Jeremiah fell in step with him, signaling the remaining men to go back to their camp. At the Chevy, Jeremiah slipped behind the wheel and started the engine, waiting for The Reverend to tell him where to go.

"North, Jeremiah," he finally said. "The trail that cuts off the road to the falls that the Godless follow when they want to fornicate and use drugs. Take us there. I want to see this Pagan for myself."

"Yes, Reverend," Jeremiah answered, shifting into drive and pulling away with a squeal of tires.

Driving fast, he covered the distance to a small turnout in only a few minutes. Putting the vehicle in park, he locked it up after The Reverend exited ,then followed the larger man into the dark forest. The path was originally a game trail that local kids had found and used for easy access to the falls. The waterfall was a favorite local spot to go drink, smoke pot and try to get girls out of their clothes. Not much more than a foot and a half wide, the path was just beaten earth that wound through the heavy foliage.

It was very dark in the trees, the leafy canopy blocking almost all of the light from the moon. No matter, The Reverend knew the sun would be coming up soon. Besides, he had taken this path plenty of times with local girls, and they had always taken their clothes off for him. Whether they had done so willingly or not was beside the point as far as he was concerned.

The Reverend killed a female demon that leapt out of the forest at him, the blade flashing out of the scabbard almost inhumanly fast and stabbing deep into the demon's chest, piercing its heart. He never even broke stride and sheathed the blade without bothering to wipe the blood from it. Minutes later the path opened out, and they stopped on a small rock shelf that overlooked the falls. Below a figure could be seen making its way down the steep slope that abutted the waterfall.

Reaching the valley floor, I found a good spot behind some large boulders at the edge of the pool the waterfall splashed into. Raising the rifle, I checked the area and found nothing. Next, I checked the top of the slope, which was clear, then settled in to wait. I expected at least one of the men tracking me to fall victim to the traps I had set. Actually, I'd consider it a bonus if more than one got caught. After the first man got impaled, I expected them to be careful enough to either find or avoid the additional traps, but I could always hope for the bonus.

The night was passing and the roar of the water spilling over the edge of the falls and crashing into the pool at my back had a lulling effect on me. When I felt myself starting to relax, I scanned the area again with the rifle, took a small drink from my canteen and forced my mind to stay focused.

It wasn't long before a scream from above reached my ears. This was the scream of a man in great pain, not the scream of an infected female. One down, four to go. I only wished I knew which trap they had tripped. Less than a minute later another voice screamed out into the night, and I smiled to myself.

I didn't know for sure, but I was willing to bet someone had tripped the first trap on the path, then the others had moved off the path into the brush and tripped the one I had set there for exactly that reason. Listening with anticipation, I hoped for another scream but wasn't surprised that it remained quiet. Raising the rifle, I sighted in on the top of the drop-off and waited.

It seemed like a long time but was really less than five minutes before two figures appeared at the edge. They were to the side of the path and well concealed in the brush, but I could still see them with the scope. They stood there for a few moments; then each took a knee as they surveyed the valley ahead. Where was the last guy? There had been five men tracking me. Two screams from the traps and two on the edge of the drop-off.

It was possible someone had tripped the final trap and been impaled and killed when they slammed into the tree, but I didn't think so. I watched and waited, shifting the rifle when the sound of a loose stone tumbling down the slope reached my ears.

Scanning the slope, I couldn't see anything. Had the two at the top dislodged a rock, or was someone making their way down the slope in brush too thick for me to see into. This was a night vision scope that amplified the available light to enable me to see. It wasn't a thermal imager that would let me see the heat produced by a body.

I thought for a moment as I continued to scan, still finding nothing, and shifted back to the two men at the top. Both now had rifles raised and pointed down into the valley. Neither was aiming directly at me, so I knew I hadn't been spotted, but they also gave away what was going on. Someone was coming down the slope, and they were acting as overwatch, ready to provide covering fire if he was attacked. Well, I could take care of that.

Clicking the safety on my rifle off, I sighted on the man to the left. This shot would be the reverse of the shooting I'd done earlier to take out the infected who were still scattered around the area, dead. One hundred and fifty yards uphill this time. Shooting uphill was more difficult than down as there was a tendency to shoot low because of not accounting for the gain in altitude the bullet had to achieve while it simultaneously was dropping due to gravity.

There was no wind at my location, but I could see the branches moving around my targets and estimated there was close to a ten mile an hour breeze at the top of the slope. Adjusting my aim for the uphill shot, then for the wind, I relaxed and squeezed the trigger. The man straightened up from the impact of the bullet then started to pitch over the edge.

Dirk Patton

I didn't waste time watching the corpse
tumble down the slope. This would have given the
second man time to move. Shifting my aim, I cursed
to see that he had immediately flattened himself out
on the ground, and the cross section of target had
shrunk significantly. I could see his head, shoulder,
arm and rifle as he scanned the valley for the
location of the shot that had killed his friend.

I had one more shot, two at best, before he
zeroed in on me and began returning fire. That
wouldn't have worried me nearly as much if there
wasn't another man making his way down the slope
who could also engage me once he reached the
valley floor. OK, two more shots at the most and
time to move.

Taking my time, I sighted in on the target.
The leaves were still blowing at what appeared to
be the same amount, so I made the same windage
adjustment I had for the previous shot. The
problem was I had been shooting for a target the
size of a man's torso, and now I was trying to hit a
target the size of a head. I'd lost probably seventy-
five percent of my margin of error. Oh well,
worrying about it wouldn't help.

Adjusting for the elevation, I calmed my
breathing and sent a round on its way. Miss. Damn
it. But, I had seen the round strike the rocks
directly in front of the target, so I only needed a
slight elevation change. I saw, analyzed and reacted

to all of this in far less than a second, sending a second round on its way before the target could change position. In the scope, I watched the head snap back before falling to the ground, and the rifle slipped out of the lifeless hands and crashed into the brush on the slope below.

Not sitting still to congratulate myself I moved, running across the clearing and taking up a new position behind a tree. Rifle up, I scanned the slope but still couldn't see any movement. However, I could see where the man coming down the slope had to come out when he reached the valley floor, and I sighted in and held on that spot and waited. And waited. And waited.

This was a game I knew well. Patience. Wait out your enemy. Make him get impatient and move first, then strike. Waiting, I thought about the man who was on the slope playing the same game and realized that they had finally sent someone after me with some training. Possibly it was a civilian who had learned patience hunting deer, but I doubted it. If you haven't been in combat and learned lessons like this, you probably won't have the self-discipline to wait for the right moment.

I had been waiting for close to half an hour when I heard movement in the brush somewhere to my rear. Shit. Infected? Probably, because it didn't sound like what was moving was making any effort at stealth. Not moving a muscle, I kept my eyes focused on where I expected my enemy to appear and my ears focused on the sounds behind me. There was a snuffling sound and a growl that didn't sound like infected. Animal?

My mind started trying to come up with whatever wildlife might be encountered in the Tennessee woods, but I couldn't get past the old children's song about Davey Crocket killing a bear. A bear? Seriously? Was Davey Crocket from Tennessee? I couldn't remember, and whatever was making the noise was slowly drawing closer and sounded big.

I flipped the selector switch on my rifle from semi to burst mode. 5.56 MM bullets are not big or heavy. In fact, they are almost exactly the same diameter as the ammo used in .22 rifles. The only substantial differences being the mass of the bullet, the size of the shell and amount of powder used to propel it out of the barrel. 5.56 is dramatically faster and harder hitting than .22, but it was never intended for large game such as a bear. If this was a bear, and it decided to attack, my only hope was that I could put enough rounds into it in burst mode to make up for the lack of stopping power of the small bullets.

Another grunt from behind me and then a tearing sound followed by a crack like sticks being broken. It sounded no more than twenty yards away. OK, fuck it. I had to look. Slowly I turned my head, moving no other part of my body. Not far away a large Black Bear was standing on the back of one of the infected I had killed earlier, busily tearing an arm out of the socket. Great. All I needed was a bear with a taste for human flesh.

The bear's back was to me, so he obviously was unaware of my presence. Or he just didn't give a shit; I reminded myself. Bears are pretty much at the top of the food chain and if he did know I was there he probably wasn't too worried about me. I wished I could say the same.

I risked taking my eyes off the bear for a moment to turn back and check on the guy on the slope, but there was still no sign of movement. Turning back to the bear, I considered my options. Assuming he didn't know I was there, I could try to disappear back into the brush and get the hell out of there. That would leave an armed opponent and a bear running around loose behind me.

Maybe I'd get lucky, and the bear would find and eat the guy on the slope. Chastising myself for wasting time on ridiculous thoughts, I turned back to watch the bear tear the arm completely free from the body. The prize in his mouth, he ambled over close to the water and laid down, pinning the arm between huge paws as he started stripping flesh off the limb.

Dirk Patton

OK. No time like the present. Moving as slowly as I could, I shouldered my pack and started backing away from the clearing; rifle pointed at the bear in case he decided I looked tastier than the meal he was working on. One slow step at a time I pushed farther back into the brush, carefully moving branches and vines so I wouldn't make noise that would alert either the bear or my enemy to where I was.

I paused when I backed up against the valley wall that was almost a sheer cliff at this point. I could no longer see the slope where the man had been waiting, but I doubted he was going to come out into the clearing and tempt fate with the bear. Moving farther down the valley along the wall, I kept my pace slow and deliberate. After about 100 yards the wall softened into a slope and ahead was what looked like a game trail cutting up into the forest.

Scanning with the rifle and seeing nothing noteworthy I kept moving, pausing at the spot where the game trail reached the valley floor. There in the soft soil was the bear's tracks, but there was also a set of boot prints that were fresher. One of the boots had stepped on top of a bear print. Freezing in place, I raised the rifle scope to my eye and searched the valley floor but couldn't see any threats. Had the man on the slope been able to move laterally and circle around me while I was playing the waiting game?

Crucifixion

I pictured the terrain around the waterfall in my mind and discounted the possibility. Eons of river flow and flooding had cut the valley into sheer walls at that point. Unless my enemy was an accomplished rock climber, there was no way he could have circled me. But then, why couldn't he be? Only my own preconceived ideas prevented him from being able to scale the rock face and move around me. Idiot!

Moving away from the game trail I put myself back into the thicker brush, carefully avoiding a patch of blackberry vines that were lined with thorns that would grab clothing and skin and make a racket. The pack on my back was heavy and cumbersome, but I needed what was in it and didn't want to drop it and have the bear tear it apart to get the MREs inside. Stepping around a tree, something caused me to freeze in place. I hadn't heard or seen anything, but something, call it a sixth sense, warned me to stop.

I think I've mentioned I'm not a superstitious man, and I don't get into the whole metaphysical thing. I believe in what I can see or feel… or shoot. But I also know that if you spend enough time in combat situations, you start to develop some type of awareness of danger. Don't ask me how or why it works, but it's saved my ass a couple of times, and right now all the hair on my arms was standing straight up on end. Slowly I took a step back and pressed up against the tree.

Looking, listening and smelling the night air I couldn't detect anything. Behind me, the roar of the waterfall continued as it had for thousands of years. There was a gentle breeze blowing down the valley, and it brought the smell of the infected bodies lying dead by the water to me. I couldn't hear or smell anything else.

Deciding it was time to shed the pack I kneeled down very slowly, released the straps and lowered it to the ground without a sound. Free of the weight I felt re-energized but stayed frozen on one knee. Finally, at the very threshold of hearing, I thought I could detect a rasping sound from just ahead.

At first, I thought I had only heard something because I was listening so hard, but then it repeated. It was the sound of fabric moving against the trunk of a tree. The person making the noise was probably leaning against a tree and had shifted position to get a better or different view of the forest. He was close. As in only one or two trees away. Had he detected me, was that why he had moved?

I wanted to raise the rifle and use the scope but wasn't about to make that much movement and give myself away. Silently I lifted the rifle sling over my head and just as cautiously placed the rifle on the ground with the pack. Drawing the Kukri in one long, slow motion, I got it into my hand without any sound then slowly lowered myself until I was on my stomach on the forest floor.

Using knees and elbows, I began inching forward, worming my way around the tree and inching towards the one where I thought the noise had come from. When I was only a few feet from the tree, I stopped and stared at it. What I had thought was a knot sticking out of the trunk was actually a knee sticking out beyond the profile of the tree. Got you, fucker!

The knee told me which direction the man was facing, and I angled for the other side of the tree. Taking five minutes to cross four feet I was at the base of the tree, right behind him. As carefully as I've ever done anything I gathered my feet under me and stood up without so much as a whisper. Taking a breath, I stepped around the tree and encircled the man's neck with my left arm.

He was well trained and started to react and probably would have succeeded in throwing me over his shoulder, but I stabbed with the Kukri into the small of his back. All twelve inches of the blade entered his body, the tip poking out through his abdomen. Holding the blade in place, I exerted pressure with my left arm on his throat which was trapped in the crook of my arm between my bicep and forearm.

I held tight enough that no sound escaped his mouth as I withdrew the Kukri and stabbed a second time into his side, angling the blade in between his ribs and up into his heart. The body went completely limp, and I pulled my blade out and lowered it to the forest floor.

"That's a nice blade you have there."

The deep voice startled me as I hadn't detected anyone else. Stepping forward, I held the Kukri out at my side, ready to defend or attack. The man that stepped out a couple of trees away was massive and had a long blade held in his right hand as well.

"Why don't you put that blade down and let's have a chat?" The new arrival goaded.

"Why don't you come over here and try to take it away from me?" I suggested, shuffling sideways to make sure I had room behind and on both sides to move.

That was the last thing I remember doing as a heavy object slammed into the back of my head, and everything went black.

When I woke up, the sun was hot on my skin and my entire body ached, but the pain in my hands and shoulders was excruciating. My eyes didn't want to open and when I was able to force them they felt like they were full of sand and ground glass. My mouth was so dry my tongue was stuck to the roof of my mouth, and I was having a hard time breathing.

Gathering myself, I squinted in the bright light and saw a large, primitive camp. Numerous large canvas tents were set up not too far in front of me and beyond them was a sea of small camping tents in all different colors, shapes and sizes. Realizing I was looking at the camp from an elevated position; I let out a string of low curses when I saw a small forest of human heads impaled on stakes like I'd seen on the road just before the ambush. Taking stock of my situation, I just stared when I realized what they had done to me.

I had been crucified. I was up on a cross. A rough rope circled my wrists, tightly binding them to the horizontal arm of the cross. All of my body weight was being held up by these two ropes. I groaned when I tried to flex my hands, cranking my head around to see what was causing so much pain. I just stared in shock when I saw the nail head protruding from my right palm.

After a long moment, I checked my left hand and saw another nail. In a near panic, I checked my feet, but they hadn't been nailed. I didn't understand why but I wasn't about to look the gift horse in the mouth. It took me a few minutes to resolve myself to what had happened to me and start assessing the rest of my body.

I had been stripped naked before being nailed to the cross and as I took inventory of my injuries I could feel the sunburn across my body. Looking up at the sun, I guessed it was mid-afternoon which meant I'd been hanging in the hot summer sun for at least eight or nine hours.

"You're awake."

I looked down and saw a young woman dressed in a simple white shift and sandals looking up at me. She held a small bucket and a long pole and was constantly flipping her head to keep her long hair out of her eyes.

"Where am I?" I croaked.

"You're a guest of The Reverend," she answered. "Praise God. Praise The Reverend."

I just stared at her. The Reverend? Great. I'd rather fight an army of infected, and a whole city full of anarchists then mess with religious zealots. There's a level of crazy in the world, and I'd always found the craziest of the crazy used religion to justify themselves and control their equally crazy followers. Just fucking wonderful.

"Water?" She asked, setting the bucket on the ground.

She maneuvered the long pole which had a ladle taped to the end of it. After dipping it into the bucket, she raised the ladle to my mouth. Tilting my head forward I greedily drank the water, then two more times, stopping only because my stomach started cramping. I didn't want to throw up the water I'd been able to drink. I was severely dehydrated and needed to get some fluids in me so I could figure a way out of the mess I was in.

"Thank you, Sister Carla."

A loud, deep voice boomed out as a very large man emerged from the tent closest to me. From my uncomfortable perspective, he looked to be a good deal taller and larger than me. I'm no slouch in the muscle department, but he was huge. Arms and chest swollen from many hours in the gym and perhaps a little chemical assistance as well. His hair was long and spilled down his back, held in a loose ponytail by a simple band of leather.

Despite his size the feature that grabbed and held my attention was his eyes. They were the eyes of a fanatic and reminded me of some of the Muslim fanatics I'd encountered in my day.

Dirk Patton

The girl bowed her head and quickly picked up the water bucket and scurried away. The man, I was sure he was The Reverend that the girl had mentioned, walked over to me. He strode with confidence and the aura of absolute certainty and authority. Taking up position in front of me, he stood with his feet spread well apart, massive arms crossed over his equally massive chest, and tilted his head back to look me in the eye.

"You're quite something," he said. "You killed over thirty of my disciples last night, including four Marines and a SEAL. They were all good men and didn't deserve to die, but God and I praise their sacrifice."

"They weren't that good, or they wouldn't be dead," I answered, my smart mouth speaking before I thought about what I was saying.

If I had expected anger as a response, I would have been disappointed. The Reverend thought about what I said for a moment then laughed a deep, rumbling laugh. All things considered, I would have preferred anger.

"Oh yes, you are going to be fun." He said, turned and strode back to the tent where he disappeared inside. Even after he was out of sight, I could still hear his rumbling laughter. Oh shit.

The afternoon wore on, and I drifted in and out of consciousness. The pain in my hands was a

236

constant, but I had determined that the nails had been driven in between the bones. Again I didn't understand the care that had been taken to not seriously cripple me.

Not that this helped much at the moment, but if I survived, at least I shouldn't have permanent damage. That was all well and good, but the first order of business was to survive. During one of my more lucid moments, I analyzed my situation.

I didn't know where I was but suspected I wasn't far from where the original ambush had occurred on the road. I was injured, nothing immediately life threatening unless they left me hanging up here in the sun without water for a few more days, but I was still in relatively good shape. On the negative side, I was naked and unarmed. All things considered, it could have been worse. Much worse. But I needed to be thinking about how to escape and not focus on the negatives.

I had tested each of the nails that were piercing my hands, but they were solidly embedded into the wood. The heads of the nails weren't very big, and I believed if I had to I could tear my hands loose, but that would get me nothing as my wrists would still be tightly bound to the cross. The amount of damage that would cause and the probable accompanying blood loss was also something I needed to avoid if at all possible.

Besides, I was something of a curiosity to the people in the camp, and it was rare that there weren't at least half a dozen people standing below and staring up at me. No one offered me any more water and my body had quickly consumed all that Sister Carla had given me earlier. I felt weak and light headed, whether from dehydration or blood loss I couldn't tell, but while I didn't have any illusions that I'd be able to rip my hands free, untying the ropes binding me and hopping to the ground to fight my way out of the camp was a pipe dream.

Conserving my energy, I tried and finally succeeded in putting myself in a partial meditative state. This didn't get me any closer to freedom, but it did help me compartmentalize the pain and discomfort and shut my racing mind down to rest for a while.

The sound of a tool box being dropped on the ground snapped me back to reality sometime later. The sun had dipped below the forested hills, and it was dusk in the camp. Fires dotted the landscape, and the smell of game cooking caused my stomach to growl loudly in protest.

My hands screamed in pain when two burly men started doing something at the base of the cross that caused it to shake violently; then it was falling backwards with me still nailed and tied to it. When the impact with the ground came, I bit my lip to keep from screaming. I wasn't about to give them the satisfaction.

They walked up to my right hand first, one of them placing a knee on my wrist while the other one used a claw hammer to extract the nail. To say the pain was from a realm I've never experienced would be an understatement. Bolts of white hot fire shot up my arm, and I drew blood as I bit harder on my lip. A few moments later the process was repeated on my left hand, and I nearly lost consciousness, my vision narrowing to a dark tunnel and my hearing limited to my own pounding heartbeat.

When I came back from the edge they had already cut all the ropes holding me to the cross and each had grabbed an arm and lifted me to my feet. After all the hours on the cross, my legs weren't functioning, and I would have collapsed if they hadn't held me up.

Behind me I started hearing the voices of a crowd, growing in quantity and volume as apparently more people arrived. I was spun around, and frog marched across a large clearing to the center of a circle made up of hundreds of people. Whispers of "murderer" and "Pagan" rippled through the crowd but they stayed where they were and seemed content to call me names and stare at me. Moments later they all bowed their heads as one and started chanting.

"Praise God. Praise The Reverend. Praise God. Praise The Reverend."

The chant continued, growing neither louder nor softer, and eventually The Reverend walked into my field of view. He was dressed simply in black shoes, slacks, and a black dress shirt as he came to stand in front and look down at me.

He was a truly massive and impressive specimen. Night had fallen, and the people in the front row of the circle held torches to illuminate the clearing, and his fanatic's eyes danced in the torch light. Finally, he turned away from me and faced his followers, a large smile on his face as he raised his hands in the air. They immediately fell silent, and all eyes were on him as he stalked around the circle and looked into the crowd.

"Praise God!" His voice boomed across the clearing. "You, my friends, are His Chosen. You have survived the horrors and destruction brought on our world by the Pagans, and you have done so because He chose you!"

A cheer erupted from the crowd and more chants of "Praise God and Praise the Reverend" were shouted.

"God has also chosen me to lead you through these trying times," he was interrupted by more chants praising God and him and let them go on for almost a full minute before raising his hands for silence again.

"All of you know about all of the good men that died last night. Good men that were simply following my instructions of what God wanted them to do."

He kept walking around the circle as he spoke, and he had the voice and presence to command the full attention of the assembled people. In fact, they looked at him with nothing less than complete love and devotion in their eyes.

Glancing at the two men that still held my arms I could see the same look in their eyes as they listened. Carefully testing my legs, I was happy to find that the feeling had returned, and I could stand on my own, but chose to remain slumped in their grip for the time being. Why let them know I was stronger than they thought?

"This man," The Reverend roared and whirled to point at me. "This Pagan. He is responsible." More mumblings of "murderer" and "Pagan" rippled through the crowd and started to grow into a chant until cut off by The Reverend's raised hands. "He killed our brothers, and I have brought him here before you to face justice. He must answer for his crimes against God and you, the Chosen."

He appeared to swell in size as he stood in the center of the circle and slowly turned as he looked to the crowd.

"Here he stands. God has judged him guilty but asks you, the Chosen, to pass sentence on him. Tell me, now, here in front of God. What say you?" He boomed out the last, standing stock still with his right arm raised as he pointed a finger at the surrounding people.

"Pit! Pit! Pit!" The chant was deafening, the people in the crowd emphasizing each shout of the word with a thrust of their fist into the air. The Reverend spun in place, smiling and laughing while the people chanted, eventually raising his arms.

"The Chosen have spoken!" He roared.

As the crowd screamed and cheered, he waived several men forward into the circle and moved to the side. With only torch light to see, I had failed to notice that in the center of the area was a giant, round wooden plate lying on the ground. The selected men rushed up to it and started folding it back in sections, revealing a gaping hole in the ground thirty feet across. Cover out of the way, they grabbed torches from the crowd and stuck them into the ground around the perimeter of the pit, casting light down into it.

I was jerked forward and dragged to the edge of the pit where I got a good look. Eight feet deep and the upper inside foot of the walls were lined with rows of sharpened stakes pointed up at a forty-five-degree angle. Below those stakes, looking up at me, were three infected. Two males and a female.

Thinking there's no time like the present, I started to stand to break free of the two men holding me. But The Reverend had circled behind and with a massive shove to my back, sent me flying through the air into the pit where I landed on my face in the dirt.

24

Rachel had kept Betty and the group of kids moving, covering a couple of miles from the bottom of the waterfall when she finally called a halt. A few minutes earlier she had heard faint screams from behind and was sure they hadn't been the screams of infected. Not a praying woman, she still said a silent prayer for John's safety.

She'd had a couple of opportunities to contemplate trying to survive without him, most recently when he'd been shot while rescuing her, and she didn't think she'd last long. Besides, not that they were a couple or ever could be, but she had to admit to herself that she had feelings for him.

She knew she could never act on those feelings though as he was so committed to making it to Arizona to find his wife. Katie was a lucky woman to have a husband who was so devoted to her. Rachel felt a momentary pang of jealousy but quickly pushed that emotion down and told herself to stop being ridiculous.

"... great tits!" Rachel heard the very end of a whispered comment between the two teenage boys that were behind her.

Turning she met their eyes and held her index finger up to her lips in warning to be quiet.

They both looked properly mortified, one of them blushing so hard that she could see the red spots on his cheeks even in the dark. The comment didn't bother her. Not like it would have in the civilized world before the attacks. Boys will be boys, and she knew how she looked and the effect she had on men.

Rachel had brought the group to a halt in a large clearing that butted up against a sheer rock face. Heavy forest shielded them on the other three sides, and she felt this was as good a place as any to wait for John to catch up. She spent a few minutes getting the kids settled and admonishing them to stay quiet. Betty made the rounds as well, offering words of comfort to the frightened kids.

Soon they were all sprawled out on the ground, most of them choosing to immediately curl up and go to sleep. Rachel was tired too, but between worry about John and concern over letting her guard down, there was no way she could sleep. Finding a large tree that had fallen over she settled down with her back against it, positioned between the forest and the kids with the rifle at the ready across her lap.

Dog stretched out in the dirt at her feet and closed his eyes, but his ears never drooped as he too kept watch. After a few more minutes of checking on the kids, Betty came over and lowered herself to the ground next to Rachel with a groan.

"Are you alright?" Rachel asked, her eyes never stopping their scan of the forest.

"Just a little tired, dear. When you get to be my age, a long walk through the woods isn't as much fun as it used to be." Betty smiled and leaned her head back on the fallen tree. Moments later her breathing deepened and Rachel could hear soft snores coming from the older woman.

"You and me, Dog," Rachel mumbled. Dog thumped his tail on the dirt a couple of times but didn't bother to open his eyes.

Sometime later Rachel startled awake in bright sunlight, immediately cursing herself for having fallen asleep. Looking around, she took a quick headcount, relieved to find all of the kids still sleeping. Next to her Betty still snored, having slipped to the ground and curled up with her head pillowed on her right arm. Dog was awake and alert, sitting a few feet to her front. He turned his head and looked at her, then turned back to watch the tree line.

Slowly climbing to her feet, Rachel stooped to pet and hug him before moving into the edge of the forest and finding a bush to squat behind. Business finished, she returned to the clearing and stood looking around. The sun was well up and the day was already hot. Insects buzzed in the trees and somewhere a woodpecker went to work on a tree, making a racket that sounded far too much like a machine gun. She guessed it was nearly noon. Where the hell was John?

Worry washed over her. Was he ok? Why hadn't he caught up with them hours ago? When she had sat down earlier, she had expected him to show up within an hour, just appearing so suddenly and quietly that he startled her. But he wasn't here, and it had been hours. Too long unless something had gone wrong. She remembered the faint screams she'd heard the night before, trying to remember if they had sounded like a man screaming.

She couldn't remember, but it didn't matter since she didn't think there was anything that could make John scream out like that. Not that he didn't feel pain, but he was the most self-contained man she had ever met, and she didn't believe it had been him. That meant he was probably the one causing the screams. That sounded more like him, but then why wasn't he sitting here with her?

An hour later, the sun directly overhead, Rachel couldn't take it any longer. Good news or bad, she had to know. No more than John could have left her; she couldn't go any farther without finding out what had happened to him. Betty was awake by now, but the kids still slept the way only teenagers could. Rachel sat down next to Betty and discussed the thoughts in her head with the woman.

She was undecided if it was wise to take the kids back with her to search for John. But if she didn't take them they would be left completely unarmed with no way to defend themselves from infected or worse. After a long conversation about their options that she knew would have driven John absolutely insane, she and Betty walked around the clearing and woke the kids.

It took them half an hour to get the kids up and ready to go. Rachel had each of them individually go into the bushes to relieve themselves. She sent Dog with each of them to provide protection while they were at their most vulnerable.

Digging a couple of MREs out of her pack Rachel prepared them and portioned them out amongst the kids, so each got a few calories into their bodies. As a group, they went to the river and drank their fill while Rachel stood watch over them, rifle at the ready. Finally, everyone was ready to go, and they started retracing their path of the night before.

The valley seemed so much less intimidating with the sun shining brightly. A couple of times Rachel had to remind herself that the infected didn't care if it was day or night. They were just as likely to attack regardless of the time of day. Fortunately, they didn't come across any, and the kids were moving quietly and fairly quickly, mostly refreshed after the sleep, food and water. As they approached the pool at the base of the falls, Dog trotted ahead, and Rachel saw him turn his head, nose lifted into the air.

She brought the group to a stop and watched Dog sniff the air. After a moment, he turned and trotted into the woods, nose to the ground. Moving forward, Rachel reached the point where he had cut into the brush and stood watching him. Dog sniffed the ground some more and changed direction, trotting up to a large tree where he found something to hold his interest. Motioning for the group to stay put, Rachel followed him into the brush.

After a few steps, she could see what held Dog's attention. John's pack lay on the ground at the base of a tree. As she got closer, she spotted his rifle lying next to it. Rachel's steps faltered with fear of what she'd find, but she gathered herself and pushed forward, stopping to examine the abandoned pack and weapon. Looking around, she spotted a pair of legs sticking out from behind another tree a few feet away.

With a lump in her throat and a knot in her stomach, Rachel forced herself to walk over to the body, nearly crying from relief when it wasn't John. The corpse's shirt was soaked with blood that had dried black and already the insects were hard at work on the body. Choking down the bile that threatened to rise up from her stomach, she surveyed the area and quickly moved over to a patch of ground that was heavily disturbed.

Three distinct sets of boot prints were visible as was an impression in the soft soil left by a body. Twin drag marks in the dirt looked like they had been left by a pair of boots as a body was picked up, then two sets of tracks headed away to the north. One of them, which had already been very clear because of how deep they were in the valley floor, were now noticeably deeper as if that person had suddenly become much heavier.

Rachel put two and two together and arrived at the conclusion that someone had been knocked out or killed here then carried away. She didn't think killed, not imagining that someone would carry away one corpse and leave another. Staring at the size of the prints she tried to remember how big John's feet were and decide if he was the one carrying someone, but while she thought the prints were too big for him, she wasn't sure.

An idea popping into her head she rushed back to the tree where the pack and rifle still lay in the dirt and cast around until she was able to identify John's tracks. Definitely smaller and also a different tread pattern than the ones that exited the area. Picking up the rifle, she hustled back to where the group was waiting and selected the largest boy. She guessed he was somewhere around fourteen, but had gotten a lot of his size early and was nearly six feet tall with broad shoulders and thick legs. Leading him back to the pack, she helped him lift it up and settle it on his back.

"Jesus, this thing is heavy," he said but didn't offer any other complaint.

Rachel gave him her best smile, the one she knew could make most men melt, and was gratified to see him set his face in a stern expression as he straightened up and hooked his thumbs into the straps to help manage the weight.

"I believe in you," she said with another smile and led the way back to the group, following the tracks, the boy right behind her with a spring in his step at the flattery.

"Betty, do you know how to shoot?" She asked, walking up to the older woman.

"I've been known to pick up a rifle from time to time."

"Good. Know how to use this?" Rachel held up John's M4. Betty looked at it and slowly shook her head.

"I do," one of the girls in the group stepped forward. Rachel and Betty looked at her in surprise. "My dad and brothers taught me. I've been shooting since I was eight, and I know how to use an AR."

Rachel looked the girl up and down, still surprised. She was very pretty, slim and athletic with long hair that hung nearly the length of her back and was pulled into a thick French braid. She had an earnest look on her face and after a few moments of Rachel's scrutiny, she cocked one hip out to the side and held her hands out. Hesitating a moment longer, Rachel finally placed the rifle in the girl's waiting hands.

Smoothly, and apparently well practiced, the girl made sure the rifle was on safe then dropped the magazine to check the load, pulled the charging handle far enough back to see if a round was in the chamber, releasing the handle when she saw the glint of brass, slapped the magazine back in place, thumb checked the fire selector lever to ensure it was on safe and looked up at Rachel with a smile.

"What's your name?" Rachel asked, returning the smile.

"Nora. Nora Patterson." The girl answered, working the rifle's sling over her head and making sure her hair didn't tangle in it.

"Nora, can you shoot another person if you have to?"

"Yes I can," she answered without hesitation.

Crucifixion

"I don't mean the infected," Rachel stepped closer to her, looking down into the shorter girl's eyes. "I mean another normal, living human being."

"If that's what I have to do, then that's what I have to do." Nora held Rachel's eyes until Rachel relaxed and smiled at her.

"Let's hope that isn't necessary."

Rachel rallied the group and put Nora at the rear, reminding her to keep a close eye out for anyone or anything following, then set off on the same path the heavy prints had taken. They skirted around the clearing where all of the dead infected were being feasted on by a loud and raucous bunch of crows and started climbing the steep valley wall.

It didn't take them long to reach a flat, rocky outcropping that looked down on the pool and Rachel paused to check below them. The animals of the forest were feasting on the dead bodies, including a small pack of coyotes and Rachel was glad they had skirted the area.

At the far side of the outcropping, a narrow trail led into the forest and the heavy tracks were clearly visible in the dirt. Checking to make sure the group was staying tight and Nora was still watching their rear, Rachel followed the tracks and headed up the path, Dog ranging ahead of her with his nose in the air and tail straight up. A short time later they reached the edge of the forest, a small dirt parking area backed by a ribbon of asphalt to their front.

Rachel brought the group to a stop and after listening and visually checking the area for five minutes she stepped out of the trees. The tracks had led here, but the dirt was packed so hard they had mostly vanished once the person making them had stepped out of the trees. Searching the dirt, she spotted tire tracks that looked fresh, slowly walking around the area with her eyes glued to the ground.

Rachel was by no means an experienced tracker, had never tracked anything in her life, but she was a smart woman and after examining the area for a bit she thought she knew what had happened here. A vehicle had approached from the west and pulled onto the dirt. Faint scuffs and partial tread patterns led from each side of the tracks directly to the path in the forest then came back from the path and led to a spot centered between the tire marks, then back to each side. She thought about it for a minute, still staring at the marks in the dirt.

The tires were large which meant a truck or SUV. Coming back from the trees and going to a point between the tire tracks meant they took something and loaded it into the back. Now she knew which way the vehicle was pointed. Following the tire tracks, she saw where the driver had started a U-turn as he pulled back onto the pavement, the tires spinning in the dirt and digging a shallow furrow as they threw fresh dirt across the ground. They had gone back to the west. Back in the direction they had come from. The direction where she and John had been ambushed on the road.

What now? Rachel didn't like the idea of hiking down the pavement with the group of kids. They would be way too visible and too easy to surprise. Looking around, Rachel didn't care for the possibility of staying in the trees, either. The underbrush along the road was thick with all kinds of vines and bushes, and without a beaten path like they'd just followed, it would be next to impossible for them to move through the woods.

Not for the first time she wished John was here to make the decision. He'd know what to do. Rachel's thoughts were interrupted by the sound of a suppressed rifle firing in the woods. Turning in the direction of the group she raised her rifle and dashed onto the path.

Betty and the kids were bunched up as close to the mouth of the path as they could get without actually spilling out onto the turnout. Rachel pushed past them and saw Nora aiming John's rifle back down the path. She looked in the direction the girl was aiming and saw a dead infected male lying in the dirt.

Movement caught her eye, and she looked back down the path in time to see Nora shoot another infected as he stumbled around a bend and started towards them. Momentarily filled with pride that a girl had stepped up and was defending them, Rachel snapped herself back to the situation at hand. No time for feminism. Those days were over, and as much as she didn't like it, she knew that once again most women would need a big, strong man to survive. Nora just might be one of the exceptions to that rule.

No more infected appeared and after a few minutes, Nora lowered the rifle but kept her attention focused on the forest. Rachel pulled a full magazine out of her vest and handed it to the girl who jammed it into the back pocket of her skin tight jeans. Moving back past the group to the edge of the trees Rachel stopped next to Betty and explained the situation to her. Betty listened carefully, nodding as Rachel spoke.

"I think I know where he might be," Betty said. "There was some religious nut that called himself The Preacher, or something dramatic like that, that set up shop on some state-owned land a few miles from here. Last I heard he had about fifty followers, and they lived in a bunch of tents back in the woods. I don't know of anyone else around these parts that would have any interest in taking someone. Everyone else would hunker down and ignore what was going on, or they'd be the kind of people that'd invite you into their home and share their dinner with you."

"Do you know where this camp is?" Rachel asked, a thrill of hope running through her. For the first time, she thought she might actually find John.

"Honey, this guy, and his followers are bat shit crazy if you'll pardon the expression. Well, they were before the world turned upside down. Now, I can't even imagine."

Betty was frightening her, but at the same time, Rachel wasn't about to abandon John.

25

Two hours later the afternoon was wearing on, and they were still sitting just inside the trees at the dirt turn out. Rachel had always been a confident woman, but the one area she was weak was in making a decision. She knew this about herself and had worked on it all her adult life, but all too often she tended towards inaction as a way to avoid making a decision that could potentially be the wrong one.

She was sitting in the dirt, Dog at her feet and Betty sitting beside her. Nora was still watching the rear and every time Rachel checked she was alert and ready to defend them if any threat appeared. Rachel was really starting to like this young woman.

"There's not been a car the whole time we've been here," Betty observed.

"You think it's ok to head down the road?" Rachel asked, hoping for Betty to make the decision for her.

"I don't know, honey. But we can't keep sitting here. Eventually, someone or something is going to find us. I'm not sure which would be worse at this point, but we need to start moving soon before it gets dark."

Crucifixion

Rachel thought about that and slowly nodded her head. She asked herself, for the hundredth time, what John would do if he was here. Actually, she knew they'd already have been down the road and found the camp, but the voice of doubt kept plaguing her thoughts. Finally, Rachel got mad.

She got mad at the Chinese for having attacked America and starting this. She got mad at John for running around the forest like Rambo and getting himself captured. She got mad at the people that had captured him, but mostly she got mad at herself for sitting in the trees like a frightened lamb.

She had stayed with John since the day of the attacks and had fought by his side, saving him at least as many times as he had saved her. What the hell was she doing sitting here and wasting time? Had she already waited too long to save him?

"Let's move," Rachel said to Betty, bouncing to her feet.

She extended her hand and helped Betty off the ground then turned and got the kids up and ready to move with a few terse commands.

Sensing the tension that comes before action, Dog was on his feet with his tail held stiffly at alert. He was ready. A minute later the group emerged from the trees and headed west on the pavement. They hugged the shoulder and Rachel

259

had cautioned each kid to be ready to dive into the brush if they heard a vehicle approaching. Walking in single file, Rachel and Dog led the way with Nora bringing up the rear.

Now that Rachel had made a decision her adrenaline was pumping, and she moved with long, fast strides. She started outdistancing the group as Betty couldn't move as fast, so she had to reign herself in. She knew she should conserve her energy as much as possible for the impending fight, so she forced herself to slow down. Dog wasn't so pragmatic and kept trotting a few yards ahead before turning and trotting back to Rachel, then repeating himself. He was primed for a fight.

They started passing the impaled heads that lined the road, Betty and the kids staring at them in horror, and close to 45 minutes later they reached the site of the ambush that had put her and John on foot. The road was littered with spent shell casings, brass glittering in the late afternoon sunlight, and their Humvee along with several civilian vehicles had been pushed off the road into a drainage ditch.

As they walked past the Humvee Rachel glanced over at the machine gun and was amazed to see the barrel was now curved downwards. Not a lot, but enough to be noticeable and also to render the weapon useless she imagined. Remembering what John had told her about melting the barrel she was still amazed it had actually happened. Part of her had thought he was being dramatic even though she believed he knew what he was talking about.

Two hundred yards beyond the far edge of the ambush they discovered a muddy track that cut off the asphalt and disappeared into the forest over a rise. The track appeared to be well traveled as it was churned up from the passage of aggressive off-road tires, and all the disturbances appeared to be fresh. Turning onto the path, Rachel slowed her pace and whispered to Betty to remind the kids to stay absolutely quiet.

Walking down the path, they crested the rise and kept going as it wound its way through the trees and underbrush. Rachel didn't see anyone, but it wasn't long before she started smelling meat cooking and her stomach gave an involuntary rumble. Coming to a stop, she waved the group off the path into the trees and melded into the forest with them.

They moved a few dozen yards away from the track and came across a narrow game trail cutting through the forest in the same direction as the path. Stepping onto it Rachel led the group at a decent pace for another ten minutes until the game path took a sharp bend to the right.

This was opposite the direction they needed to travel to stay with the track and Rachel abandoned the trail and pushed back into the woods in the direction the smell of the cooking fires was coming from. Dog easily moved through the heavy underbrush, but Rachel had to slow as she pushed through, careful to not make any more noise than absolutely necessary.

Finally, the brush thinned and they reached the edge of the trees. In front of them was a large clearing, at least two acres, and much of it was occupied with camping tents. Directly in front of them was the track that led from the road. It ended to the right in a large area where dozens of all different types of vehicles were haphazardly parked. At the far edge of the camp, Rachel could see several larger tents that looked like they were probably military surplus and had once been command tents.

Set amongst them a large cross towered over the camp. People were moving everywhere in the camp. Normal looking people, going about their business. Cooking food. Fetching buckets of water from the small creek that ran along the edge of the camp. Children playing. Children. Rachel's resolve weakened at the thought that children might get hurt during John's rescue.

"Oh my God!" Rachel turned and saw Nora looking at the camp through the rifle scope. "Oh my God!" She repeated, eye glued to whatever she was seeing.

Crucifixion

"What?" Rachel and Betty asked at the same time, staring at the young girl.

"Look at the cross," she answered, her voice shaky.

Rachel raised her rifle, but the scope she had did not have any magnification, only a red dot for aiming. She called the boy over that was carrying John's pack and dug through it until she found a pair of binoculars. Raising them to her eyes it took her a moment to find the cross, then another moment to focus the glasses. When they came into focus, she said exactly what Nora was still repeating.

She had found John. He had been nailed to a cross that was standing amongst a small forest of impaled heads. She was unable to tell if he was still alive. Several emotions blasted through Rachel at that moment, everything from disgust to pity to rage. Rage won out. The kind of rage that made her want to wipe out every living soul in the camp. She now understood how John could do the things he did and still sleep at night.

The sun was low on the horizon, and soon they would have the cover of darkness to move around. Rachel didn't know yet how she was going to rescue John, but she was working on it. Her biggest fear at the moment was that he was too severely injured to be able to move, and they would have to carry him. She knew from experience just how big he was and knew there wasn't anyone in the group that could carry him.

Maybe four of the kids working together, but they would need to be able to move fast. This thought coincided with her looking at the parking area as she scanned the camp with the binoculars. Parked off to the side of the area was a short bus, painted white with hand-lettering along the side that read Primitive Baptist Church.

"Betty, you said you were a bus driver. Right?"

"Yes. Why?"

"Do you know how to hot wire one if the keys aren't available?" Rachel answered the question with a question.

"I don't, no. But young Mr. Hillman over there had a bit of trouble with the police this past spring, and I expect he can."

Rachel lowered the binoculars and looked at the kid Betty was pointing at. The boy was scrawny and had kept to himself as much as possible since Rachel had joined the group, but she had caught him stealing longing glances at Nora, who studiously ignored him. He maintained a perpetual scowl on his face and was glaring back at them, knowing he was being talked about but unaware of what the conversation was. Rachel stood up, staying in a crouch, and moved over to squat in the dirt next to him.

"Hi," she said. "What's your name?"

"Jared Hillman." He answered. "What do you want?"

The anger and attitude the boy carried with him was evident in his tone and in his expression.

"We need your help. Do you know how to hotwire a bus?" Rachel stared at his eyes and saw the look of surprise cross his face before he shut it down in favor of the scowl.

"I can start anything with a motor," he said, sitting up straighter and puffing out his chest.

"Good!" Rachel beamed and put her hand on his shoulder. "I'm going to need you soon. Don't go anywhere."

The kid smiled for the first time and nodded his head. Working through more of the plan in her head Rachel went back to sit next to Betty and lifted the binoculars back to her eyes. After seeing what she needed to see she motioned the Hillman kid over to her.

"Alright, Jared. You and I are going to sneak through the brush and into that parking lot. See that white bus off to the side?" Rachel asked, pointing and handing the binoculars to the kid. When he nodded, she continued. "I'm going to get you into that bus, but I don't want you to do anything other than hide for now. Some time later you'll hear gunfire, and that's when I want you to get it started and have it ready to go. Can you do that?"

"Damn straight!" He answered, cracking a smile and glancing around to see if Nora had noticed that his help was needed.

"Is there anything you need to break in or get it started?"

The kid reached into his pocket and pulled out a multi-tool that had everything from a knife blade to pliers to a screwdriver.

"Got all I need right here."

"Good. Let's go." Rachel patted Dog on the head, telling him to stay and set off through the brush with the kid close behind her.

It didn't take them long to reach the edge of the parking area, and they worked their way across by moving from vehicle to vehicle. The bus was parked at the edge of the lot closest to the camp, and there was a good 40 yards of open space between it and the closest vehicle. Pausing, Rachel looked at the open ground and at the movement in the camp just on the other side of the bus.

Crucifixion

"What's wrong?" The kid asked.

"I don't know how were going to sneak into the bus without anyone seeing us," Rachel answered, doubt creeping into her mind over the decision to hide the kid in the bus.

"I'll just walk over," he said. "The trick is to look like you belong and know what you're doing."

Before Rachel could say anything Jared stood fully erect and started strolling across the dirt lot to the bus. He moved slowly and casually, head down and feet dragging with each step, just like you'd expect a sullen teenager to move. Several of the people moving around in the camp glanced his way but ignored him and went on about their business.

Mouth hanging open in surprise, Rachel watched as he walked right up to the bus like he had all the reason in the world to be there. The multi-tool was already in his hand and in less than fifteen seconds he had jimmied the door lock. Climbing into the bus, he pulled the doors closed behind him, moved towards the back of the bus and waved at her through one of the side windows before disappearing from view.

Rachel stared in surprise for a few moments before she smiled and started making her way back across the lot to the edge of the brush where the group waited, but paused when a thought struck her. Even if they did get John away from the camp, made it onto the bus and drove off what would keep the people in the camp from pursuing them.

Looking around the lot with an evil smile, Rachel kneeled down and pulled her T-Shirt over her head and started tearing it into long strips. With a handful of strips, she moved through the parked vehicles and randomly stuffed a strip of fabric into the gas tanks of more than a dozen of the trucks. Task completed she worked her way back to the group, greeted by the thumping of Dog's tail and the appreciative stares of all the teenage boys.

Digging a spare shirt out of her pack she worked it over her head then looked around the group and asked if anyone had a lighter. Two of the boys quickly dug disposable butane lighters out of their pockets and held them out towards Rachel. Taking both lighters, she selected one of the boys, the one who had blushed when she overheard his comment about her breasts earlier and brought him over to the edge of the brush.

His job was to wait for explosions and gunfire; then he would run through the parking area, setting fire to each of the strips of fabric Rachel had placed in the fuel tanks on his way to the bus where he would wait with Jared for the rest of the group. She had him repeat her instructions and satisfied he understood she marshaled the swiftly dwindling group and started off through the brush.

Crucifixion

They spent the next twenty minutes moving around the perimeter of the camp, getting closer to where John was nailed to the cross. Rachel could picture how she wanted this to go, but her plan fell apart just as they reached an area that was close to the cross. As they watched two men walked up to the cross, removed a couple of bolts from the base and let it fall backwards to the ground, John still attached.

They then removed the nails from his hands with a large hammer and cut the ropes that were binding him to the rough wood. While this was going on, people started assembling in a rough circle to his rear, and it looked like the entire camp was in attendance. Again, Rachel experienced some doubt, but the rage she had felt earlier returned as she watched the two men drag John inside the circle made by the people and hold him there while a giant man started talking about God and how God had found John guilty.

Thinking hard, Rachel turned and was momentarily distracted by the heavy bag tied to the side of her pack swinging and banging into her arm. It was the bag John had told her to fill with grenades when they were bailing out of the Humvee. Grabbing it, she spilled the contents on the ground and counted ten grenades. Gingerly picking one of them up she inspected it and quickly saw how it worked.

There were six kids remaining in the group after having left Jared in the bus and the other boy ready to start the fires. She wanted to keep Nora available on the rifle which left five. Gathering them into a tight group, she quickly explained what she wanted and looked closely at them, getting an acknowledgment from each that they could do it. Handing two grenades to each kid, she sent them on their way, telling them to hurry.

What was she forgetting? Something nagged at the back of her head, but she couldn't pull it out so dismissed the distraction and turned her attention back to the assembly just as several men were uncovering a large pit in the ground and setting torches into the dirt around its perimeter. The people were chanting 'Pit' at the tops of their lungs and as she watched the giant strode up directly behind John and using both hands shoved him forward to disappear into the pit.

When I hit the ground at the bottom of the pit, I landed on my face then rolled and wound up coming to a stop on my back against the legs of one of the infected males, spitting out a mouthful of dirt. He snarled and leaned down to grab me as the female screamed and charged, the other male stumbling around trying to change direction and come after me. As the male above me bent down, I grabbed one of his arms, ignoring the searing pain in each of my hands, and yanked hard.

Pulling him off balance, I raised my knees and deflected him into the female as she dove for me and the two of them went down in a tangle of limbs. Above me, the crowd roared in excitement, but I ignored them and scrambled to my feet and to the other side of the pit where the second male greeted me with outstretched arms.

Ducking his embrace, I tripped him with a leg sweep and turned back in time to deflect the female into the wall of the pit. They were all dangerous, but the female was the higher priority because of her speed. I took half a second to look around for anything I could use as a weapon, but the pit was all smooth dirt. In the time I had taken to glance around the female had regained her feet and was charging again.

This time, when I tried to deflect her, I was hampered by the grip of the male on the ground who had snaked a hand out and grasped my ankle. The female slammed into my chest and started tearing at my bare skin with her splintered nails. Raising an arm to protect my face I lashed out with an elbow and knocked her aside, broken teeth falling from her mouth when she landed on the ground. I stomped down with my free foot and heard the male infected's arm snap and the grip loosened enough for me to break free and move away.

The other male was closing in, and the female was back on her feet, screaming as she prepared to launch herself through the air at me. The male with the broken arm had struggled back to his knees, and I grabbed him by the upper arms and yanked him to his feet, facing away from me, just as the female sprang forward. She impacted the male's chest, and the three of us tumbled to the ground with me on the bottom of the pile.

The male squirmed like a beetle on its back as the female tried to reach around him to continue slashing me. Summoning energy reserves I wasn't sure were there, I pushed off with my right arm and leg and rolled the three of us over so the female was on her back with the infected male and me on top of her.   The other male loomed over me, and I slithered sideways and kicked out, shattering his knee and sending him to the ground.

Crucifixion

I reached around the male and fumbled to get a grip on the female's throat but had to jerk my hand back when I felt the male's lips on my arm as he tried to bite me. The female was screaming and fighting to escape, but she had over four hundred pounds lying on top of her and for the moment at least she wasn't going anywhere. The crowd was in full throat, and I absently noted the sounds of bets being shouted out and accepted as I raised up and started raining elbows onto the back of the male infected's neck.

He was a big man, larger than me, and in my weakened condition, the impacts weren't having any effect. I thought about wrapping up his head in my arms and breaking his neck but dismissed the idea because I didn't want to put my flesh that close to the female's snapping jaws.

The male with the broken knee had crawled within an arm's length of me, and my skin crawled when his fingers brushed my naked hip. Kicking out I caught him in the nose with the heel of my foot, breaking it, but otherwise having no effect on him. Forced to scramble sideways out of his reach, my weight shifted, and the male underneath me was able to roll to the side and slip me off his back.

Continuing my roll across the floor of the pit I came up against the wall and looked up at the stakes embedded in the earth at the top of the pit. Scrambling to my feet, I continued the motion and leapt high, well... high for me, and grabbed one of the stakes in the lower row. The pain in my hands was unbelievable. I nearly let go, but the scream of the female sent a new surge of adrenaline into my system, and I was able to push the pain down due to sheer panic. Hanging from the stake, I started bouncing and felt it give slightly.

Bouncing harder, the stake shifted a little more then pulled free from the dirt wall of the pit. I now had a weapon, but when the stake came loose, and I fell back to the floor of the pit I stumbled and went down.

The female had finally extricated herself from underneath the male and charged directly at me, rushing across the pit on all fours like an animal. Prepared this time I met her, getting a forearm under her chin and on her throat. Twisting with her, I used her momentum to drive her to the ground and put all my weight into a push on her throat.

Feeling her larynx collapse, I spun away from her clawing hands and tripped over the male with the broken knee. I automatically stuck a hand out to break my fall and almost passed out from the pain when all of my weight came down on my left. Rolling away from the male, I protectively pulled my throbbing hand to my chest and lurched back to my feet.

Crucifixion

The male on the ground changed direction and crawled towards me while the other one stumbled around the far side of the pit for a second before righting himself and coming in my direction. The female also rose to her feet, unable to scream with a broken larynx and barely able to rasp a breath in and out. I grasped the stake in both hands, leapt over the male on the ground and charged the female who met me halfway across the pit.

I held the stake in front of me and as the female and I met adjusted its position and succeeded in driving it deep into her mouth. Using my legs to drive forward I held the blunt end of the stake against my chest and kept churning forward until she went limp and fell away from me. The stake had gone into her mouth and pierced the back of her throat, the sharp tip eventually coming out of the back of her neck as the bulk of it embedded in her vertebrae. She was finally dead.

A huge roar sounded from the crowd when she went down and losing betting slips fluttered down into the pit like a heavy snowfall. I was backing up to face the still mobile male when the first explosion ripped through the night and silenced the crowd. A heartbeat later more explosions sounded, and the roars of excitement from above turned to screams of terror.

When John disappeared into the pit, Rachel told Nora and Dog to stay close and started moving forward. The kids with the grenades had gotten into position quickly, spacing out in a large semi-circle surrounding the crowd that was pushing in to look down into the pit. Their roars of excitement made her blood run cold as she imagined what was waiting in the pit for John.

Stopping a few yards behind the back edge of the crowd Rachel looked to her right and spotted one of the kids she had sent off with grenades in hand. The girl looked at Rachel then looked to her right and watched for a few moments. The crowd roared again, even louder, and the girl looked back at Rachel and nodded her head that they were ready.

Another roar from the crowd, shouts of happiness and disappointment both obvious, and Rachel looked directly at the girl as she raised her arm high over her head. The girl's eyes were fixed on Rachel's arm and when it dropped she yanked the pin out of the grenade she was holding and tossed it forward, deep into the ranks of the crowd.

A few seconds later the grenade detonated with an ear-shattering blast and bodies flew through the air in all directions. The crowd fell silent as everyone froze for a heartbeat, then there was the start of a stampede away from the point of the explosion. The people who were trying to get away hadn't taken more than two steps when more grenades tore through the crowd, the explosions each coming from different points around the circle.

Now the crowd screamed as one and everyone was trying to go in a different direction as no one could tell where the destruction was coming from nor where it would strike next. Rachel let the panic grow then raised her arm and signaled the girl for the second wave. A few seconds later five more explosions ripped through the crowd, and all semblance of order evaporated.

Frightened people ran in all directions in their desperation to get to safety. People were knocked down and trampled as panic reigned and in moments, a nice wide path opened up in front of Rachel and Nora leading directly to the pit.

Dashing forward, Rachel skidded to a halt at the edge, raised her rifle and shot two men that were running towards her from the far side of the circle. Nora had run with her and had dropped to one knee, shooting into a small group of men that were pushing their way towards them through the stampeding crowd. Rachel heard Dog growl, and a moment later he leapt into the pit before she could stop him.

Spinning and looking down she saw Dog impact the chest of an infected male and knock him to the ground, immediately tearing into his throat.

She noted John on the ground fighting with another infected then had to turn her attention back to the battle above ground.

Nora had picked off all the men that she had engaged, but two more small groups armed with pistols and hunting rifles had formed up and were getting ready to start attacking. Rachel started shooting at one group while Nora kept the other group's heads down. The first explosion from the parking lot was massive, turning night to day.

The attackers paused to gape at the furiously burning vehicles and the woman and girl took advantage of the moment and dropped most of them. Three shots later and the disorganized group Rachel had been fighting was done, and she was able to turn her attention to the pit.

Three dead infected lay in the dirt. A female with a wooden stake sticking out of her mouth, a male with an obviously broken neck and another whose throat had been torn out by Dog. John and Dog sat in the center, John's arms wrapped around Dog's thick neck. Taking stock of the situation Rachel looked around and spotted an aluminum ladder laying in the dirt a few yards away.

Rushing over she grabbed it and dragged it back to the pit, letting it fall over the edge as she had to return fire on a man who had popped out from behind a tent. Another explosion from the parking lot ripped the air, then two more so close together they almost sounded like one. The man fell, and Rachel glanced around, glad to see the grenade kids running towards the bus, Betty bringing up the rear. That's what she had forgotten. There was no one to help her with John.

She started to shout at the group to come back but checked herself when John poked his head over the lip of the pit. Rushing over she helped him the rest of the way up the ladder then stepped back as Dog came bounding up the steps, blood from the infected he had killed flying off his muzzle as he moved.

Rachel turned her head to call Nora so they could head for the bus, but the words died in her mouth when the young girl flew backwards and landed in the dirt at her feet. A large, red hole was in the middle of Nora's forehead and blood poured out of the back of her shattered skull and started soaking into the dirt. Rachel stared for a moment before John tackled her to the ground, a bullet cracking the air just over her head.

"There, to the left of that pile of wood," John yelled at her and pointed out the sniper.

Raising the rifle Rachel fired until the magazine emptied, not caring that she had sent ten rounds into the body after she'd already killed the man. When she realized the rifle was empty, she dropped it in the dirt and leaned over Nora, tears streaming down her face.

"Rachel! We have to move. Now!" John grabbed up the rifle, nearly dropping it from the pain in his hands, and shoved it into her arms. "Reload and let's go."

Rachel mechanically dropped the empty magazine and slapped a new one home, slowly rising to her feet. John looked at the tears streaming down her face and then down at the dead girl. Fighting back the pain he scooped her body up in his arms and stuck his face in Rachel's.

"What's the plan?" He shouted over the roar of another explosion from the parking area. Rachel shook her head and refocused on the moment.

"Bus in the parking area." She said, raising the rifle and firing at a man running in their direction. The bullet caught him in the shoulder, and he spun to the ground and quickly started crawling away. "Follow me."

They set off, Rachel in the lead with Dog at her heels. John brought up the rear, moving more slowly with the burden of the body cradled in his arms. They had to cover a hundred yards to the bus but had only gone twenty when The Reverend stepped into their path. He was a fearsome sight. He had obviously taken some shrapnel wounds from one of the grenades, and his shirt was in tatters. His torso was covered in blood and his face a mask of pure rage.

He held a wicked three-foot blade in his right hand and stood with his legs wide apart, silhouetted by the vehicle fires. In his other hand, he held John's Kukri. Raising both above his head, he screamed and charged.

Before John could react, Rachel brought the rifle up to her hip and fired in burst mode, repeatedly pulling the trigger. The impacts of the bullets on The Reverend were obvious, but it took three bursts of three rounds each before he slowed. Raising the rifle to her shoulder, Rachel put a final three rounds into his face that blew out the back of his skull. Walking over to the body, she bent and retrieved the Kukri then stood up and spit on him.

"Fuck you!" she said in a low, venomous voice, kicking the body for good measure before running for the bus.

We quickly covered the final distance to the bus and rushed through the open doors. Betty was waiting behind the wheel and leaned into the lever to close the doors as soon as we were aboard. I stumbled with my burden in the center aisle of the bus when Betty hit the gas and would have fallen to the floor except for the hands of the kids that reached out and grabbed me and held me upright until I got my balance back.

Moving to the back of the bus, I gently laid the girl across one of the back seats and collapsed onto the other. Rachel dug around and found a small towel that she draped over my privates, then dug some more under a seat and found a rough woolen blanket that she used to cover the girl's body after removing my rifle and laying it on the floor under the seat. That task completed she looked over the bus and after appearing to count heads twice reached out and placed her hand on a boy's shoulder.

"Jared. Where's the boy with the lighter? I'm sorry, I don't know his name."

"Trey," one of the girl's volunteered.

"He was lighting the gas tanks like he was supposed to and one of them went out. He went back to re-light it and just when he got to the side of the truck it exploded." The boy answered her question.

Rachel cursed and lowered herself into the seat next to the boy. I glanced around the bus and did a quick head count. There were now only six surviving kids. I wanted to know the details, especially about the girl who had been killed rescuing me from the pit, but that could wait. Climbing to my feet I held the towel over myself and side stepped, bare-assed, up to the front to check on Betty.

"How we doing, Betty?" I asked, stepping down onto the first exit step so I could talk to her without bending over.

There was also a short bulkhead there that shielded me from the rest of the bus. I'm hardly what you would call a modest person, but I didn't particularly enjoy running around in front of a bunch of teenagers with just a small towel covering my crotch.

"If I was only twenty years younger we'd both be doing a lot better." Betty glanced sideways at me and grinned with the familiar twinkle in her eye. "We've got half a tank of gas, and those crazy people don't have any vehicles left to chase us. We're going to follow this road for a bit then turn north to Murfreesboro. Should take us about an hour if the good Lord's willing and the creek don't rise."

I couldn't help but grin when she used one of my mother's favorite sayings. Leaning down, I kissed her on the cheek and headed to the back of the bus. Resuming my seat, I was surprised to see a large boy walk up and set my pack down on the floor next to me. I thanked him and dug through, finding a spare pair of underwear.

After the third attempt at pulling them on, I dropped them on the floor, and Rachel helped me get them over my feet and up in place. For not the first time in my life, I was reminded of how much better it feels to have some clothing on. Modesty restored, I plopped back onto the seat as Rachel reached out and took each of my arms in her hands, holding me by the wrists as she examined my damaged hands.

"We've got to get these cleaned and do something to stop the bleeding." She said and bent down to dig the medical kit out of my pack.

The first thing she held up was a morphine auto-injector, but I shook my head. As bad as the pain was I couldn't afford to be loopy on morphine if we ran into another fight. Shaking her head in doubt, she put the spring loaded syringe back in the med-kit and spread the rest of the items out on the seat next to her. Waving one of the girls over

Crucifixion

Rachel handed her a small flashlight that she aimed at my hands.

This was the first good look I'd gotten at my hands, and I was shocked at how bad they looked. The nails they had driven through me had been large, so large in fact that when they were removed the wounds failed to completely close back together, and I could look all the way through each hand. Worried that my earlier assessment of the degree of damage may have been optimistic, I experimentally made a fist with each hand.

I can honestly say the pain was the worst I've ever experienced in my life. Worse than a dislocated shoulder. Worse than a broken jaw and nose. Worse than getting shot. I leaned my head back on the vinyl covered bench seat as Rachel started to work.

If I thought my hands had been hurting, it was nothing like the experience of having alcohol poured into the wounds to sterilize them. How I managed to not jerk my hands away, I can't really say, but somehow I was able to hold them out as the alcohol burned its way through my raw flesh and sweat poured off my body. What's the expression? Sweating like a whore in church? If that was the case, well... I had been a very bad girl, and the preacher was on a roll.

As I watched, Rachel repositioned the light and peered at my palms then started using tweezers to remove debris. Finally satisfied she doused me with alcohol again before slathering antibiotic ointment into the wounds. Thinking the worst was over I was ready to relax until she unwrapped a suture kit. Fuck me.

Half an hour later Rachel trimmed the final stitch, applied a thin coat of antibiotic ointment then started wrapping my hands with gauze. I made her adjust and redo the bandages a couple of time so that I would have at least minimal use of my hands. When everything was as good as it was going to get she packed everything except a fat syringe and a bottle of yellow liquid back into the med-kit.

Sticking the not very small needle through the rubber top on the vial, she pulled out the plunger and the syringe filled with some of the liquid. All of this was done right in front of my face, and if I didn't know better, I'd swear Rachel was enjoying messing with my head. Needle ready she motioned me to stand, pulled down the back of my underwear and after swabbing a spot clean with an alcohol pad she jammed the needle into me.

"OK. That last was a high dose of antibiotic." She said. "Do you know when your last tetanus shot was?"

Crucifixion

Actually, I did. I had gotten one as part of routine vaccinations for international travel just a year ago.

"Good. I don't think there's any significant damage, but there's no way you don't have some degree of nerve damage. The good news is you can open and close your hands. There may be some numbness and weakness, but we'll have to wait and see. The biggest danger right now is infection. Those bandages need to be changed twice a day so we'll keep a close eye for a while."

"Thank you, mother," I said, receiving a nasty look in response as she busied herself with cleaning up and repacking the med-kit in my pack.

While she was in the pack, she dug out pants, a shirt, socks and a pair of athletic shoes for me and helped me dress. I had no boots and had lost my vest. Retrieving my rifle from the floor I checked it then slung it over my head and cut a big chunk of the heavy vinyl upholstery from one of the bus seats. Rachel started working on it to make a sheath for my Kukri while I went back up front to check on our progress with Betty.

"How we doing, sweetheart?" I asked as I reached the front of the bus.

"Oh listen to how you talk! We're almost to the highway that goes north to Murfreesboro. We were a little farther away than I thought, and I'm having to keep this old pile of junk under 40, or it feels like the whole front end is going to shake itself to pieces."

Betty never took her eyes off the road, leaning slightly forward to peer into the gloom that was as good as the weak headlights could do. As poor as they were I was kind of glad the speedometer only read 35. A cheap, dollar store compass was stuck to the dash, and it showed we were driving directly south, but less than a mile later the road curved and swung around to the east. At the very edge of the lights, I could just make out the stop sign that must be at the highway we were looking for.

Turning my head to check on Rachel and the kids I didn't see the female infected that ran right at the front of the bus, bouncing off the right front fender. The sound of the impact jerked my attention back to the road and brought gasps from the kids. Rachel rushed forward and stood next to me, peering through the windshield.

Ahead, the road we were on ended at a T intersection, connecting with a state highway. A small green sign that read 'Murfreesboro' pointed to our left, but no distance was indicated. Betty hit the brakes and Rachel, and I had to brace to keep from being thrown into the dash and from the back of the bus I heard a yelp of protest as Dog slid off the seat he was sleeping on.

Crucifixion

The old bus shimmied to a stop thirty yards shy of the stop sign, and we all stared through the cracked windshield. The lights didn't do a good job of lighting up the highway we wanted to turn onto, but they were good enough for us to see the hundreds of infected marching along it in the direction we wanted to go. We were immediately noticed, and dozens of males and females peeled off from the group and headed in our direction.

28

The narrower road we were sitting on was quickly filling up with infected. A few females raced ahead of the slower males, and in seconds were at the grill and spreading out along the sides of the bus pounding on the thin sheet metal walls. Sounds of panic came from the kids, and Dog ran forward and stuck his head in between mine and Rachel's legs.

"Back up!" Rachel said, anxiety causing her voice to raise an octave. For a moment, I agreed with her, but...

"Wait," I said to Betty, who had already shifted into reverse. We sat there with her foot on the brake and the bus's back up alarm beeping loudly. "If we go back, where does this road go?"

"It winds around a bunch of small valleys then turns south and down to Alabama eventually," Betty said, hand still on the shifter.

"Forward! Push through them and turn for Murfreesboro!"

Betty and Rachel turned and looked at me like I was crazy. It wasn't doing us any good to just sit there so I repeated myself a little louder, waving at the gear shifter with my bandaged hand.

Crucifixion

"Trust me. Just get us moving and I'll explain."

Betty didn't waste any more time. Moving the shifter back to drive, she slowly accelerated. The males in our path were either knocked down then run over, the bus's worn suspension squeaking as the whole vehicle swayed from each body we drove over, or were pushed aside where they lost their balance and fell to the ground. Unfortunately, they were back on their feet in no time and in pursuit.

The females stayed with us, running alongside and pounding on the bus as Betty kept our speed under ten miles per hour. Maintaining a steady speed Betty turned onto the larger highway, and the bumping and swaying got worse due to the sheer number of infected in our path.

"The herd coming up from the Gulf," Rachel said a moment later, turning to look at me.

"That's what I'm thinking. I think it's a safe bet that the defenses the military was setting up at the southern Tennessee border were compromised when the second outbreak hit. These infected are only a little ahead of schedule based on what we heard Max say the other day. I'm guessing this is the leading edge of the herd. The healthiest and fastest males and a lot of females. If we'd gone back and followed that road south, we'd have run into the main body of the herd."

Indeed, there were quite a few males on the road, but the majority of the infected we were encountering were females. Both sides of the bus were now lined with females as they pounded in frustration at not being able to get to us. Two of them were clinging to the large mirror mounted on the right front fender but for the moment, I wasn't worried about them as it was taking all their effort and concentration just to hang on.

Betty was still poking along not moving any faster, and I wanted to tell her to accelerate, my mind screaming at me that we needed speed, but there were just too many infected on the road for us to risk going faster. The impact of bodies was a near constant sound and for as far as the weak headlights could shine there were infected in front of us. By now most of them had turned, having heard the noise of our engine, and were either standing and waiting for us or coming directly at us. If the bus broke down, we were royally screwed.

We continued bulling our way through the herd for the next ten minutes. The press of bodies against the old bus alternately thinning out before thickening again. To its credit, the bus kept moving, but I was hearing a grinding noise from somewhere in the drivetrain that was starting to concern me. I kept glancing between the dash and the road in front of us and was not happy to see the engine temperature gauge hovering just below red.

A quick glance up and I saw the problem. Infected were plastered to the grill, blocking the normal air flow across the radiator that would cool the engine. Our speed was so slow that both males and females had managed to grab onto the front of the bus and were clinging to us. Overheating would also bring us to a dead stop. Glancing back and up at the ceiling of the bus I spotted the vents in the roof I expected to be there.

These old busses didn't have air conditioning so the manufacturers had cut large vents into the roofs and covered them with translucent plastic domes that could be raised a few inches to allow hot air to vent out. Striding back to the third row of seats, I waved the kids sitting there out of the way and straddled the aisle, standing on the edge of the seat on either side. A small handle, just like older houses had for opening their windows, stuck down and I grabbed it with my damaged hand and cranked several turns.

The cover over the opening was hinged at the front end, and the crank moved a rod at the unhinged end that pushed it open to a forty-five-degree angle, the crank stopping when the cover reached the limit of its travel. The opening itself didn't look very large, but I thought I could work my shoulders through and get my upper body above the roof so I could shoot the infected off the grill.

Turning my rifle muzzle down, I used the stock to batter the cover off its hinge and out of the way. Opening ready, I shifted my feet until I was standing on the tops of the backrests, and rifle in hand shoved an arm and shoulder through the opening. That was as far as I got. I was just too large to work my head and other arm and shoulder up through the roof. Cursing, I retreated and started trying to think of a way to enlarge the opening. Rachel had come back when I'd started battering the cover out of the way and stood looking at me trying to figure out if I'd gone nuts.

"What are you doing?"

"The infected hanging on to the front of the bus are blocking the radiator, and we're going to overheat," I said, dropping back into the aisle.

Understanding dawned on her face and Rachel shooed me out of the way. Climbing up onto the seats, then the backrests, she wormed her head and shoulders out of the opening. That was as far as she got, the backrests she was standing on not high enough for her to get her upper body above the roof line. With only head and shoulders in the clear, she couldn't effectively use her rifle.

Stooping, I moved in between her legs, wrapped an arm around each thigh and took her

294

weight onto my shoulders as I stood up to my full height. Rachel crossed her ankles across the small of my back to stabilize her perch and she gained over a foot of elevation and was in a good shooting position. I was facing the front of the bus and watched out the windshield as she started picking off the infected riders with head shots.

Unfortunately, it wasn't a one and done exercise for as soon as she shot an infected that fell away from the grill and under the wheels of the bus, another one took its place. Rachel kept up the fire. She was slow and methodical with her shooting and as far as I could tell she didn't miss a single shot.

A couple of times female infected climbed over the mass of bodies riding along with us and made it onto the hood, charging Rachel's position, but she was able to drop them before they climbed fully onto the roof. I was getting occasional glimpses of the engine temp gauge over Betty's shoulder when she swayed to her left as we ran over bodies, and while the temp was still high, it had stopped flirting with the red zone of the gauge.

Rachel kept up the shooting for what seemed like hours but was closer to fifteen minutes. I was focused on staying as steady as I could as I supported her while the bus rattled, shimmied and swayed and it didn't register at first when her rate of fire started slowing. When I did notice, I was relieved to note the infected in front of us were thinning out. Then they were gone, seemingly as if a line had been drawn. Rachel shot the last one hanging on to the grill then shifted and dispatched the two females that were still clinging to the mirror on the fender.

"Spin me in a circle. Slowly." She shouted down through the roof.

I made a slow circle, feeling her body tense slightly as it absorbed the recoil of another shot, then I completed the circle and was facing front again. Rachel uncrossed her ankles, and I took this as a sign she was ready to come down. Sliding my aching hands down her legs, I guided each foot to the top of a backrest as I squatted.

When I felt her weight shift off of me and onto her legs I ducked out from under her and reached up to help her down. Holding her just above the hips, I steadied her as she worked her body back into the bus then stepped away so she could drop down into the aisle.

"Good shooting!" I said with a grin.

She smiled, pleased with the compliment, and then led the way back to Betty. A glance at the speedometer showed we were up to over twenty-five. Looking out the windshield, I was pleased to see nothing but dark pavement ahead of us. Looking back at the dash, I noted our current mileage on the odometer.

Crucifixion

"How far do you think, Betty?" I asked.

"Not sure. Maybe another twenty miles to the center of town, but we should start getting to the edge of town in about ten to fifteen miles."

"Half an hour, roughly," I commented.

"Maybe longer," Betty replied. "This old tranny isn't sounding so good, and I think I'd better slow down a bit."

I watched as the speed dropped to twenty, and Betty seemed satisfied for the moment even though the grinding sound from beneath my feet was growing louder. She held our speed steady, driving through the dark night. Twice we saw animals dash across the road in our headlights, a coyote moving fast and a skunk moving as fast its short legs could propel it.

The road carved gentle curves through the heavy forest, and we had been driving for fifty-five minutes, only covering eighteen miles, when we came out of a curve and saw the roadblock just ahead. Red road flares defined a line across the pavement in front of a line of six-wheeled military transport trucks. Behind the trucks, I could see the red and blue pulses of police lights flashing in the night. Lined up behind the trucks was a row of men armed with all varieties of hunting rifles and shotguns.

They saw us at the same time we saw them, and a moment later dozens of weapons were pointed at us. Betty slowed, finally stopping the bus a few yards short of the line of road flares. Behind me, I heard rustling as all the kids shifted around trying to get a better look through the windshield. Dog growled, and I placed a calming hand on his head.

He went silent, but I could feel the tension in him like a wound spring ready to release. Betty moved the gear shift into park, and we sat there for a long moment before a voice sounded out in the night, amplified through one of the police car's PA system.

"Step out of the bus without your weapons and your hands in the air." It commanded. Rachel looked at me, and I shook my head. No way was I going to disarm myself.

"It's OK," Betty said, having seen the exchange between Rachel and me. "I think I know that voice. Sit tight."

Rachel and I stepped back out of her way, and she leaned into the door lever to open the doors. They moved a couple of inches and stuck. Stepping around Rachel, I added my weight to the lever, and they popped free of whatever was obstructing them and slammed open.

Crucifixion

The glass that had been cracked by the female infected shattered and fell to the pavement. Betty smiled at me, patted me on the arm and stepped out of the bus where she was immediately spotlighted. Raising a hand to shield her eyes she called out towards the roadblock.

"Is that Jonathan Jackson I hear?"

There was silence for a moment, then the same voice without benefit of the PA system answered, "Ms. Jasinski?"

"Indeed, it is, and I have a handful of youngsters and a couple of survivors on this bus."

Within moments, the spotlight shut-off, and four men emerged between two of the trucks and walked forward. All four were wearing police or sheriff uniforms, I couldn't tell which, and the one in the lead rushed up to Betty and hugged her. She hugged him back, and they talked for a minute, her gesturing to the bus and him nodding his head as she talked.

Conversation completed Betty came back to the doors and called all of us out. I stepped aside and let Rachel lead the kids out, shouldered into my pack and followed the last kid out with Dog at my side. Moving over to where Betty stood with the four cops I nodded a greeting as I approached.

My rifle was slung in front of my body, my hand on the pistol grip which was a natural carrying position for me and not intended as a threat, but two of them placed their hands on the butts of their holstered pistols as I approached.

"I come in peace," I said as I came to a stop directly in front of them.

I caught a look from Rachel out of the corner of my eye but ignored her. Betty introduced us, but I declined to shake hands due to my wounds and heavy bandages. It turned out that Jonathan Jackson was a sergeant with the Murfreesboro Police and had grown up two doors down from Betty. I could tell from his body language that her endorsement of me was all he needed to accept my presence. He was full of questions and Betty was starting to tell him our tale, but I interrupted the reunion.

"Sergeant, we've got a lot of infected on their way here right now. Eighteen miles back, probably less than that by now, there's a big herd with lots of females at the front that is headed right here. They'll swarm over this roadblock in a hot minute and keep on going right into town. Please tell me you've got better defenses set up closer to town."

He looked shocked and turned to Betty, who just nodded her head in validation of what I was saying.

"We've got three hours at the most," she confirmed.

Standing there in the dark, his features washed with the red flickering light from the flares I could still see the panic and indecision on his face. He glanced over his shoulder at the other three officers, all younger, and they looked just as panicked.

"OK, tell me your situation here. Who's in charge?" He just stared at me until Betty reached out and grabbed his arm, shaking him.

"I guess I am," he said, looking at the other officers for support. They nodded agreement. "We've lost a lot of people and the mayor, the city council, the Chief of Police, they're all dead, and I haven't seen or heard from my lieutenant in days."

"OK, then." Time to take charge. "What's this road block all about?"

"Uh, well," he stammered. "We've been hearing about some crazy shit The Reverend is pulling so we thought we'd better set up here in case he and his followers decided to come to town."

"The Reverend is dead," I said. "What you need to be worried about are the millions of infected that are headed this way. We just drove through the leading edge of the herd that's coming up from the gulf. How many people are we talking about in town? Can you evacuate?"

"No way!" He shook his head for emphasis. "We've got refugees from all over the countryside, women and children, and there's no way we have even close to enough vehicles to evacuate to Nashville."

"What about the National Guard?" I asked, waving at the trucks blocking the road.

"They all got pulled out of here by the regular Army and went south," he answered. "I heard rumors they were setting up a defense down on the 'Bama border, but that's all I know. These were trucks left behind at the armory that we grabbed for the roadblock." Shit. Was there any good news? These people were about to get overrun.

"What's left in the armory?"

"I don't know. It's locked up tight, and we didn't try to get in."

"Get me to the armory," I said and turned to Betty. "Miss Betty, thank you for everything."

"Don't thank me, young man. Save us. That will make it worth everything."

Minutes later I was in the front seat of Sergeant Jackson's cruiser, Rachel and Dog stuffed in the back behind a wire barrier, and we were screaming through town with lights and siren. Behind us were the other three officers, each in their own car and we made a very conspicuous convoy that was attracting a lot of attention. Everywhere I looked were people. Mostly families.

They were camping on the front lawns of homes, in the parking lots of businesses and as we roared past a large park, I could see a sea of tents covering every inch of open ground. Fuck me; this was just one big buffet waiting for the infected to show up and select the all you can eat option. I glanced over my shoulder at Rachel, and she met my eyes and shook her head. There were just too many people and the infected were way too close. The Sergeant was right. There was no way to evacuate in the amount of time we had, but we could still save a lot of these people.

Minutes later we flew past a rail yard, the cruiser nearly catching air as we blasted over multiple sets of rails embedded into the asphalt. The rail yard was massive with a long row of orange cargo cranes stretching away into the distance looking like skeletons of dinosaurs in the dark. I looked at the hundreds of railroad cars sitting on dozens of tracks that crossed the area and had an idea.

"Sergeant, do the tracks from this yard go to the west?"

"Yes, they do. Not quite sure where, but they head west out of town." He glanced over at me as he drove.

"OK, we're going to see what we can find at the Armory to slow down the infected. I'll deal with that. I want you to find whoever you need to find to get a train hooked up and start loading people on it. There may not be enough vehicles to evacuate, but you can sure as hell shove a lot of people into those livestock cars."

For some reason, my mind flashed on another time in human history when men dressed all in black who thought they were the master race, shoved livestock cars full of people, to haul them to their doom. I didn't like the thought and shook my head, ignoring Rachel's question of what I was thinking.

Once past the rail yard Sergeant Jackson slowed enough to make a tire screeching left into a huge parking lot that was full of civilian vehicles that had been driven there by the National Guard soldiers who had been called up. He gunned the car down a long row of what was mostly pickups then came to a tire-smoking halt in front of a large building that looked like it had been built during WW II.

A large sign read 'Tennessee National Guard Armory' and under it was a large yellow sign with the radiological symbol that advised the building was a fallout shelter. Next to it was another faded sign that was white with the symbol for Civil Defense barely visible on it.

Piling out of the car I trotted to the double front doors which were locked tight. The doors were steel and built to the specs one would expect from a cold war era fallout shelter. I rushed back to the car where my pack sat on the front seat and dug through until I found the remainder of the plastic explosive breaching charges. Back at the door, I pulled out the rope-like charge, but my hands couldn't work the material and remove the waxed paper from the adhesive side.

Thrusting it into Rachel's hands, I talked her through how to set it up and where to place it, where to insert the detonators and we all moved away from the doors and took shelter behind Jackson's car. Thumbing the remote, I involuntarily turtled my head into my shoulders when the explosion ripped through the night with enough force to shatter the windows on the side of Jackson's car that was facing the building as well as the closest row of parked vehicles.

Dirk Patton

Standing up, I rushed into the dust cloud and up to the damaged doors. The right door was still hanging by part of a severely damaged hinge, and the two doors were still attached to each other by the padlocked chain that had been fed through each handle. A swift kick on the right door and the overstressed hinge gave completely, the heavy doors falling to the ground with a loud bang.

I stepped quickly into the building, Dog at my side with Rachel and the cops following. Moving through the structure, I came to an area in the back that was fenced off with a heavy duty chain link fence that went all the way to the ceiling. The double gate was reinforced but was only secured with a standard duty padlock you could pick up at any hardware store.

Inside the cage I could see row after row of older weapons, older defined as what appeared to be twenty-year-old M16 rifles which would have been passed on to the National Guard as the regular Army upgraded to the M4. Stepping back, I waved everyone around a corner and fired two bursts from my rifle into the padlock which shattered and fell away.

"Sergeant, get on the radio and get those Deuce and a Half's - the military trucks at the roadblock – on the way over here. Also, have someone start rounding up able-bodied men."

Crucifixion

I moved into the cage as Jackson started making radio calls and issuing orders. Besides the rifles lined up neatly in racks, I found dozens of crates of loaded magazines, more crates of bulk ammunition and another rack of pistols. Yanking cabinets open, I was happy to find uniforms, boots, belts, vests, and more goodies.

Grabbing replacements for what I had lost, I quickly changed clothes, laced up a new set of boots and loaded my new vest down with magazines and a shiny new Ka-Bar knife. My Kukri was strapped horizontally to the small of my back in the new sheath that Rachel had fashioned for me from the vinyl seat material from the bus.

I took a moment to look for a pistol to replace the one I'd lost when captured by The Reverend, but all I was finding were the new 9 mm pistols the Military had switched to. Not my preference, but you fight with what you got. Outfitted again I went to check up on the loading of the rifles into the truck.

Jackson had worked quickly, and a veritable mob of men and women had shown up, quickly forming a bucket brigade that was passing rifles, crates of magazines, ammo, and grenades out to the waiting truck. As I was watching a couple of crates at the back of the cage caught my eye, and I walked over, very happy to find two M60 machine guns.

Both looked well used but well maintained. Stacked next to them were thousands of rounds of ammo, ready to go. I whistled to get the attention of the work gang leader and pointed at all the crates I was standing next to. He nodded and immediately sent half a dozen men in my direction to start grabbing and loading.

Dog and I followed the chain of frightened looking people who were passing the crates along to the waiting trucks and squeezed our way out the doors into the night air. Rachel stood at the edge of the parking lot, watching men load the truck. Another truck turned into the lot while we stood there, pulling up behind the first one and waited to start loading.

I looked around and saw hundreds of people streaming into the parking lot. I didn't have a watch, but I've always had a good internal clock and knew we'd already spent half an hour of our three-hour window before the infected arrived. People kept pouring in as word spread amongst the townspeople and refugees that a fight was on their doorstep. Watching the people file in I looked up to the horizon where the cranes in the rail yard were faintly visible in the moonlight and had another idea. Looking around, I spotted Jackson and trotted over to him.

Crucifixion

"I need the guys that work in that rail yard," I said, pointing in the general direction. "Preferably a foreman."

"Jim Roberts," he said without hesitation. "He's inside on the bucket brigade."

"Get him," I ordered, pushing Jackson towards the doors and turning back to look at the rail yard, my head whirling with ideas. Less than a minute later he returned and tapped me on the shoulder. I turned around and found myself looking at the top of the head of a skinny, balding man.

"I'm Jim Roberts. You needed something?"

"That rail yard. Lots of freight in there in those big metal shipping containers?"

"Yeah. We're the busiest freight yard east of the Mississippi except for Chicago. Why?" He was looking at me like I was an idiot wasting his time.

"You have forklifts big enough to move them around?"

"Yeah. So what?" He was getting irritated but curious too. Jackson and Rachel were pressing in to listen, and I saw realization dawn on Rachel's face.

"Grab as many men as you need and start moving those containers to set up a wall south of town. Place the containers end to end. When you get a wall say a half a mile long, you'll need to start stacking them up. I've seen the infected come up against buildings and start piling on top of each other until they made it all the way to the roof. Can you do that?"

He got the idea and smiled.

"Use Forrest Avenue," Jackson interjected. "It's four lanes wide, and there're not any residential areas south of it. It runs perfectly east and west." I nodded and looked at the foreman.

"Hell yes, I can do that!" He turned and started to run off, but I stopped him for a second.

"You've got to work fast. That wall is our only chance to slow them down long enough to get people loaded onto the train," I said.

He looked at me for a moment to see if I was serious. Realizing I was he ran back into the building yelling names at the top of his voice. A minute later he ran back out the door with three men on his heels.

"I need some military vets," I said to Jackson. "Preferably Army or Marine, but I'll even take a Coast Guardsman if he has experience with an M60 machine gun."

Crucifixion

An older grizzled man wearing jeans and a Hank Williams, Jr. t-shirt was standing not far away and spoke up when he overheard the conversation.

"Wilbur James, USMC." He said. "Vietnam in '67 and '68. Reckon I know an M60 about as good as anyone around here. What do you need?"

"I've got two M60s and need gunners that know how to use them," I said. "Know anyone else?"

"Yes, sir. My grandson. He served two tours in Afghanistan with the Corps."

He turned his head and shouted towards the crowd. Moments later a much younger version of him pushed through the press of bodies to stand next to Wilbur, who gave him a five-second version of what was going on.

The M60s and their ammo were just starting to come down the bucket brigade, and I pointed the James boys at them. Wilbur assured me he had it under control, and he and his grandson set off to intercept the machine guns, redirecting them to waiting hands that carried them across the parking lot to a couple of battered Chevy trucks. Meanwhile, the first deuce and a half was fully loaded and started to pull off so the second could pull forward and start loading.

"I'm going to the wall. Find someone to take over here and start getting that train put together and loaded." I said to Jackson and thumped on the door of the first truck.

The driver braked, and I pulled open the passenger door and waved Rachel and Dog inside. Cab full, I shut the door and climbed up on the running board with an arm hooked through the heavy bracket that held the side mirror.

"Hang on a second," I said to the driver who nodded.

"Hey!" I shouted out over the heads of the crowd.

A few people looked my way, but there were still dozens of conversations going on, and I didn't have the crowd's attention. I looked at the driver, and he leaned on the truck's horn and held it there for ten seconds, stopping every side conversation and drawing the crowd's attention.

"There are thousands of infected on their way, not much more than a couple of hours away." I deliberately understated the size of the herd that was bearing down on the town. "We're building a wall on Forrest Avenue to slow them while we get a train loaded up to evacuate the town, and we've got a lot of rifles we're getting out of the Armory with no fingers to pull triggers. I need anyone with military experience first, then anyone that knows how to shoot to meet me on Forrest Avenue.

"We have to defend the wall. We can slow them enough to save the people in this town, but I need every able bodied person that can help."

People looked at each other, some frightened, some determined. From the back of the crowd a small, young woman shouted out over everyone's heads.

"I was in the Army in Iraq and can shoot. I'll be there!"

Everyone cranked their heads around to look at the woman, then a young man with only one arm spoke up too. Soon the whole crowd was shouting their support. I waved to them and told the driver to get us to Forrest Avenue as fast as he could.

Forrest Avenue turned out to be Nathan Bedford Forrest Avenue. He is best known for being the first Grand Dragon of the Ku Klux Klan but was also a brilliant general for the Confederacy during the Civil War and a son of Tennessee. Despite all of that I was quite surprised to see a street named after him in the hyper-politically correct times we live in…. er, lived in, I corrected myself.

Not much time or place for political correctness when the people trying to kill and eat you ran the gamut of color and ethnicity and could care less if you were black, white or purple. We were all finally and truly equal. Somehow I didn't think this was the dream Dr. King was talking about. All of this ran through my head as the truck pulled to a stop in a parking lot for a large home improvement store that sat at the intersection of Forrest Avenue and the state highway we had followed into town.

People were streaming into the parking lot by the dozens, and I knew I needed to get them organized. We were fast running out of time. Jumping down from the truck's running board, I turned to Rachel when she dropped to the ground next to me.

Crucifixion

"Did you see the hospital we passed about half a mile back?"

"Yes. Why?" She asked, adjusting her rifle sling to free her hair which she then whipped up into a quick braid to keep it out of her face.

"My hands are killing me. I can't grip anything. Would you run back and see if you can find something that would numb them? Something that would be a local. No morphine or valium or anything like that."

"On my way," she said, turning and dashing back up the road, Dog running at her side.

I looked around at the quickly assembling throng and didn't waste a moment detailing several men to unload the trucks and organize the weapons. I was mentally cataloging and prioritizing what else needed to be done when a loud horn sounded from behind. I turned to see the largest forklift I had ever seen approaching down the highway with a huge, steel shipping container held a few feet off the ground in its forks. Behind it were three more forklifts with similar burdens. I trotted over to meet the one in the lead, stepping up on the side of the massive vehicle that was driven by Jim Roberts.

"Where do you want it?" He shouted over the roar of the diesel engine.

"Smack in the middle of the intersection, running east and west," I shouted back, pointing at the location and gesturing with my bandaged hand.

Jumping down from the forklift, I stood back and watched as Jim dropped the first container on the asphalt. The first piece of the wall, forty feet long, ten feet high and ten feet deep was in place. I saw Jim raise a walkie-talkie to his mouth, and less than a minute later three more containers were in place, and we had 160 feet of wall in place. The forklifts spun around and charged back towards the rail yard. The men were still unloading the truck and organizing the cargo, and I walked over to the large crowd and raised my hand in the air. They went quiet and pressed forward to listen.

"Glad to see all of you here!" I shouted. "We have about two hours at most before the first infected start arriving and a lot to do to get ready. First, I need everyone experienced with a military rifle to move over by the deuce and a half."

I pointed at the truck and about three hundred people separated themselves from the main group and moved to the area I indicated.

"OK, next we need about a thousand sand bags."

Immediately a heavy set man stepped forward from the front ranks of a large group of boys. A quick look at their jackets and I realized it was a high school football team.

"We've got that," he said. "Where do you want them stacked?"

"To the right of the stacks of weapons." I pointed, he nodded and trotted off with eighty football players at his back.

"We need ladders to get to the top of the containers."

An early middle-aged woman stepped forward.

"I'm Jess. I'm the manager of the Home Depot right there. Lots of ladders. Follow me!" She turned and headed across the parking lot, a couple of dozen people falling in behind her.

"Radios. Walkie Talkies. We need at least thirty, all on the same frequency." I called out to the group.

"I own a CB and Ham radio shop. Got you covered!"

An elderly man headed for his car at the far side of the parking lot and a couple of women joined him to lend a hand.

I spent another couple of minutes detailing groups to collect water and medical supplies; then the second truck arrived and the men that had just finished unloading the first one immediately set to work. Four more containers showed up a minute later, and our wall doubled in length. Stepping over to the group that had served in the military I shouted out asking for NCOs – Non Commissioned Officers or Sergeants – and was rewarded with about thirty raised hands. I waved them forward to where I was standing.

"We've got," I turned my head and did a quick count of crates and did the math. "Looks like seven hundred and fifty rifles. I want to put five hundred on the wall along with our two M60s. Each of you grab twenty-five shooters and make sure they seem to know what they're doing. As soon as the sand bags and ladders are here, get them a rifle and have them grab a sandbag on their way to the top of the wall."

The sand bags would be rests for the rifles and hopefully improve the shooters' accuracy.

"Doesn't look like there's enough bodies, so start picking people you know that can shoot to fill out the ranks. Get going!" I shouted.

"You six stay with me." I pointed at six older men who were standing closest to me.

Two of them had globe and anchor tattoos on their forearms. I might crack jokes, but I'd never turn down help in a fight from a Marine. The other four were from the same generation but didn't have the look, and when I asked found that two were retired Navy CPOs, one retired Air Force, and the other had been in the Coast Guard.

"We need a 250-man ready reaction force," I said, and the two Marines quickly nodded understanding and agreement.

A reaction force is held in reserve to swiftly move into an area of the battle where there is a risk that the front lines will be overwhelmed. It can often mean the difference between victory and defeat.

"Alpha, Bravo, Charlie and Delta." I pointed at each one of them in turn as I said the designator for their piece of the reaction force.

Having made a very spur of the moment assessment, I assigned Navy as Alpha and Bravo which would be the first units I called if we needed to use them. I expected them to have the least experience in a firefight and be the least effective, so I'd throw them into the grinder first. My two Jar Heads were Charlie and Delta. Again the two Marines nodded their understanding of what I was doing, and the four of them set off to start rounding up shooters.

I was left with the Air Force and Coast Guard non-coms and assigned one to put together a group to load the loose ammo into magazines. I had the other oversee the filling of the sandbags, and when the football team was done with that, he would conscript them to be ammo runners for the shooters, collecting empty magazines for the crew doing the loading and delivering full magazines back to the top of the wall.

Everyone was scurrying around, and I was surprised how quickly all the people had jumped in to help. Of course, they'd all had a couple of weeks of the apocalypse to get used to the idea that everyone needed to pitch in if anyone wanted to survive. Besides, there was a reason Tennessee was called the Volunteer state.

More containers arrived and were quickly placed. The forklift drivers showed their skills, maneuvering the large containers into place with an apparent ease that I knew only came from years of experience. The wall was quickly spreading out, and I was starting to feel a tiny little glimmer of hope but reminded myself that the containers were only ten feet high, and we still had a lot of work to do and almost no time to do it in.

Ladders started arriving and were put in place to give access to the tops of the containers. Grabbing one of the men that was heading back to get another ladder I told him to find as many cans of white spray paint as he could get his hands on, then sent him running. My plan was to have five hundred shooters spread along the top of the wall, each shooter needing about five feet of space, so I needed 2,500 feet of wall completed before the infected arrived. I did a quick count and came up with sixteen containers, or 640 feet.

Wanting a look, I strode to the closest ladder and climbed, grimacing at the pain as I gripped the rungs. As I reached the top of the ladder and stepped onto the roof of the container a rumble of thunder sounded behind me. I turned and while I couldn't see the clouds in the dark sky I could see the play of lightning through the clouds. Shit. All we needed right now was a storm. I turned back to the south and looked down the highway. No infected were in sight, but I knew that wouldn't last long.

I spent a couple of minutes on top of the container, watching Wilbur James and his grandson carry the two M60 machine guns up a ladder. They set them up to bracket the highway, each one settling in about seventy-five yards on either side of me. I nodded my approval, and as each of them started working with a couple of teenagers they'd brought along to act as gun crews I turned to look back to the north.

Four more containers were arriving, and the forklifts split when they reached the wall, two going to the right and two to the left. Another four containers. Another 160 feet. Two vehicles with red and blue flashing lights were fast approaching, and I climbed down the ladder to meet them as another rumble of thunder, closer this time, rolled over the town. The air felt heavy and charged with energy, and I expected we were in for a hell of a storm.

When I reached the ground, an ambulance led by Sergeant Jackson pulled to a stop. The driver side door of the ambulance opened, activating the dome light, and I could see Rachel and Dog climb down out of the vehicle. A large pickup truck that I hadn't noticed pulled in next to the ambulance and the driver, one of Jackson's officers stepped out and waved me over.

Crucifixion

Curious I went to the back of the vehicle where he was standing and couldn't suppress a big grin. In the bed of the truck was a crated 60 MM mortar and half a dozen crates of mortar bombs. The officer was smiling too and used his nightstick to break off the lid on one of the crates of bombs. The crate held twenty HE – high explosive – bombs nestled into wooden cut outs and padded with shredded cardboard.

"Thought you'd like this," he said, looking at the grin on my face.

"You have no idea," I said, pointing at a spot a hundred feet behind the wall and in the center of the highway. "Can you put it all right there?"

"You got it," he said and jumped back into the truck to move the weapon to the middle of the street.

Dog had trotted over and was nudging my hip with his head. I absently scratched his ears and turned as the man with the cans of spray paint came running up, pushing a rattling shopping cart half full of spray cans.

"Where?" He shouted to me without breaking stride.

"By the ammo supply." I pointed. "Grab someone to be ready to help you and stand by. We need a few more containers first."

He nodded and ran to where I had indicated, pushing the cart to rest against the tall tires of the truck, then looked around for someone who wasn't doing anything.

A screech of tires sounded in the parking lot, and an aging Buick came to a stop. The man that owned the radio shop waved from behind the windshield then he and the women who had gone with him jumped out and started loading up their arms with stacks of walkie talkies from the trunk. He walked over to me, and I picked two of them, handing one to Rachel.

"Sorry, it took so long. We put batteries in each one and set them all to the same frequency. They're ready to go."

"Excellent. Hammond!" I shouted to the Coast Guard NCO, who was making sure the football team was stacking the sandbags neatly as they were filled.

He trotted over, and I pointed at the radios and told him to make sure each NCO received one. He nodded, grabbed one for himself and waved for them to follow as he set off to get our communications distributed.

"Alright, in the ambulance," Rachel said, grabbing my left arm and pulling me towards the vehicle.

Crucifixion

She led me to the back and opened the doors, climbing up inside and sitting on a padded bench that ran the length of the wall. I joined her, and Dog jumped up as well, giving Rachel a look when she kicked him out and made him wait on the ground just outside. Rachel opened a drawer and pulled out a pair of medical scissors that she used to cut the bandages off each hand. Thunder rumbled louder while she worked.

"I'd better do something to waterproof these when I re-bandage," she said without pausing in her work. "Sounds like we're about to get soaked."

Bandages off she examined my wounds under the bright lights in the back of the ambulance and nodded to herself. From another drawer, she produced more antibiotic ointment which was liberally smeared onto my wounds. Standing up, she dug through her pocket for a key she used to open a couple of locked drawers.

Leaving the key in the lock, she picked through and pulled out two different syringes wrapped in paper and a couple of different vials of liquid, one clear and one cloudy and yellow. While she was getting what she needed, Sergeant Jackson walked up to the back of the ambulance and stood next to Dog.

"Are we going to be ready?" He asked.

"We have a chance," I said with much more conviction than I felt, but I wasn't going to let anyone see a shred of doubt. Right now my outward confidence was as important as any preparation we were making. "How's the evacuation going?"

"The railroad guys are getting a train hooked up, and I've got men going through town and sending people to the passenger terminal. I've got to get back in a few, but I got a call from the hospital that they were under attack, and I had to run over."

He watched as Rachel inserted the smaller needle into the vial of clear liquid and extracted enough to fill the syringe.

"You know she took the key for the narcotics cabinet there from an EMT at gunpoint, then stole the ambulance. All of this after she threatened to shoot one of the doctors in the balls."

I looked at him then turned and caught Rachel grinning as she held my right hand and prepared to insert a needle.

"He taught me everything I know," Rachel sassed, then the needle went into the raw flesh of my hand, and liquid fire flowed into me.

"Fuck me," was the only reaction I made, but I wanted to jump, yell, scream and flap my hand in the air like a maniac. Fortunately, I didn't, as moments later the pain started easing and blessed numbness began to spread across my palm. Several injections later Rachel turned my hand over and did the same thing on the back.

Finished with my right she moved and started working on my left. While she worked, I tested the hand, making a fist and squeezing, then wiggling each finger individually. Not perfect, but at least the pain was gone for the moment. Finished with my left, she started bandaging me back up.

"Sergeant, is his pack still in your car?" Rachel asked without looking up from her work.

"Yes, ma'am. Do you need it?"

"Please."

Rachel finished the bandaging then slipped a latex glove onto each hand to protect the heavy gauze and used medical tape to seal the cuff of each glove around my wrist so water wouldn't run down inside. More thunder, much closer, and Jackson returned and deposited my pack in the ambulance. Rachel opened it and looked through until she found a pair of thin leather gloves that she handed me. Slipping them on I secured the Velcro tabs at the wrist, so they were tight and tried my hands again.

I was able to open and close my hands most of the way, but more importantly I could grip my rifle and pistol without pain. Without much pain would be more accurate. I reached behind my back and drew the Kukri, but wasn't confident I could grip it tightly enough to be effective with it. Oh well, good enough for now.

"One last thing," Rachel said, filling a much larger needle and syringe with the yellowish liquid.

"Oh shit. Really?"

"Yep. Stand up, turn around and drop your pants." She said with a grin.

"I've been waiting for you to say that to... Ouch!"

Rachel jabbed the needle into my ass, probably harder than she would have if I hadn't been a smart ass. As bad as the needle was, the antibiotic hurt like hell when she pressed the plunger. A moment later, syringe empty, Rachel pulled the needle out and swabbed the spot with an alcohol pad then pulled my underwear back up and snapped the elastic waistband into place.

"Just because you were crucified doesn't mean you need to get a God complex. And, you need a shower," she said, slapping my ass on the exact spot she had just injected then started straightening up the supplies she had used.

Crucifixion

The loudest peal of thunder yet sounded, and Dog whined and jumped into the ambulance with us, willing to risk Rachel's wrath rather than stand out in the open. He pushed up against me and shoved his head behind me to look at Rachel from a safe distance.

"Sounds like we're all about to get a shower," I said, properly put back in my place. I pulled my pants up and buckled my belt.

Stepping down from the ambulance I looked up at the wall, and an idea struck me. I turned to Sergeant Jackson just as the first rain drop fell, splattering directly on my nose.

Wiping the water out of my eyes, I asked him, "How many fire trucks in this town?"

"Three," he said after a moment's thought.

"Get them here. Now." I said, turning back to the wall and starting to count containers.

Four more had just arrived, and the forklifts were roaring back into town to get more. I heard Jackson on the police radio issuing orders and heard the acknowledgment that the fire department was on their way. He wished me luck and took off to make sure the evacuation was progressing smoothly.

I didn't think there was any way we could stop the infected; rather my plan was to hold them at the wall for a while. Hopefully long enough to get all the people in the town loaded onto a train that would head west towards Kansas City.

It took me a few minutes to finish counting and by the time I was done four more containers were arriving. I added them to the total and came up with forty-four containers. 1,760 feet. We were getting there. I dashed forward and climbed the first ladder I came to and looked up and down the top of the wall.

It was already impressive, but not enough, I knew. Turning to my left, I started jogging along until I came to the end of the final container. Ahead I could see Forrest Avenue curve to the south and decided this was far enough. Running back, I reached the center of the wall just as four more containers arrived. Climbing down, I trotted to Jim's forklift and gave him updated instructions.

Only one container was going to the left, east, and it was going to be at a forty-five-degree angle to the wall, the far end of it angling south. I had noticed the terrain quickly grew very rugged as I had jogged east, and I expected that the more difficult terrain would help to keep the infected funneled along the highway. I hoped.

Crucifixion

Climbing back down, I found the paint guy, waiting right where I'd asked, a woman standing next to him. I started explaining what I needed as soon as I walked up to them.

"I want the wall broken up into numbered sections. Every three containers make up one section. Start at the far east end and the first three containers are number 1. The next three are number 2. Got it?"

They both nodded their heads.

"On the top of each container, I want the number of that section painted every ten feet, so you'll paint a number four times on the top of each container. On the face of each container, right in the center, paint the same number very large so it can be seen from a good distance. Repeat back to me what you're doing."

They repeated it back correctly, and I sent them on their way, the woman running east along Forrest Avenue pushing the shopping cart, the man rushing up a ladder and heading east along the top of the wall. I wanted the numbers every ten feet so in the heat of battle if someone needed help they didn't have to look far to find their location.

Looking around I was pleased to see a large group of women seated on the ground, surrounded by crates of loose ammo and empty magazines. They were loading the magazines and stacking

331

them into waiting crates. The football team was organized and kept moving the full crates to the side and placing empty ones back within easy reach of the women. I dug the walkie talkie out of my pants pocket and raised it to my mouth and pressed the transmit button.

"All NCOs attention. All NCOs attention." I gave them a moment to hear their radios and listen, then started transmitting again. "Get your shooters armed and on the wall. First unit on move all the way to the east, then let's fill from there. Each unit spread out across three containers. Let's go!"

There was almost immediate movement from the large group that had been sitting quietly out of the way. A man I recognized as one of the NCOs stood up, and twenty-five people stood and followed him to where the rifles were neatly lined up by the two deuce and a halfs. As each man, and woman moved down the line they grabbed a rifle, moved forward where they were handed half a dozen loaded magazines, continued on to grab a sandbag that was held out to them by one of the football players then climbed a ladder and headed east.

The next NCO had his group lined up behind the first one and ready to go. Satisfied things were working for the moment I called Rachel on the radio and told her where to find me. It took her a minute, but she trotted up with Dog at her side.

Crucifixion

"I need you right next to me," I said. "There will be things that need done that can't get done over the radio once the shooting starts."

"Whatever you need," she said.

"Thanks. And I want you to keep Dog with you." Rachel nodded, and we stood and watched the shooters continue to arm themselves on their way to the wall.

Containers were still arriving, Jim waving as he roared by with another section of the wall. Behind the last forklift three bright red fire trucks arrived, swinging into the parking lot and coming to a stop, side by side. I walked over, Rachel and Dog trailing me, and met the fire captain when he swung down from the lead truck.

He introduced himself, and I shook hands with him, suppressing the wince that wanted to form on my face when he squeezed my hand. I looked at the three trucks and quickly explained what I wanted. He grinned, nodded and climbed back into the cab of the truck and got on the radio to explain to the other firemen what was happening. I headed back to the wall and climbed a ladder to the top, Rachel following as Dog sat at the bottom of the wall and watched us.

The rain had started, big drops but not a lot of them and lightning lit the night like a strobe light. The thunder wasn't far behind, the bass boom so loud it rattled the metal container I was standing on. Shit. Metal in a thunderstorm. Maybe not my best idea, but it was all we had. The infected should be arriving very soon, and we didn't have time to do anything else.

The shooters were moving quickly and efficiently, and the wall was quickly getting lined with people laying on their stomachs, rifles resting on sand bags and pointing to the south. Diesel engines roared behind me as more containers arrived. More engines added to the noise as the fire trucks maneuvered into place and I turned to watch.

The largest fire truck, one of those impossibly long ladder trucks that has to have a pivot point in the middle and another driver at the very back, came to a stop on the side of the highway and across Forrest Avenue, front bumper only yards from the wall. With a whine of hydraulics, it extended two giant legs on each side that would stabilize it when the ladder was raised. Firemen scurried around the truck, two of them dragging a thick hose across the pavement and connecting it to a fire hydrant.

Other firemen set about raising the ladder, and I could see the captain himself sitting in the basket at the top of the ladder. He waved then hit a switch that turned on a bank of brilliant halogen lights. The lights were fifty feet in the air and aimed over the wall and lit up the highway like it was noon. The other two trucks, both ladder trucks but smaller, positioned themselves to either side of the big truck, directly behind the two machine gun emplacements, raised their ladders and turned their lights on too. The result was a two hundred and fifty-yard width of wall that was as well-lit as any stadium I had ever seen at night.

More containers arrived, and the shooters kept filing up the ladders and into their sections. Lightning flashed again, close enough that the thunder rattled my fillings almost before the lightning faded. The rain started falling harder, and the wind picked up a little, blowing out of the south and driving the rain directly into the faces of the shooters.

I lifted the walkie-talkie to my mouth and reminded the NCOs to enforce fire discipline, making sure their people were firing single shots only, not full auto. That done, I didn't know what else to do at the moment, so I stood in the rain and waited for the first infected to appear on the highway.

I didn't have to wait long. The first infected appeared at the edge of the light cast by the fire trucks, a female that had already broken into a sprint even before we could see her, apparently enraged by the bright lights. Nearly every rifle on top of the wall opened up and kept firing until the body was pulped into mush. I immediately got on the radio and screamed at the NCOs to get their units under control. As a group I estimated they had just blown through four or five thousand rounds of ammunition to kill one infected.

Up and down the line I could hear the NCOs yelling and cursing and couldn't help but smile as the moment took me back to my youth. The rain was coming harder now, the lighting and thunder a constant. A young boy ran up to me, breathless and slipping on the wet metal roof of the container I stood on. I reached out to help him regain his balance, but he managed it himself and stuck another walkie talkie out for me to take.

"So you can talk to my dad, I mean Jim Roberts," he said, turned and dashed off and slithered down the ladder the way I used to be able to move. I raised the radio and identified myself.

"Major, we've got you close to three thousand feet of wall built. Do you want us to turn the corner or start stacking?" He was shouting over the roar of the forklift's diesel engine.

"Turn the corner but head south with the wall a couple hundred feet before you start stacking. I want them funneled into the rifles." I answered.

"You got it."

I raised the other radio and sent Alpha unit of the ready reaction force to the west end of the wall, telling them to provide security for the forklift drivers while they were placing the containers. While I did this a dozen more females appeared in the lights, but this time, only the shooters on the containers directly to their front opened up. These were the shooters stationed on the container I was standing on and most of them were picking their shots and making them count, but there was one that was popping off rounds as fast as he could.

I went over to where he lay prone on the container and kicked him on the bottom of the foot to get his attention. He stopped firing and looked over his shoulder, then started to swing his rifle around and stand up when he saw me. Reaching, out I pushed the rifle back onto the sandbag, pointed in a safe direction and squatted next to him and told him to watch how the people on either side of him were shooting. He nodded and turned back to watch them before facing front again.

The next wave of infected was larger, close to a hundred females this time. They sprinted into the light screaming so loud I could hear them over the rain drumming on the wall, only the thunder and sounds of rifle fire drowning them out. The firing was slightly more disciplined this time, and all hundred were cut down well short of the wall. Firing died out, and everyone seemed to be holding their breath, waiting.

The rain intensified, and I was thankful for the lights. Without them, in the pouring rain, we wouldn't have been able to see the infected until they were piling up against the wall. I paced up and down the wall, nodding to the NCOs as I moved through their area. Rachel stayed with me, and Dog paced us on the ground, looking up at us as he moved, distinctly unhappy at being left out of the action. I paced as far as the eastern machine gun, manned by Wilbur, squatting down next to the old vet.

"Gunny?" I asked him.

"Yes, sir. I was." He replied, hands on the M60 and eyes trained out on the far edge of the light.

"Knock the sir shit off, Gunny. I'm John," I said, also keeping watch on the front.

"Yes, sir." He responded with a grin.

Crucifixion

"Smart ass, Jar Head."

"Yes, sir. That I am, sir." He laughed, then straightened up as bodies appeared downrange.

Female infected burst into the light, running flat out, and I didn't see a back edge of the group. Slapping Gunny James on the shoulder I stood and unslung my rifle as the shooters engaged. The sound of rifles firing blanked out all other sounds, infected bodies dropping well away from the wall, but more females hurdled the dead and kept coming. I sighted in on a running figure and dropped it with a head shot and kept finding and dropping targets until I had burned through a magazine.

Changing magazines, I strode to the west along the wall, checking on the NCOs and shooters. Several shooters were frozen, just staring at the screaming females running at us and I pulled them out of line and sent them down the ladders, telling Rachel to go down and find replacements. She scampered down the ladder like a monkey, Dog meeting her at the bottom, and started moving through the people at the bottom finding volunteers.

I only pulled six people off the line, and I was surprised that the number was so low. Lots of people think they can pick up a rifle and go into combat because it looks so easy in the movies. But

Dirk Patton

until you've had an enemy trying to kill you, and you have to pull the trigger to save yourself and the man next to you, no one really knows how they'll react. Some people are built for it; some aren't.

Rachel was back with six new shooters in short order, and I pointed them at the NCOs who quickly plugged them into place. Football players were already dashing up and down the line, gathering empty magazines and leaving full ones, and I glanced down below to make sure there was still a crew loading magazines. Satisfied I turned my attention back to the front.

The wave of infected was thickening, and there was already a two-foot high pile of bodies downrange, and it was growing, but the volume of females was increasing, and they were slowly pressing their front edge closer to the wall. Raising a pair of binoculars, I looked to the sides of the highway and saw females moving through the forest, their speed tempered by having to fight through the underbrush.

The shooters in front of them were engaging, somewhat more successfully than the ones focused on the highway. The herd kept increasing in numbers and soon the highway was a solid mass of infected bodies. Males were now in view and were pushing and stumbling forward, often gaining a lot of ground as the shooters were focused on the much faster females.

Crucifixion

I was just turning to run down the wall and tell Gunny James to join the fight when his machine gun started firing. He was targeting the mass of bodies at the far edge of the lights, and a moment later his grandson joined him, and two streams of fire reached out and started chewing up the infected. Bodies were torn apart; limbs severed, and heads exploded, but the infected still pressed forward.

They knew no fear and had no self-awareness to warn them that what was happening to their comrades was about to happen to them. Soon every weapon on the wall was firing, and the piles of bodies in front of the wall continued to grow, and the leading edge crept closer.

Raising the binoculars, I checked the edges of the pavement again. Infected flowed through the woods in numbers too large to count, but the shooters were spread along a nearly half-mile front and were keeping them back for the moment. I looked to the east where the terrain should be working in our favor, and for the moment saw nothing moving.

Back to the highway, I watched as the press of infected bodies continued to increase as they flowed forward and over their dead brethren. The males were stumbling over the difficult footing, but the females seemed to not even notice they were running on fallen bodies rather than a nice smooth road. Inexorably the herd pushed forward against our fire and were now no more than fifty yards from the wall.

The firing kept up, and we were burning through thousands of rounds a minute. I ran to Gunny James' position and checked on his ammo supply. He was an old hand and was doing a good job of maximizing what he had. Running the other way, I was pleased to find his grandson was just as frugal. If I survived this, I was going to find a Marine and apologize for having snuck onto Camp Pendleton where I painted the battle cannon on display at their welcome center a shade of hot pink. Maybe.

To the west, I could see Jim Roberts and his crew setting the first upper row of containers. The shooters on the container already in place had to move out of the way while the new container was stacked in place, then a ladder on the end got them on top of the new container, and they were now twenty feet off the ground. Looking at the front edge of the herd pushing in I knew we'd get overrun before the second level of the wall was in place.

Turning, I went to the nearest ladder, waiting for one of the football players with an armload of full magazines to finish climbing up then raced to the ground and straight back to where the police officer had dropped off the mortar for me. Rachel was at my side, and Dog ran with us, taking up a guarding stance when we stopped at the waiting crates.

Using my Ka-Bar, I pried off all the lids then quickly started setting up the mortar. The 60 MM mortar is really simple. There's a round base plate that lays on the ground onto which you set the closed end of the mortar tube. The mortar tube is just that, a tube with a closed end and a fixed firing pin at the bottom. It's only about four feet long or so and about a foot from the muzzle an adjustable bipod is attached. The bipod has an azimuth adjustment built into it for setting the elevation of the mortar.

When you get it where you want you simply pick up a mortar bomb, align it at the mouth of the tube, let it go and be sure you move behind the plane of the muzzle. The bomb drops down the tube where its explosive propellant strikes the firing pin, ignites, and it is propelled out of the tube like a bullet out of a rifle. The biggest difference here being that the tube is not rifled as the mortar bombs are stabilized with fins. The idea is they are shot in a high arc and fall down onto your target. 60 MM mortars are one of the smaller sizes the US uses, but they still pack quite a nice punch when all you're using them against is flesh and bone.

Mortar set up, I adjusted the azimuth to seventy-five degrees, made sure Rachel and Dog were behind the tube, then dropped the first bomb and spun away to avoid the muzzle blast. There was a deep thumping sound and I turned to look down range. A few moments later there was a bright flash and loud explosion from beyond the wall. Grabbing the radio, I called the NCO responsible for the section where I'd been standing and asked where the bomb had struck.

"Your distance is good, hitting about a hundred yards down range, but you need to adjust left. That one hit in the trees."

I turned the mortar a few degrees to the left then sent another round on its way. A moment later the NCO called and told me I still needed a few more degrees to the left. Making the adjustment I let another round fly and waited for the report.

"Spot on Major. Right on the yellow line if we could see it. Fire for effect!"

I started sending a round every ten seconds, wanting there to be enough delay for the hole I was blowing in the herd to fill back in with more infected. After six rounds I adjusted right a couple of degrees and sent another six rounds with the same timing, then moved to the left and sent another six. Telling Rachel to stay with the mortar and make sure it wasn't messed with, I ran for the wall to see what effect I was having.

Climbing a ladder, I noted that the firing by the shooters hadn't slowed and was dismayed when

I reached the top of the wall. I looked at a solid sea of infected and they were now within thirty yards of the wall. What the fuck? The NCO for that area saw me and ran over, looking almost comical as he ran flat-footed to keep from slipping on the rain-slicked metal.

"Each shell kills dozens and blows a huge hole in their ranks, but they flow into it in seconds and just keep on coming."

"Damn it. OK, I'm going to send up a couple of the reaction units and step up the rate of fire. We've got to hold them until this wall gets raised."

I turned and flew back down the ladder, not waiting for a response. Running for the mortar, I keyed the radio and told Bravo and Charlie units to deploy to section 12 which was the center section. The two NCOs acknowledged as I reached the mortar.

"Feed these to me as fast as I can fire them," I said to Rachel. "And for God's sake, don't drop one."

She went a little white, but nodded and pulled a bomb out of its case to have it ready to hand to me. I started firing as fast as I could feed the bombs into the tube. Every tenth round I adjusted a little to the right, then back to center, then left. I was keeping up a good rate of fire, explosions from the far side of the wall coming every two to three seconds. When I was about half way through my supply of rounds, I paused to check on the wall building.

The stacked sections were getting closer but were still a long way off. The rate of fire from the wall had not lessened one bit, and I was starting to worry we were going to run out of ammo before we even got the wall raised to twenty feet. Pushing the worry aside, I started feeding the mortar again, the explosions resuming with the same frequency. I was in a rhythm; hang, drop and turn, grab new round and repeat and was caught by surprise when I held my hands out, and Rachel didn't have a bomb ready for me.

"That's all there is," she said, straightening up and stretching her back.

I looked at the empty crates, still surprised, then shook it off and headed for the wall. Rachel and Dog ran with me, Dog rushing ahead through the pouring rain and not about to be left out again he bounded up the ladder ahead of us. Great. Who was going to carry his big, furry ass back down?

Back on the wall I stared dumbfounded at the sea of infected. They had reached the base of the wall and were pushing in; the bodies pressed so tightly together they appeared to be a solid mass. Mounds of bodies from my mortar assault were piled high on the highway, but the infected just flowed over and around them as they moved forward. As the herd had made contact with the wall, it had started spreading out to the sides.

The heaviest concentration had been following the highway and while some had been in the woods to either side most had stuck to the easier path the asphalt afforded. Now, as they spread, the woods for a hundred yards to either side of the highway was packed with bodies, and they were still spreading. They were also starting to pile on top of each other at the base of the wall, and it wouldn't take much piling up for hands to be able to reach the ten-foot high edge of the containers.

As I was thinking this there were shouts of alarm from several places along the wall as shooters suddenly saw hands reach up and grab the metal rod that ran along the top edge of each container. Most of them were able to quickly dispatch the infected with shots to the head, but a couple were caught unprepared when females made big leaps, reaching over the edge to grab a hapless shooter and drag him into the churning mass in front of the wall.

Moving right up to the front edge, I looked over and then scanned up and down the length of the wall. The second level was still too far away, and we were only minutes away from the infected breaching our defenses and pouring over the wall and into the town. A female leapt up from below, screaming like a banshee as she tried to grab my leg. Stepping to the side, I kicked her in the face while she was still in the air and her body did a back flip before landing in the herd below.

"Grenades, grenades, grenades!" I shouted into the radio.

All up and down the line I saw and heard the NCOs passing the order, and the sounds of rifle fire sputtered out as each shooter started pulling pins and tossing grenades over the front lip of their container. The explosions ripped up and down the wall, competing with the thunder but not winning. As planned, each shooter tossed two grenades then went back to their rifle.

The effects were devastating on the infected bodies that were pressed against the metal containers. Unfortunately, when they fell the ranks of infected behind them just used their bodies to gain more height as they clawed and scrambled to reach the people on top.

The only advantage for us was the herd was pressing in so tight the females couldn't get a run to leap at the wall, and were hampered in even being able to jump straight up. This didn't stop them from trying and right next to me one succeeded in leaping high enough to grab a shooter's arms and start dragging her over the lip. This was the young girl that had been the first to speak up earlier when I'd asked for volunteers.

She screamed when the female latched onto her arms and started tugging, and I dove across her body to anchor her to the top of the container. Fumbling for my pistol which was trapped between our bodies I felt her slip a few inches on the wet metal, then Dog bounded over me and bit down on one of the infected's forearms. I don't know how strong a German Shepherd's bite is, but I know it's strong enough to break the two bones in the forearm and destroy the surrounding muscle.

The female's hand slipped off the shooter's arm, and Dog moved out of the way as my pistol finally came free and I shot the infected in the head. The girl scrambled back from the edge, adrenaline-fueled panic giving her enough strength to move me with her.

Rolling off her and standing up I raised the radio again and called for the firemen. This defense had been Gunny James idea, and when he'd proposed it, I had liked it immediately. All up and down the wall firemen carrying red plastic five-gallon jugs of gasoline mixed with liquid soap charged up ladders and stepped to the front edge of the wall where they started pouring poor mans' napalm onto the infected.

Each fireman walked the length of a couple of containers as he poured, soaking the raging bodies below. One by one as their containers ran out they tossed them back to the town side of the defenses where a crew gathered them and started refilling with gas then more soap. Waving the shooters back from the edge, the firemen pulled out road flares and sparked them with the igniter in the plastic cap before tossing them down onto the napalm-soaked infected. All along the wall fires ignited with a whoosh, the mixture sticking and burning even in the pouring rain.

Napalm is one of the nastiest and probably most frightening weapons that man has ever devised. It's really quite simple, just gasoline and any type of gel that will mix with the gas and cause it to stick to anything it touches while not affecting the flammability of the fuel. Military grade napalm is a bit more complicated than that, but for our purposes, four and half gallons of gas mixed with half a gallon of thick, liquid soap worked perfectly.

Crucifixion

Thousands of infected instantly became walking torches, the mix sticking to their clothing and skin and burning so hot that the infected's flesh started separating from the bone. The bonus was that as they burned, any other infected they came in contact with had some of the gas rub off and start burning them. Flames and heavy black smoke shot above the front edge of the wall and all of the defenders had to move to the back edge. I was glad it was raining, and all my people were soaked. The water helped protect them from the heat of the fire.

Gunny James' suggestion had given me another idea, and as the front ranks of the infected burned, I called for the next wave over the radio. Moments later to either side of me I heard the two smaller fire trucks crank up their diesel engines. As I watched, they rolled forward, each with a ladder extending over the wall, thirty feet in the air. Next to each truck sat a trailer with a big plastic tank on it, we had appropriated from a landscaping service. Each tank normally held two hundred gallons of weed killer the landscapers would use along the sides of roads, but that had been dumped, and the tanks pumped full of gas from a truck stop's underground tank.

Now, each pumper truck's hose ran to these tanks rather than a fire hydrant and the high-pressure nozzles at the tops of the ladders started spraying gasoline across the herd of infected in front of the wall. Both quickly ran through their supply of gas, the men manning the nozzles on the ladders sparking flares and throwing them in long arcs out into the herd. First, one new fire erupted with a loud whoomp, then the second flare hit and ignited the fuel. The fire spread throughout the ranks of the infected and soon there was a sea of flames extending from the wall out to nearly a hundred yards. The smell was horrendous.

Despite being on fire and their flesh literally cooking and falling off their skeletons, the infected continued to push forward. They truly felt no pain nor did they care about mortal wounds. Despite the number of infected, I had fought I felt a thrill of fear and not a little disappointment that not even the instinctual fear of fire still existed in these creatures.

There truly was no way to stop them other than killing them. I looked up and down the wall and could tell all the men and women manning the defenses were thinking similar thoughts. Looks of panic and terror were on almost all the faces, and that's when I knew we were about to lose the battle and the town.

"We've got to get these people's heads back into the fight." I had grabbed Rachel and pulled her close enough for her to hear me. "If we don't they're going to start breaking and running and this wall will fall before the train is loaded and out of here."

Rachel didn't look to be in a much better frame of mind than the defenders, but she nodded and turned to look at me.

"What do you want me to do?" She asked.

"Go east along the wall. Encourage. Use their fear and emotions to get them mad. Right now they're afraid. Get them pissed off, or at least get them fighting!"

Rachel nodded and headed east as I started walking west, Dog at my side.

"We're holding them! Don't let up now! We have to buy time for the evacuees! There's no one but us to do this. Don't let these fuckers win! We fight together, and we can stop them long enough for our people to escape!"

I was yelling as I moved down the line, looking up to see that the second stack of containers was finally getting close. The ex-military heard my words, and with looks of resolve started picking up their rifles. The NCOs were also working to rally the shooters, and soon sporadic firing started up, but there were still a lot of civilians on the wall, and they didn't look so sure.

One burly man dressed like a truck driver stood with a dozen other similarly dressed men, and they all stared at the flaming herd. He turned as I approached, fear on his face which quickly turned to anger when he saw me. He stepped forward to meet me, the men pressing in at his back.

"It's time to cut our losses and get the hell out of here!" He challenged, looking over his shoulders for support from the other men.

The first thought that flashed through my mind was to shoot him in the head and get on with fighting the infected, but just as quickly as I thought it I dismissed it. He wasn't the enemy; he was just scared. He hadn't trained for this, had never dreamt of this in his worst nightmares. Until now the most violence he'd probably every experienced was a bar fight or two. I kept walking forward and stopped a couple of feet in front of him, resisting the urge to put my face in his.

"And go where?" I asked him in a calmer voice than I felt like using. I have little patience or sympathy for people who break and run when things get tough and was summoning all of my self-control. "You think that herd out there is just going to go away and not keep coming if you run? What about the women and children in the town? What happens to them if we don't hold this wall?"

Everyone on the wall knew we were just there to buy time, and they also knew loading thousands of people onto a train would take every second of the time we were fighting for. The man was really scared and was turning that fear into anger towards me. He started to step forward; hands balled into fists at his side.

I really didn't want to fight him, and I was tired of wasting time with him. I was half a second away from pulling my pistol and shooting him when one of the men behind him reached forward and put his hand on the man's shoulder. He met my eyes and I saw understanding, not anger.

"Rick, it's time to get it together. We've got to help. My wife, daughter, and granddaughter are trying to get on that train. The man's right. We've got to hold this wall for a while."

Rick's shoulders slumped as soon as he knew he didn't have any support from the other men. After a long moment, he lowered his eyes and turned back to look at the herd. Nodding my thanks to the man who had interjected I kept moving down the wall.

I didn't have to go far before reaching the vertical end of a container that was the easternmost edge of the second stack. A ladder was leaned up against it, and I climbed up to the next level. Twenty feet really isn't that much higher than ten feet when you're trying to stop tens of thousands of raging infected, but I got an immediate psychological boost from the gain in elevation.

Looking at the defenders, I could tell they felt the same way. They were already setting back up on the sandbags and sending shots into the infected. Looking towards town, I saw four more containers coming my way, and I went back down the ladder and headed back to the center of the wall. Damn, but maybe we could hold out long enough.

As Dog and I moved back east, I looked out over the wall to the south. Thousands upon thousands of infected had died in the fires, blackened bodies littering the area. But as unstoppable as the sea the infected from farther back in the herd were pushing forward, their crushing feet and the steady downpour turning the dead into a thick, soupy black pulp.

The defenders were slowly rallying, the rate of fire picking back up as the next wave of infected approached. Females raced out in front, but the carpet of bodies was so thick and uneven that they had to slow to maintain their balance. This made them easier targets and the shooters were cutting them down well short of the wall. But right behind them was a relentless tide of solidly massed bodies that rifle bullets alone could not stop.

Soon, the sheer volume of the herd had pressed to the wall again, and we had to repeat the napalm attack. The second stack reached the center of the wall and kept moving east as Jim Roberts and his crew worked without pause. As I watched the results of the napalm from atop a newly installed container, I reflexively ducked when there was a thunderous explosion to my right and behind the wall.

I spun my head to see the fire truck and trailer full of gasoline fully engulfed in a massive fireball. The defenders on the wall in front of and thirty yards to either side were immediately consumed by the fire, other shooters to the right and left of the fire were running for their lives along the metal containers. One of them slipped on the rain-slicked metal and skidded over the wall into a thousand waiting hands.

"What the hell just happened?" I asked no one in particular.

"Lightning strike," Rachel answered me.

She had been standing to my left and facing that direction when the explosion had occurred. I looked up at the sky, rain washing across my face and said a few choice words. Focusing back on the task at hand, I called ready reaction force Delta and sent them to help plug the hole in the defensive line the explosion had created.

To my left, the other truck finished spraying its load of gasoline and out of the corner of my eye I saw another flare arc across the heads of the infected before igniting a large swath of the herd. I only watched the fire for a moment before looking back in the direction of the explosion. Not only had we lost a lot of shooters caught in the fireball, we'd lost the lights on the fire truck.

That quadrant of the battle was now barely lit by light from the fires and what little spilled over from the larger truck directly to my rear. I sent Rachel to tell the firemen to move that truck fifty yards to the right. She passed one of the football players that was an ammo runner, and he came directly up to me, panting, soaked and looking exhausted.

"Major, Mr. Hawkins asked me to tell you that we've only got about five minutes of ammo left, then we're out." I nodded, thanked him and turned back to watch the herd press forward as he raced off. Fuck me, was there ever going to be any good news?

I got on the radio with the NCOs and told them to pull half their shooters off the line to conserve ammo. They weren't happy about it, many expressing their displeasure the way only an NCO can, but they did what I told them to do, and there was a noticeable drop in the volume of fire. More napalm was mixed and used, and more gas was sprayed from the fire truck and ignited. Without the fire, we would have fallen long ago, but even with it, we were only delaying the inevitable.

The infected continued to press in and pile up at the base of the wall. Leaning out to check I was not happy to see they were above the point where the upper containers sat on the lower, which meant they were more than ten feet off the pavement. The rain was finally slackening, and the thunder was moving away, now more of a rumble than a sharp crack from every lightning bolt.

A few minutes later Jim Roberts and his crew placed the last container to make a full second row, and he drove his forklift over beside the larger fire truck and honked the horn to get my attention. I turned to see him gesturing with a walkie talkie and dug the one his kid had brought me earlier out of my pocket.

"...last one. What's next? Want us to start a third row?" I caught most of his transmission.

Turning to Rachel, I asked her to call Sergeant Jackson on the police radio she had to check on the status of the evacuation. It took her a couple of tries to get a response.

"We need another hour," Jackson shouted over the crowd noise on his end. I had Rachel tell him he had half an hour which she did then stuffed the radio back in her pocket.

"Let's start a third, Jim," I said into the radio. "This time split your crew and start at the ends, working your way in. We've got to hold for at least another hour so that train can get out of here. Any way you guys can move faster? Are there more forklifts?"

"There's plenty more forklifts, but I don't have guys to drive them. I lost a lot of good people to this shit."

"If I find you drivers that know how to operate a forklift can they operate these monsters, or is there something special about them?" I was starting to feel a glimmer of hope. Surely there were some guys here that had driven a forklift before.

"Nothing special other than just how damn big they are and how careful you have to be with a load this big and heavy, but considering the alternative, I'll take anyone that can drive."

"Stand by." I lowered the radio I was using to talk to Jim and raised the radio to put a call out to all the NCOs. "I need forklift drivers. Now. Find me ten bodies that have driven a forklift before."

I repeated myself a couple of times to make sure all the NCOs heard the call over the weapons fire and screams and snarls of the infected.

Soon, a handful of men were trotting towards me, and I waved them down the ladder and pointed at Jim, still sitting in the idling forklift. Eight men wound up climbing on and clinging to the forklift as Jim hit the throttle and roared off back to the rail yard. One of them was the burly man I'd had the confrontation with earlier and I was glad I hadn't shot him. I didn't think we had time to build a third row the complete length of the wall, but if we could get sections of it raised to thirty feet and concentrate the infected into more of a choke point, we might be able to hold them off a little longer.

The extra drivers helped speed up construction of the wall, but not by as much as I'd hoped. Their inexperience with the sheer size and weight of the loads they were handling slowed them down. One of them managed to lose a container off his forks as he was driving to the wall and precious time was wasted getting the obstruction out of the road so the work could proceed.

Despite the issues, twelve drivers still got more containers from point A to point B in the same amount of time and the wall quickly started growing to 30 feet from the far edges in. The infected kept pushing forward and piling up on top of the bodies of the ones we were killing as well as crushing other living infected under them in their frantic desire to reach us.

The second fire truck's pump failed, most likely due to running something as highly corrosive as gasoline through it. We were now limited to filling jugs with our homemade napalm and dumping it over the wall on the heads of the infected. This helped, but we no longer had a way to knock down any of the bodies farther out that were pressing in.

Crucifixion

As the wall rose and moved in, I had the NCOs start pulling their shooters off and back to ground level. Ammunition was collected and redistributed to those that were still on the wall fighting. The shooters that came off the wall took the opportunity to drink water and eat some food that had been scavenged from a large grocery store a couple of blocks down the road behind us.

The forklifts finished placing another section of wall and roared off to bring more containers. We now had a thirty-foot wall running in from each edge, but the center section was still twenty container lengths short of being raised. Eight hundred feet of only twenty feet of wall. I stepped in between two shooters and could see the grasping hands of the infected only a foot below the edge.

We weren't going to make it. I had halted the napalm. It had become ineffective as we could only burn the infected closest to the wall and the herd had now piled up to the point that it seemed we were just making an easier path for those in the rear to climb forward on top of the burned bodies. I grabbed the police radio from Rachel and called Jackson to check on the status of the evacuation.

"One train is gone, Major. We're loading the second one. Had a problem when some people resisted being loaded into livestock cars, but I got them in, and we're loading up the last of the hospital right now. Ten minutes at the most."

Dirk Patton

"Copy. I want you and everyone else on that train when it pulls out. If the last one is ready, I've got one last trick to delay the infected so all the defenders can make a run for it and get out. Do you have an engineer that will be waiting with that third train for us?"

"10-4, I do. Rick Simmons is already in the engine and waiting. There're half a dozen livestock cars hooked up, doors open and waiting for you."

"Copy that. Thank you. Call when your train is pulling out."

Handing the radio back to Rachel, I looked around for the forklifts, but they weren't back yet. Glancing back to the front, I saw fingertips brushing the top edge. We were in a bad spot now. If we didn't shoot, then the infected would grab onto the top edge of the containers and start climbing up into the midst of the shooters. If we kept shooting them, we were just creating another layer of the pile for the ones in back to climb on and get closer to us.

Not shooting just wasn't in my DNA. Raising the radio, I called for a couple of the units that had already come off the wall to come back up and fill in the open space between the shooters that were still fighting. They came running and started plugging themselves into the line. The volume of firing increased and the infected were beaten back a few inches. Not much, but every inch we won was more time for our escape.

Horns sounded behind me as a convoy of forklifts rolled up. Another twelve containers arrived, ready to go into the wall. The NCOs coordinated moving their shooters out of the way as each new container went into place, but it was a slow process. We had a lot of shooters in a shrinking area, but the NCOs did a good job and in only a few minutes the eight-hundred-foot gap had been reduced to three hundred and twenty feet.

I watched with satisfaction as the containers thumped into place, several infected females that had made the leap onto the top of the wall when the shooters pulled back crushed under the massive steel boxes. That satisfaction quickly went away as I started hearing voices calling out that they were out of ammo.

Running up and down the remaining gap in the wall, I started pulling the ones out of ammo off the wall and sending them to the train station. If they didn't have any more bullets, there wasn't anything to be gained by keeping them here. Rachel was circulating through the volunteers on the ground below and sending everyone that was not actively involved in the defense to the train as well. Dog was still on the wall with me, shadowing my footsteps as I ran back and forth.

Dirk Patton

Grabbing one of the shooters that was out of ammo and on his way to a ladder I sent Dog with him to get carried down. Dog was talented and a hell of a fighter, but as good as he was there was no way he could climb down a twenty-foot ladder. He gave me a hurt look but allowed the man, with some help, to lift him up on his shoulders and secure him in place with a donated shirt that tied him to the man's body. The guy probably thought I was a moron for having let Dog come up on the wall in the first place, but he scampered down the ladder without complaint, Dog tied to him and looking at me with hurt eyes that I was sending him away.

The infected kept pressing forward, and they now seemed to be surging like the tide. One moment hands would be over the edge and trying to grab on, the next they would disappear below. Like 'the tide' was a good analogy as the hands always came back and were a little higher each time. The shooters had slowed their firing and were now only shooting infected that made a successful grab onto the edge of the container.

Unfortunately, the number of them that were doing this was increasing and the number of defenders laying down their rifles when they fired their last round was also increasing. We needed five more minutes, but we weren't going to get it. Two partial crates of grenades were sitting on the top of the wall, and I started pulling pins and tossing them over the edge, hoping to disrupt the push against the wall even for a few moments.

The effort was partially successful, and we gained probably another thirty seconds. The damn things flowed into and over any space created by the explosions so quickly that the hundreds killed by my efforts weren't even significant.

Out of grenades, I did a quick count and saw that we were down to about a hundred shooters that still had ammo. This was bad, but not as bad as it could have been. The distribution of ammo had been fairly equal, and these last defenders had been shooters that picked their targets and made their shots count. They hadn't wasted ammo on body shots that did little to slow or stop the infected; they had aimed and made every round count.

I was willing to bet every single one of them was either ex-Army or ex-Marine. We had momentarily settled into a static battle, the defenders shooting the infected that were in position to breach our defenses as fast as they arrived. If only we had a few thousand more rounds of ammo, we could hold static for a few minutes, but wishing wouldn't get me anything.

A forklift horn sounded from the rear again, and I breathed a huge sigh of relief as I turned to look. That sigh turned into a scream of warning that no one could hear. A large pack of infected females was racing down Forrest Avenue from the east, heading directly towards the lead forklift driven by Jim Roberts.

The females had apparently worked their way through the rugged terrain at the east end of the wall and with the defenders having been pulled off due to the wall being raised and an ammo shortage there had been no one there to stop them. I raised my rifle to sight in on the lead infected, lowering it with a curse a moment later. They were well over four hundred yards away, and moving fast.

A four hundred yard shot with an M4 rifle is certainly possible, but at night from a standing position at a fast moving target; I knew I couldn't make the shots and would end up only wasting valuable ammo. Rachel had noticed me aiming the rifle and turned to look at what I had seen, also raising hers when she saw the infected. She quickly lowered the rifle and started running towards the approaching forklift, waving her arms over her head and pointing at the threat.

Jim finally got the message, but it was too late. I saw the forklift swerve as he tried to avoid them, but they were too close. Three of them leapt onto the side of the machine and swarmed the driver's seat, but Jim wasn't there. When they leapt, he had bailed out the far side of the open cab. Unfortunately, the swerve he had started was the new path the forklift followed.

Despite a deadman switch for safety that applied the brakes automatically if a driver's foot stopped pressing it, the giant machine with its massive load couldn't stop on a dime. Slowing, but still moving at a good pace, the forklift carried the container directly into a fueling area of the truck stop where we had been getting the gas for the napalm and fire trucks.

The lower leading edge of the forty-foot-long container made contact with two islands full of fuel pumps at the same time, and even though the forklift was braking the forward momentum of all that mass was still great enough to shear all the pumps off their mounts and shove them along the ground in front of it before finally coming to a full stop. For a moment the scene was frozen in place, nothing happening; then I saw the first flames.

I started to open my mouth to scream a warning but before I could even form a word the fire found the fuel in the underground storage tanks. The explosion was unbelievable. I've been on battlefields where both artillery and air dropped ordnance – bombs – were detonating, yet I've never experienced anything close to the force of this blast.

The entire truck stop, the container, the forklift and everything and everyone within a one-hundred-yard radius just vanished in a searing ball of flame. This was probably comparable to the fuel explosion that had happened on the flight line at

Arnold Air Force Base, but I had been much farther away from that one. This one knocked me on my back, and I would have slid over the edge of the wall and into the sea of infected if one of the defenders hadn't grabbed me.

Sitting up, I stared at the column of fire and smoke shooting up from the explosion, then remembered to look for Rachel and Dog. The fire did a good job of lighting up the whole area, and it didn't take me long to spot them. Rachel was on her back, certainly having been knocked back by the pressure wave from the blast, Dog standing next to her. She wasn't moving, but neither was anyone else.

When the explosion had ripped through the night all of the shooters on the wall had stopped firing and turned to see what happened. They were still staring at the inferno, but the infected hadn't been distracted and were using the lull in our defense to push forward. Several females made it onto the roof and fell on the prone shooters, ripping into flesh with nails and teeth. They were quickly joined by more and I raised my rifle and started firing into faces only a few feet away.

I was screaming for the shooters to get back in the fight, but they were probably as deaf from the blast as I was. Slowly they started turning back to the front, but we had given too much momentum to the infected. More shooters were falling to female leapers and all along the gap hands were now solidly grasping the edge.

"Fall back!" I screamed, running up and down the line.

Every few feet I was shooting an infected that was either already on the wall or about to clear the edge. Quickly the remaining shooters scrambled backwards and started rushing down the ladders, a couple of them slipping and falling to the asphalt below where their screams of pain were added to the overwhelming sounds of the fire and the battle. Soon there was only me and three other shooters remaining on the wall, clustered in a tight group at the top of one of the ladders, facing a swiftly growing number of infected.

I looked over my shoulder at the fire captain sitting high in the air at the top of the ladder, saw him looking at me and made a slashing motion with my arm. Seconds later a tightly focused stream of very high-pressure water started jetting out of the chrome nozzle that was mounted at the top of the ladder with him.

The water pressure was so great that it not only knocked the infected down, it sent them cartwheeling through the air and back out into the herd. The captain controlled the placement of the water jet like a maestro and even though we got a good soaking from water splattering off of infected bodies he never touched us. In a few seconds, he had bought us enough room to start down the ladder.

One by one the shooters disappeared over the edge until I was the last defender standing on the wall. Waiting for the ladder to clear, I didn't want to push my luck by adding my weight to that of the three men already on it, I shot five more infected on one side while the water jet swept through dozens of them and sent them tumbling.

Finally clear I stepped onto it, grasped the outside of the ladder and moved my feet outside the rails and started a fast slide twenty feet to the ground. I had forgotten about my damaged hands, and I had just started the slide when they reminded me that they weren't one hundred percent. Somehow I managed to hold on but descended way faster than I wanted and hit hard enough to lose my balance and fall flat on my back. Fuck that hurt.

Forcing myself up and on my feet, I did a quick check of the top of the gap in the wall, glad to not see any infected faces staring back down at me. The captain worked the water jet back and forth, aimed a few feet above the top of the wall so that any infected was blasted in the midsection and shoved back. Shouting at everyone to run for the train station I rushed to where Rachel was still flat on her back in the middle of the street.

Running up, I slid to a halt on my knees and leaned over her, Dog whining as he pressed closer to her still form. Her eyes were closed, and she didn't respond when I called her name. I checked the pulse in her neck, letting out a relieved sigh when I found it beating steady and strong. She was laying in the same position you would use if you were making a snow angel and were just making the top arc of the wings.

Her torso was straight and her head and neck aligned with her body so I didn't think she would have a spinal injury. She had just been knocked flat by the pressure wave from the explosion. I hoped.

I checked around us, and the water jet was still holding the infected at bay, but even from here I could tell that the rate they were now climbing into the gap was quickly going to overwhelm the captain's ability to knock them all back. It would start with a trickle of infected leaking through the opening then grow to a stream and eventually become an unstoppable torrent that would flood the town and kill anyone still here.

We were only a few yards from the ambulance that Rachel had stolen and even though I was reasonably sure her neck and back were OK I decided to take advantage of what I had available. Rushing into the back, I grabbed a cervical collar out of a bin on the wall and a backboard that was clipped to the other wall. I had just gotten the collar on her when Dog sprang to his feet with a growl and leapt over me.

I spun to see him collide with a female that had rushed around the side of the vehicle, tumbling across the pavement with her. Another female was moments behind the first and ran around the edge of the ambulance with a scream and dove at me as I squatted on the ground.

I had enough time to turn slightly and take the impact from the body on my shoulder, twisting to keep the female away from Rachel. The woman attacking me was big. She was probably close to my height and nearly as heavy and had a strength that came from rage. We rolled on the ground, each of us fighting for a solid grip on the other, but unlike me, she was also trying to get her teeth into the fight.

Still rolling, I finally got a fist full of her hair and started trying to pull her jaws away from me, but she managed to get her mouth on my right forearm and locked on tight. Her bite was strong enough to paralyze the muscles in my right forearm, and all I could do was use the strength in my upper arm and shoulder to control her head. She raked at my face, opening long bloody furrows and kept clawing until she found something solid to grab.

There was a sharp pain then my left ear suddenly burned like acid had been poured on it and I could feel warm blood running across my face and neck. Releasing her hair, I managed to break her grip on my ear and bat her hand away, then started pounding the side of her head with my free hand. Each blow sent waves of pain from my damaged hand up my arm, but I kept hitting, hard and fast. After several blows, her bite on my right arm loosened and I kept pounding, aiming for the softer spot right at the temple.

I must have hit her a dozen times before she let go of my arm. I stopped hitting her and got my left hand on her throat, tucked my legs up between us and used them to push her off me. She hit the asphalt, rolled and Dog was on her as soon as she came to a stop. He consistently amazed me at the speed and power he possessed, and this time was no different. In a flash he had landed on her chest and before she could do anything he lunged his head down and ripped her throat out, standing on her until she quit moving.

Looking around, I didn't see any more immediate threats as I scooted across the wet and bloody pavement to where Rachel still lay unconscious. When I leaned over her a surprisingly large stream of blood started pouring off my chin and onto her shirt. Not wanting to waste time but needing to staunch the bleeding I ripped my shirt off and wrapped it tight around my head and ears like a turban.

Blood still dripped on Rachel as I carefully worked her onto the backboard, but there was nothing I could do about that at the moment. With her fully on the board, I used its Velcro straps to tightly secure her as immobile as possible. Keeping a close eye on my surroundings I was happy that Dog was doing the same, and I lifted the head of the backboard and dragged it across the parking lot to the back of the ambulance. Laying the end on the floor inside the vehicle, I rushed to lift the foot, shoving the whole thing into the back before running back to where Rachel had fallen and retrieving her rifle, which I tossed in back onto the gurney that was locked to the floor.

I had just closed one of the doors when the siren on the big fire truck started wailing. Turning I saw that the water cannon had stopped, and females were starting to pour through the gap in the wall. The problem was readily apparent. A large piece of flaming debris from the explosion at the truck stop had landed on the big hose that connected the truck to the fire hydrant, and though the hose is very tough it had finally burned through, and the end was whipping back and forth as it sprayed water.

The females quickly swarmed the truck, and while the driver in the cab was safe for the moment, they were on the truck and up the ladder like a pack of monkeys. The fire captain didn't even have time to get unstrapped from his seat before they were on him and tearing him to ribbons. Slamming the other door, I whistled for Dog, and we piled into the cab of the ambulance. The keys were in the ignition, and I started the engine, females slamming into the back and sides of the vehicle before I could get it into gear.

Transmission in drive I jammed the accelerator to the floor and smashed through the females that were piling up in front of me. Heading north on the highway, I steered a wide path around the roaring truck stop fire, feeling the heat from the flames even inside the cab of the truck with the windows rolled up. A small mirror mounted to the dash let me keep an eye on Rachel as I drove, gunning the ungainly vehicle farther into town and away from the wall, pursued by thousands of females.

The rail yard was just ahead and to my right was the station for passengers that Sergeant Jackson had used to stage the evacuation. As I turned onto the road that ran in front of the station, I could see there was still a group of several hundred people waiting to board. Damn it! There was no time. The infected were only half a mile behind me and coming fast.

Crucifixion

I felt for the police radio then remembered it was in one of Rachel's pockets. Slamming to a stop, I scrambled into the back and ran my hands over Rachel's pockets until I found it, ripping it out and pressing the transmit button.

"Jackson! Infected have breached. That train needs to go now!" I shouted into the radio as I climbed back behind the wheel.

I had hoped to make it to the train where I could get some help with loading Rachel onto a car, and we could escape on the rails. Now, not only was that not going to happen, there were going to be people left behind that would die when the infected reached the station.

"Say again? There's still people on the platform." I could hear the chaos of frightened people in the background when he transmitted.

"You have to leave them and save the people that are already on the train. There're thousands of females coming, and they'll be here in less than a minute."

I let out a long, slow sigh and wanted to pound the steering wheel in frustration but settled for reaching across the cab and wrapping my arm around Dog who leaned into me and rested his head on my chest. Watching in the side mirror, it was only about thirty seconds before I saw the fastest females appear on the road no more than a quarter mile behind me. They were in a full sprint. I had stopped a few hundred yards from the platform and could see the people waiting to board turn all at once when the screams of the approaching females reached their ears.

"Now, Jackson! You're out of time!" I said into the radio, then dropped it into a deep cup holder molded into the dash.

I knew we needed to start moving to stay ahead of the herd, but I couldn't put the ambulance into gear. I was exhausted. Mentally, physically and emotionally exhausted. This didn't stop me from being able to physically drive us out of there, but I felt like I had failed these people. Most of the men and women still standing on the platform were shooters that had stayed on the wall until the last minute. Shooters I had recruited.

I've had men under my command die before, and as I sat there, I recognized it would probably happen again, and there wasn't a damn thing I could have done differently. That didn't make it any easier, and all I wanted to do was step out of the ambulance and face the approaching herd and kill every single one of the damn things.

Checking the mirror again I saw that the females had already covered half the distance and more were pouring into the street at the intersection. Looking back up, I saw the train start to move. Several men in the group were picking up the women who had fought with them and were throwing them through the air to waiting hands that caught them and pulled them to safety on the train.

Three women were saved this way as the train picked up speed, but a fourth fell short and landed under the train car to be run over by the steel wheels' moments later. After that, no one else tried.

There was movement at the edge of the group closest to the swiftly approaching herd, and I saw Sergeant Jackson step clear of the people around him, face the infected and rack a shell into the chamber of the shotgun in his hands. Another man I recognized as the vet who had lost an arm stepped up beside him, a fire axe swinging lightly in his one hand. As one, the group turned to face the coming death. Pipes and boards, anything they could find to fight with, in their hands.

The train continued to pick up speed as the leading edge of the sprinting females reached the ambulance and raced past me, focused on the survivors standing under the train station's lights. With the herd only a few hundred yards away I could see Jackson raise a hand to his mouth a moment before I heard his voice on the radio.

"Thank you, Major. I wanted you to know we got two trainloads of people to safety, and Ms. Betty and her kids were on the first train. There's still people in the town, but we saved thousands. Good luck to you." His voice was steady and strong.

Less than a minute later the infected were close enough for him to fire the first round from his shotgun, obliterating the head of a female with long brown hair. I couldn't stand to watch anymore and dropped the transmission into drive and accelerated away, females pounding on the sides of the ambulance and being crushed under as I drove. Tears streaming down my face, I kept my eyes forward as I passed the massacre at the train station and sped away into the dark.

Crucifixion
Continue the adventure with Rolling Thunder: V Plague Book 3, available from Amazon.

91238175R00213

Made in the USA
Lexington, KY
20 June 2018